If you go in a bookstore and they don't stock it, ask for it, even if you have read it. Someone else hasn't!

Have fun! There's plenty of room in the merry band for everyone, if we try.

Live the Love

&

Share the Love

A. F

ISBN: 978-1-7370862-2-2 (EBook)

ISBN: 978-1-7370862-3-9 (Paperback)

First Print Edition 2021

Published by Aster Oktogonia Press

Asterius & Thesius
Walk Into the Light

Aaron Fown

One

The sea was calm, and the sun was shining. The wind was still, and the waves beat their slow quiet rhythm on the planks of our finest ship. I kept pace with my fingers. My knot and string worked that beat into a finer rhythm. Estius accompanied me on his lyre, and together we wove a sad tune. I looked around at my fellows, dressed to their finest in the early summer air, and not one met my eye. I wavered in my rhythm, for I knew our music could only move the oars faster. But then, I played on. There was no escaping my fate. I let my mind wander into the song, and wonder about how I had ended up here, dressed for a party, and doomed to die.

I thought of the day of the dark lot, and the look on my mother's face when she saw the black soot at the end of my stick. She didn't cry out, and beg and cry like so many of the parents did, squabbling in the dirt in the town square. Her chin was set firm, and her eyes were fixed on me, as she strode forth and took me by the shoulders. She said a few last words.

"I always knew you were too good to be true. No one is so beautiful and strong and at ease with everything without attracting woe to them. I am glad I had this time with you, as I am glad I have had my time with your father. I won't even curse the people of this little fishing village, so far from the place I was born. Your father is a king amongst these fishers, and I am their queen. Face your fate with dignity."

I wanted to crash into her like the waves against the shore, but two big men walked me firmly away, almost carrying me. I knew them, of course: the potter, and one of the many fishermen. Too many children are snatched back by their families in that moment, and no one wanted to fight the matriarch, nor contest with all the other parents who would rage at the unfairness of any unequal treatment of me. It would be ugly. So they bodily carried me away to the other side of town, near the council house. The rest of the kids had been given a similar treatment, and were separated, boys and girls. They were then swiftly placed on carts and before I knew what was happening they left. The temples would keep them as they would their own virgins for their workings and their rights; I figured this would be my fate as well. I was darkly comforting myself that one of my own friends, who I would often play music with, pulled the black stick before me. Misery loves company, but I was denied even that. Instead, I was hustled into the king's court, where my father, the king and the elders were in meeting.

I had eaten many meals in the council house, for it was all our house in that way. Feasts and great events honoring our goddess would happen there, and I remember spending many days gazing up at the tiny circle of the sky you could see out the top of the roof, as if the sky itself was held up by a spider's web of timbers, on a circle of ancient trees. Today the sky stared down at me like an accusing eye, and I did my best to stand proud and firm under the chamber's undivided attention.

"Thesius, my son... "

I interrupted, "I will not be spared just because I am your son. Aethra told me to face my fate with dignity and... "

"Silence!" He smashed his fist upon the table with a loud clap: the unquestioned symbol of his authority in this space. "You will not be spared," his voice cracked. There was a long awkward silence as he paused to take a drink of broth from his cup. "You make me proud, though. No begging or crying like the others. Maybe you are some sort of hero, with such poise." His eyes snapped up, and grabbed mine, pierced through me, "I trust your mother, that you were not touched by the gods in the traditional way. That she never laid with anyone but me. But we all know what you are, my son. It's clear as that golden fire on your crown. However it was done, you were never like the other children. Perhaps, in the end, you can spare us from this horror."

2

The conditions of our defeat need not be repeated in these chambers. It was carved deep on all of our hearts, written in worried lines on all of the faces of those assembled. One princeling dies in sport, and a great city bears down its wrath on our little town. Every six years we bleed out our youths at the very moment they would normally take partners and start families. In the 15 years since those events, our city had sent out three groups of youths, seven and seven, never to be seen again. One group of them had just left; we threw a party for them. What else were we to do? We assumed they were simply killed, in the King of Minos' endless revenge for the loss of his fair son. He wanted something so hard to get: virgins, in the prime of their lives. And he was so particular. The first group sent, shortly after the demand was made, was too young; they had to be adults by the standards of Crete, not by the standards of Athens. Not that they were spared, of course, they just demanded that we do better. So the selection was done before there was too much temptation, and the sacrifice was kept in the way we already had available to us. I knew all that, but apparently there was more.

"Listen, son, we have to make this brief so the town doesn't burn this place down. And, if I were so bold I think they likely should." The room liked that, it almost elicited a chuckle, but it settled to an appreciative solemn murmur. "The King of Minos is attempting to craft a god of his own to oppose ours. Our children, our blood, are just a tool to this end." He paused, to let his words have more weight, and in that moment he squared his wide shoulders, bowed a bit by age, and straightened the woven crown of olive branches, rendered in gold and silver, that signified his rank. Like all the other men, he was lightly dressed against the summer heat, and were it not for that crown, he might have been mistaken for the fisherman he once was. He was our king, but we were no great city who could shower him with finery. "I knew you were going to be selected. Athena herself came to me in a dream and told me you would be." A few in the chamber inhaled sharply at this, but it wasn't so unusual for our chosen king to speak with the goddess that protects us, who gave us her very name. "And, I knew that the grace of a child would bring me only woe."

"Frustrating, how accurate those drunken witches are." It was dad's money guy, who had given up being merely the most resourceful man in town for the privilege of having a bit more sway in where the trade went.

My father turned, and in a tone I'm sure he didn't think I could hear, grumbled, "Be quiet, and remember we are condemning my son." Latrius chose to study his sandals rather than talk further. Father returned to his tone of authority, "Our Lady of Wisdom is not happy with this dark working, nor with our unjust sacrifice, and she wants you to kill their godling before they rise in power. She wants you to go north, to Thessaly, to train with the people of the forest and their ancient teacher. And when you go on to your fate our gods themselves will arm you, to cut down the horrible maw all of our children are being cast into. Now go, my dear son, before I lose my resolve."

And, just like that, the same two men grabbed me and escorted me from the chamber, out into the harsh light. I now realized, having a full view of their faces, that one of these men had lost their daughter to the last sacrifice, and the other, a brother. And that was the last I saw of Aegeus, until the very day I left to meet my fate.

Thessaly lies to the north of my humble home of Athens. It's not a city, or even a town. More a large area of forest and plain inhabited by the Lapiths, a people who live on their feet by choice. Two days by horseback, holding on to the back of a strong fisherman, was enough time to think about everything I'd known of them. Whereas most people chose to sit in one place and farm, or row out and cast their lot, the people of Thessaly kept their food trees in many places, and so walked to and fro to them, hunting along the way. They did give worship to our gods, and they did help pay for the raising of the temples. That would be enough reason to tolerate their differences even if they did not enjoy the favor of their ancient teacher, and the boons of knowledge he gave unto all of us.

4

Lapiths would come into town occasionally, dressed simply in skins, and running swiftly on bare feet. My mother would jest they hardly knew how to use a thread but to hold two skins together, but we did trade with them for their game leather, which was far more strong and soft than what we could produce. They seemed happy, and healthy. Their great teacher had gifted them with knowledge of medicine and this, too, they traded with us. Often they would eat a great feast of fish before they left if they had healed too many on a trip, and they were very generous to share with us what was a payment for their services. But it was not their way to care for too many stores of food, so they gave. Thinking back, it seemed we often took more than they received, but they never complained.

It was a good day's journey, in the way that a journey without any temples to pass is both drab and, at its best, uneventful. On the morning of the second day, we ate dried fish and thin crispy breads, with some cheese and dried spring berries, by the embers of our dying campfire. When I realized the berries and cheese were just for the prince, I insisted my courier have some as well.

"You're the prince, it's yours."

"And, why does the king get more, anyway?"

Ailen sighed; he knew me well enough. "Because he's the king."

"A poor king might think that, but think about what the court does: they throw feasts, they make sure no one goes hungry. The king gets more because he sits up high and so he can see where it needs to go, that's what my dad says anyhow. And if I'm going to get more because I'm a prince and a golden child or some shit, then I feel like spreading it around. So, that means you get some cheese."

"Fine." He took a large chunk of the cheese out of the grape leaf with his knife, and put it on the bread with his freshly charred fish. "You know, I wish you hadn't taken that damned stick, even if the gods should will it."

"Ailen, don't... don't be profane. Even the fields can hear."

"No, our little fishing village ain't got anything going for it but some good currents and a good king and... you. You go running

5

round making everyone happy, with you being nice about everything and being beautiful and kind and the gods gotta take it all away."

"Who knows, I might not be running off to die. I mean, I'm not going to the temple to... what do they do?"

"Carefully not touch girls, I guess." Ailen knew a great deal about the workings of a boat, and very little about the workings of a temple.

"Or the opposite for the girls... I'm going to be trained by the great teacher and be a hero or something like that. Athena... said so."

"She said you're gonna be a hero." Ailen locked eyes with me.

"Yeah, I..."

"That means you're gonna go off to die, kid. Heroes die. They almost always do." I could tell Ailen was crestfallen to be a part of this, so I spoke no more of it. We packed up our light camp, and before I knew it we had rode on till noon in silence. What more was there to say?

"Hey, pretty boy, wake up."

I snapped out of my daze. The sun had set quite a bit, and was now shining well under the bit of fabric that protected the people on the deck, right into my eyes. I turned my head aside and threw up my hands instinctively, feeling a small wave of nausea pass over me.

"Hah, I get to dazzle *you* for once." It was... Miletta? I barely knew her before the selection. "We got some food. You know, so we can be well fed for the sacrifice, so nice." There were a few groans from the other chosen ones.

"Why not throw ashes on my bread?" one grumbled.

"Oh, and it gets better. Since they got some virgin magic and just know if we've been fooling 'round, we have to stay above decks, and on opposite sides, for five whole days. You know, so we don't get any ideas. They want some well fed, fully grown, wind chapped virgins." She flopped down next to me, and one of our chaperones shot her a dirty look from the prow. "Don't worry Aesther, my virgin womb is safely aside him, if I slip and fall in his lap go ahead and kick me or something." She continued, in less of a yell, "Now they got their all

6

knowing magic but I figure they don't care about all those polished sticks and stones I've been making happy husbands of the past few years. Or at least the eternal virgins at the temple of brewing thought so." This bit of too much information would probably have brought some color to my cheeks, but she elbowed me before I could be too embarrassed. It struck me that she was eye to eye to me seated, and I was pretty big. "I didn't want to leave, you know. Those ladies are a lot of fun. Oh, and I didn't want to die and be eaten by some monster, yeah." She laughed, loudly. Aesther piped up.

"Do you think it's easy for me, sailing my niece away to die? I should be at your weddi... "

"No." Another woman spoke, one of the chosen seven. Helea... daughter of the oil merchant. "I'm fairly certain you are going to have a much easier time of it than good Miletta here, unless Poseidon plans on gnashing your bones on the trip back." The sailors on deck erupted into cries of horror at this profanity until Miletta, somehow, pierced the din.

"Oh shut it, was that bad etiquette?" Miletta was capable of being quite loud, it seems, without even a hint of a break in her voice. Now I remember; her mother used to direct traffic on the docks! "Speaking his name! A woman no less! Well, how are we to address our lord Poseidon when we are using his giving ocean as a ferry way to a bloody sacrifice? Oh sure, he takes his own, but why exactly is he all clear skies about spilling blood to make another god to rival him?" At this a low murmur broke out; this was evidently a topic of much conversation back in Athens. Helea took her turn, to speak out over the murmur.

"Oh, yes, the godling we are to be fed to. It was the talk of Athens when we went through, and though it felt like I hardly knew the place, I know a good entertaining rumor when I hear one. So, should we act like it's a big secret?"

"Back when I was... chosen, dad... the King acted as if that *was* a big secret. The whole town knows now?" I returned to eating bits of fish and roasted carrot wrapped in bread while I listened. I was more hungry than I thought.

"Not only knows," this was the helmsman, Kato, "they can't stop talking about it. The King of Minos thinks he can reopen the Heavenly Gate with some sort of monster his wife gave birth to. Feed a bunch of kids to it, and reawaken the old bull god."

"Everybody in Minos saw it when it was a child, they walked it around like a normal kid I guess. They built a huge bloody temple of sacrifice under the palace for him to... what?" Miletta shot a look at Helea.

"Achieve apotheosis?"

"Or the opposite of that, whatever." They must have gotten pretty close at the Temple of Brewing, if they were finishing each other's sentences like that. Back in town, they would have rarely interacted.

"Honestly, I would be appalled even if I wasn't the sacrifice. Eaten alive, by some godling monster." That was one of the seven men. I wished I could see his face, I hate not being able to place a voice and a name. It didn't help that he sounded a bit faint of breath. Perhaps he lost the sea legs? "I wonder, why doesn't Pos... Why does he not just send us to the bottom? Spare the world the evil of it?"

"Because Poseidon is caring enough to spare Athens the horror that would happen if we don't show up." This was Helea again, with a sharp edge on her voice. "Because he apparently can't stop their ships, and he can't stop their blinding light. Maybe Zeus really does love Minos more than the people of Hellea, like they say." The name of our rolling peninsulas, an echo of her own, shrank on her lips before the name of our enemy. She clawed at her clothes, with fire in her eyes. "Or need I part my wrap and show you what their return would mean?" Everyone looked at the deck. No one needed a reminder of the scars the Minoans had left on the survivors, horrid patches of roiling pale skin that would never heal. Even years after, the ivory colored, damaged skin would never stop hurting with every movement. She was a toddler when the Minoan ships entered our harbor for the second round of their revenge, after two of our 'virgin' sacrifices, apparently, failed their test. Her mother barely escaped with Helea in her arms, but not without losing her eyesight in exchange for her child's life. Many of the survivors went blind after both attacks; pretty much everyone who looked at the light did. The whole town chipped in after that to help them out. Even though they were one of the wealthiest merchant families in town, they were still survivors, and it takes anyone a while to learn how to be useful when they lose their eyesight.

It could have been worse. When I was a child, burnt bones from the people who once lived in the stilt homes along our golden shore would still wash up at the high tide, like twisted blackened driftwood. Our previous King and fully a third of the town died in that attack. Every one of our fishing ships was set alight, and it was only my father's quick work in the aftermath, rallying the people to rebuild our fleet, that saved Athens from starvation. It's why they elected him as the new king. Compared to that, the second attack was just a reminder. I suppose they needed our blood unboiled for their sacrifice.

"I love the beard. You must have raised some eyebrows when you strode into town with that." Miletta was taking advantage of the lull to talk to me one on one.

"Father and I had... some words about it. If I am not to marry, then who am I keeping my cheeks clean for? It became a terrible bother after it grew in. It's just so much, and I was living like a hermit in the woods." Indeed, by the time I was 17 the shell could hardly cut it, and I would have to sharpen the thing every time, grinding it against the stone. If I didn't do it every other day I had to start with a blade, it was so long. Eventually I just gave up, and called it a stand. In a way, I viewed it as a sure mark of my father's parentage. They didn't used to call him 'Goaty' before he became king for his varied diet.

"You know, to be honest, I'm a bit surprised to see you. No offense, but I thought the King would get his golden child a break, especially when you didn't come with us." Was this the reason Miletta had sat within whispering range?

"I think this may still be a real secret, but... " But, I was done with secrets, "They took me off to train me to be some kind of hero. In Thessaly."

"Oh! With the centaur? That must have been some strange times!" She was struggling to maintain her low tone over her excitement. I took that as a sign that my father's court knew how to keep a few things to themselves. I was also thrilled to have the chance to change the subject. There was nothing I wanted to talk about less than Dad trying to spare me, not after that episode at our house before I left.

"He was strange, yeah. But it was mostly just slashing at bundles of reeds and learning things. Philosophy, mathematics, animal husbandry, cooking, craft, music... " I paused, and realized that listing every subject would be dull. "Chiron thought learning such things was vital for a hero. Knowing where to place the blade, and when to use it, is as important as how to use it, he would say. I never did get him to explain to me how knowing the stars and their names would help me to slay a monster, though." Miletta giggled. I was happy the little joke landed, but her smile quickly turned to a skeptical smirk.

"And... how exactly are you supposed to slay this monster? With your bare hands? I mean, you're strong and fast and, if I remember right, you hear every damn thing, but... "

"Somehow, and I don't know how, I am to be armed with glorious weapons from our gods. Athena gave me a chance to train with them, briefly. I'm supposed to have faith they will be there... somehow." I noticed that Miletta had almost fallen over, she had leaned in so fast.

"Wait, you met her, our goddess? Athena? I... wow, that's just amazing. I know you're not supposed to talk about such things but...
"

"Not just her… All types of strange and wonderful people seem comfortable in Thessaly after dark. Or perhaps Chiron attracts them, with his wisdom? But yeah, I'm not supposed to talk about it."

"Well, isn't that our golden boy, heading off to a glorious fate. Must be slightly nicer, having a spot ready in Elysium. I hope[1] you succeed for everyone's sake, back in town. Not that it'll help you or I one way or another."

"That seems… dire."

"Oh! I get it. After you kill their little baby god you're gonna walk out of their temple of blood, which they built right under the palace, past hundreds of guards armed with gods know what, and swim home?" She paused for effect, before finishing (me). "I expect miracles from my gods, not whatever that is. But hey, good luck." Even Athena herself had given me little cause to believe I would survive, but I didn't care to think about it. My face must have twisted up quite violently, because she grabbed my leg and gave it a squeeze. "Look, sorry. I've been dealing with this by making light of it. Most of us have been. You need a hug?" I nodded, and she gave me a very welcome, and warm side hug. Aesther coughed, loudly.

"Now look, uncle, my holy passage is firmly planted on the decks. But maybe you think I have a spare hole on my thigh, or maybe you think Thesius' rope is like a trawling line? Fine, I'm moving." And at that she arose and rejoined the ladies on the other side through a veil of laughter. I realized Miletta was right to make light of our situation. Her mirth was as welcome as her hug, and I found myself laughing along with the rest of the deck. We all quieted down, as the sun fell lower on the horizon. The conversation had left me with a lot to think about. So I leaned back on the deck cushion, closed my eyes, and let my meal settle. Before I knew it, the next day came.

---

[1] Take note of the capitalization. I will explain later.

Two

The flame stood caged, ringed in silver and gold. The oil in the fine copper vessel burnt clean on the wick, fed air from below by well placed holes, barely flickering in the never still air. The single strategically placed dent in the bowl glinted in the reflected light. It was the only reason this precious thing wasn't missed up above.

Am I that flame? No finer cage has ever been made than the one I live in. Here I sit, ringed in silver and gold. If I were let loose, would I simply devour everything that fell before me, merciless and all consuming? Dad would like that; I quietly laughed at the thought.

Always quiet, in my true home. Always on mouse toes, surrounded by my illicit pleasures, lit by my illicit flame. They were my last line of defense, in a way. If they ever found my true home, perhaps my father's fury would keep them from wondering where that steady flow of air was going.

This scroll bored me. More tales of the east, of times long past, that I had to painfully decipher if I wanted to make heads or tails of it. Mother found it remarkably easy to gather scrolls from grandpa's old library and send them down here, down the hole. Dad could care less about reading, and knowledge, if it doesn't point directly to power. However, Elaía didn't always have a clear idea of what would be worth pilfering. This last batch was not terribly amusing. When grandpa was on his own thieving tour, through the haunted ruins of the Heavenly Gate, he would just grab every scroll he could find, if only to save it from crumbling away to dust. I couldn't fault him for that.

Should I play a few notes? The harp, made just for me, with the strings gapped just a bit wider than the usual, laid right there. I could go to that bend in the corridor; I'm fairly sure no note can reach beyond those twists. Ah, but that's such a risk! What if one of my attendants should be braving the dark for some unknowable reason? No, best to wait for the moon to play my song.

Then what? Too many hours to sleep, too many hours to stare into the darkness and practice my peace. I twisted the furs beneath my legs in frustration.

Perhaps I will visit my old master; he always cheers me up. I killed my flame, and the darkness pressed in upon me. I placed the lamp carefully in the alcove, next to the flint and the iron. It was too much a risk to have it alight anywhere outside this room. If anyone were to smell the lamp oil on a tour, it might raise too many questions. Besides, I knew my home. The architect and his masons had made sure of that, though that was by my father's design as well. The darkness was my armor, to raise me in the darkness, and defend me from my prey.

I turned the corner, from the finished area I had been in, and simply followed the air, not even bothering to brush my hands against the wall. I did have to steady myself as I pulled myself through the more natural gap at the end of the corridor, into the chamber beyond. I could hear the burble of the stream here, far further down in the caves. It was hard to imagine that tiny trickle had carved this majestic thing, but perhaps it was greater at one point in time. Or perhaps it just had an eternity of time to work. I walked along my practiced path, staying away from the sharp rocks on either side, before squeezing through another gap, into the architect's masterwork.

At some point, long ago, this cave had been a stand-in underworld for the people of Crete. It consumed enough of the youth, seeking enlightenment, that it got a fearsome reputation, and was closed off for generations. Dad had the brilliant idea to open up this little hell and build a… what is this place? A temple? A bloody sacrificial pit? Whatever it was, it was a monument to his arrogance, built out of sight of everyone with the best things that our family could buy with their wealth, or steal with their power.

The Architect, Taitale, was one of those things stolen, taken from his home on one of the great islands to the west of here at the point of a blade. Sometimes it invites danger to get a reputation for greatness, when greater men have a mind to take what they want. Father's grand idea, to build a vast structure in this cave, under the palace? That required genius, not the mere craftsmanship and skill our existing crew had. Father had his toddler son snatched up too; the move was a brilliant one, as there was nothing he would not do to keep his child safe. As I understand it, he's locked up in one of the towers with his son now. He must be an adult by this point; not much of a childhood he had. But, that's a greater courtesy than was given to most of the people who labored to create my lovely home.

My old friend, Ma'aht, was another thing stolen, this time from the land of the Nile. He was taken in the dead of night by a band of local bandits, on the specific orders of my grandfather. Auro then secreted him away to Crete in a shipping vessel, tied up amongst rows of amphora. The people of the Nile are in some disarray at this moment, but they are older than any living civilization I know of. They know what is valuable, and worth protecting; such a theft would not have been appreciated if it were known, so secrecy was paramount. This all happened long before I was born. Stealing people and their skill is a family tradition.

He was selected for this honor for his ability with the resonance flutes, which my grandfather coveted, and his relative youth, which made him a valuable asset. If he didn't comply, build his instrument and work it, then his knowledge would die with him. His own elderly master was slaughtered before him, to get the point across. Indeed, without Ma'aht's tireless work and tremendous brilliance, neither the grand city up above nor the pit I dwelt in below could have ever been made. It would have required a band of slaves greater than all the people in Hellea to do it, and Taitale's brilliant plans would have been nothing more than lines on a parchment.

The architect's masterwork, made with endless repeating stones each twice the height of a large man, was carefully designed to befuddle and confuse. The passages would double back, and twist and turn. Several times in its expanse there were subtle rises and dips in the path that would take corridors above or below other corridors. Several paths ended in traps; most were meant not so much to kill, as to wound and terrify. If I hadn't walked these corridors countless times while it was under construction, I would be as lost as anyone else here. But, this was to be my home, and Ma'aht made sure I was at home here.

I turned another bend on my twisting path, and stepped into my real bedroom. My stomach turned at the smell, as the reeking piles of clothes, soaked in blood and slowly fermenting in the cold dank darkness, had given the room a sharp moldy air. I checked the placement, patting the piles and making sure they were in roughly the shape of a bed and a lounging area. Once some animal had got in here and made a mess of everything; that had given me quite a fright, but I fixed it before the next inspection. I checked my pile of treasures; bracelets and rings and necklaces, all finely made of gold and silver, fit for a god. All right where I had left them, except for a single ring, and my broad belt, made of interlinked hoops of metal. Both were finely decorated, but they also served practical purposes. The belt, for instance, kept my skirt on. Finally, I checked my other outfit. Torn, bloody and reeking: right where I had left it. I'd rather be naked than wear that thing every day. But, were I to go naked I would suffer from the continual cold of this cave, despite my natural gifts. I pulled my outer layer, a robe, around my shoulders, and felt gratitude for it, as I left to visit my old friend.

Finding him was easy: follow the air. I walked, twisting and turning, towards that source, before stopping at the threshold. I sat, and dangled my legs over the edge. The vastness of the chasm before me was so obvious, if you took a moment to hear it. But, in a panic, who would? This hole was the worst monster in this place. I took a moment to honor everyone it had consumed, before addressing my old friend and teacher.

"Ma'aht, old friend." He greeted me in his usual manner. "I feel restless today, torn asunder by my mind. I look forward to my task, it disrupts my monotony. But I also fear it... I know it's the moment of our greatest risk. I live in terror of dishonoring you, by fumbling the plan." I sat there, in the cool breeze, and listened to my quiet words as they bounced from one rock face to another, spanning a chasm I couldn't cross, a dozen times before they rested. He was there, he always was, and he replied in his usual manner. "I'll do my best, as always. I will play my part, and satisfy my father. And, I'll do my best to keep anyone else from joining you... I'll do better. You don't need any more company, right? You've still got me." I sat, in communion with the darkness, for a long while. I cleared my mind, and tried to consider what he had taught me. But I was consumed by thoughts of my own family instead.

I never did have the pleasure of Ma'aht's company when I was a child. He was around, of course, busily raising up the stones that mark the power and distinction of the city of Minos, and directing the quarry to build to his specifications. But those workings were not the place of a child, even one so unusual as myself. That being said, I cannot help but look back at those idle years in the sun, playing in the gardens around the palace, as being a bit of a wasted opportunity. A good teacher, in that moment, could have shown me the door to my prison before it snapped shut on me. Time seems so short in the span of human lives.

My grandfather, Auro Minos, saw fit that I was educated, and I learned to read in several languages, including a few that men had long ceased to utter. As the king saw me as the natural heir to the Heaven's Gate, he had me learn their script, and also the script of the people who had preceded us around this sea, so that I might know the ebb and flow of language as it changes over time. I had such a knack for it he introduced me to the ancient twisting script of the people who dwell far to the east of here, in their endless bewildering kingdom of a thousand kings. It also suited him that I should keep my nose to the parchment, as this task kept me busy.

He must have realized my mind would make me uncontainable if he didn't give it a task. Never was I allowed beyond the walls of the garden, except briefly on holy days, and even then only as an object of marvel for the people. If he had lived longer, I wonder how much of the world would be under our sway now? He understood people so well, myself included. I don't think he ever loved me, but he understood me well enough to control me. Control was always so much on his mind. I wish he had shared with me what he intended to do with this power, had he seen his plan through. Trying to understand him still tears at my mind, but I have no answers.

My mother Elaía, on the other hand, always did love me. How could she not? I was her child, and though I was strange, I was not so different that it caused her strife. As I grew I can recall her often opining that I was a gift of the stars, and a continuing symbol of our family's rightful kingship of the land, which was granted to us by the great childless god-king, Asterion. My name, Asterius, is a play on both of these things. My mother was born a princess, my grandfather's only child by the only woman he ever loved; a grand woman named Hylcallis, whom I never had the privilege to meet. Elaía was used to wealth and power, but the power that her father came to wield, the great power of the ancients married to a force of dedicated soldiers, engineers and scholars, awed her tremendously. Before her eyes she saw our home city of Knossos raised up from the rubble heap into a semblance of its former glory. When she was a babe, Knossos was a muddy patch of ruins, a horrible reminder of the volcanic waves that wiped clean the works of the previous kings of Crete. But by the time she strode into adulthood it possessed temples and palaces of stone to rival those of the Nile.

Before long, people came to call the city by our name. The family of Minos had not merely reclaimed the glory of the previous Cretan civilization, but the great power of the ancients, a power to rival the gods themselves! She was a true believer even before I was born, but afterwards, it seemed as if my grandpa's ambitions were heavenly ordained. She was my whole world for so long; I had her more or less to myself through most of my childhood, if only because my other family members were so busy with the affairs of the state.

My father, Arbias, distinguished himself with his tremendous prowess in sport and martial competition at a young age, and was the youngest member of the crew when he was selected by my grandfather to accompany his expedition force to the east. By the time he had achieved young adulthood by the standards of our people, he had a list of accomplishments most men would be proud to die with. Many men had died in his general vicinity to add to that list, of course. He bathed himself in blood, and his glory only ever increased for it. I suppose that might explain his own vision for how I was to be treated, so that I might gain in glory.

Over the years of talking with my mother about it, I got the distinct impression that it wasn't her that fell in love with Arbias, so much, as it was my grandfather who did. Who better to carry on the name, First in War, than this invincible warrior? The fact that he was one of the few men in his crew that seemed to have some understanding of the marvelous things they were uncovering cemented my grandfather's opinion of him. He was to marry his daughter, and be the future king. And so it was. Auro always got his way.

Of course, if Minos was to be the seat of power for the whole world, our control over Crete had to be secured first. That terrible disaster a few centuries back had shattered the previous civilization that had lived here, and the Minos family taking the reins was not fully embraced by everyone on the island. This despite the blessing of my namesake, the old God King of the Sea, whose wise rule in the aftermath of the disaster saved the peoples of both Crete and Hellea. Even now, several generations later, the eastern part of the island was not fully on board with rule by Minos. Cleaning up this resistance, and cementing control of the critical small islands that surround us, for purposes of controlling trade and staging future conquests, became Arbias' work. He threw himself into this task with his typical passion. Auro barely had to direct him, and I'm sure it pleased him endlessly that he had selected a man of such boundless ambition to be his heir. Even after this work was done he spent far more time at the eastern fortress at Zakros, or to the west at the base of the White Mountains training our forces, than at the palace here in the center of the island. I'm sure that suited mother just fine, unlike my older brother's perpetual absence, which did nothing but make her worry.

Androgeos. Thinking of him fills my stomach with frogs and moths. He was beautiful, and perfect in his form, marrying the rugged strength and stature of my father's frame with my mother's graceful face and flawless bronze skin. When I was a child I wanted nothing more than to have his face. So that I could meet the eyes of another person without them turning away. So that I could walk beyond these walls. Maybe never return. No one said no to him, even if they dared; all he had to do was smile and most everyone would go along. He came and went as he pleased. But he rarely stayed for long, and when he did I was far less a concern to him than the stream of women who would pass in and out of his chambers, or his endless pursuit of sport and martial prowess. I can hardly recall him even speaking to me when I was a child, but to make me the object of fascination to some young woman, or the object of gawking ridicule to the circle of athletes and warriors he paraded around with. Not that he was without his accomplishments. By the age of sixteen the final decision on matters of trade had fallen into his hands. Though he was a youth, he was savvy, and he was family, and was thus trusted more than the merchants under our employ. This also suited him as it gave him the means and the excuse to travel to every sporting competition around the sea. Thus involved in them, he often found great success. Nothing could stand between him and the throne, and ultimate glory. Except his own damned self, of course.

When I finally broke from my reverie, some time had passed. I arose to my feet, and placed one hand against the wall to steady myself. The chasm beckoned, but it wouldn't catch me today. I tried to judge by the ache in my muscles, and the tension in my neck, how much time had passed. A few more hours till nightfall, I would wager. I was tired enough for a nap, and it would be best to do so soon, if I wanted to make any use of the night. So I made my lonely commute, in the dark, to my bed. I didn't even bother to light my lamp again before I crawled between my furs, and fell fast asleep.

Three

On the second day of our voyage, the clear green waters of the sea were so perfect, and trouble free, I almost fooled myself into thinking this was a pleasure cruise. It had been so long since I had been on the water, and I must have missed it terribly. The crisp sea air brought forth countless happy childhood memories, and the glassy waves reflected a smile that I felt embarrassed to wear, in light of our fate. Not everyone was so lucky. Sinia, the voice I couldn't place the day before, had fully lost his sea legs, and was in misery, hanging off the side of the deck. Even when he wasn't face to the surf, he couldn't bear to show his face, probably because he was a fisherman's son. He was ashamed. After a few hours of this, I felt pretty bad for him, so I took the place next to him on the deck cushions to talk.

"Sinia? How are you feeling?" His face was buried in the space between his knees, but he looked up, considered for a moment, and spoke.

"Yes, much better. My guts belong out there. I'll leave some of me in the sea."

"I think I have something that might calm your stomach, if you wouldn't mind trying it." I began to reach for my bag, and the compact apothecary we were trained to have on hand at all times.

"Would you stop it."

"What, I... "

"Stop trying to be a hero, and fix everything. What does that get you? You're in no better place than I. Let me rest." He then returned his face to that space between his knees. He wasn't wrong. I didn't leave, but I did let him rest, as I quietly considered what it meant to be a hero.

"Your father seems to think I am to make a hero of you."

"Athena herself told hi... ."

"Men always go before the gods. Where do you think your lady of wisdom got the idea?"

I simply didn't know what to say to that. My new host coughed out a rude word, and awkwardly turned his torso before his legs decided to move in the same general direction, away from me.

"Your father is a fool, and he is disrupting everything." Without facing me, and choosing to yell from about 20 paces away to magnify the indignity, he barked out, "Red rag is on your shack. Three ladies gave up their beds for you, that should be enough for a prince, even the prince of a fish stand." And then he ran off into the woods, as only four horse legs can carry you.

In the clearing, on a rise near the brook we had been following for most of the day, stood nine or so small triangular homes, made of split wood and thatching. Each had a peak opening away from the door, to vent a fire on those rare occasions when they would need heat in the winter. Anything worse than a frost would probably send everyone scrambling to the larger communal house for the night. This larger house was of a design I had not seen; something like an arch made of timbers, joined and daubed at the seams with tar. An arched door jutted out from one side, and had its own arched roof to keep it plumb and covered. To me it seemed akin to a boat flipped on its top. Judging by the array of implements hanging outside of the one end, it also served as the village kitchen.

"I think you should go, Ailen."

"You sure, this seems like a cold reception."

"He's right though, this is imposing on them. You saw that angry crowd of women." We had passed several of the students whose studies had been disrupted on my behalf along the way, as they hoofed it back to one of the larger Lapith camps at the head of the river. They were not at all interested in our greetings, and just glared at us. It was clear that this crowd of women could have ended us easily, but chose not to, so we were a bit shaken by the experience. "Look, head home and tell dad I was accepted into Chiron's," I looked around at the tiny village in the woods, "school. Tell him all is well.

I'm sure he is having a bad time of it, with his only son being chosen and all."

"Thesius... you've been too good to us. I can't believe you've only been around for 12 years with you speaking wise like that. Athens won't be as much fun without you spreading your joy all over." He was actually choking up a bit. It always amazed me, the impression I left on people simply by being kind. "Farewell."

I waved briefly as he left, before gathering my bundle of effects against my side and walking towards the school. Four young men were waiting for me there, sitting under the small copse of olive trees that the structures encircled.

"Hey look, it's our little prince!" Everyone gracefully rose to their feet with startling, practiced speed. I had a momentary urge to run, but instead I tempered my will and walked confidently forward. Most of these boys were older and larger than me, but I stood half a chance with my face towards them, if they wanted a fight. The smallest one walked to the fore, and squared up. Looking over them, the school uniform appeared to be variations on the theme of skins and rope. Not that different from the other Lapiths, really. "Look around, Chiron's great school! All five of us, you included. Everyone else had to run away from your cursed penis."

"All the best hunters, all the best cooks." This youth was less in control, in every sense, but the first gave him room to speak, "We're all gonna be hungry, and cold all night, and... " At this point he lost track of his words and started punching the air and grunting angrily. He was larger, but seemed younger.

The first one spoke over his fellow student's assault on the air, in a more friendly tone. "Look, we're all doing our very best to not hate you. I'm Hillian. Punchy over there is Zeno, Pythius has the bad eye, and Boreo is the dark one."

I saw my opportunity, "Boreo, you must be from across the sea. We have a family in Athens that looks a lot like you. Came back on the oil ship when I was a baby, been doing pretty well. They make the best bread in town, people line up in the morning for it."

"That sounds good, I may have to try it if I ever end up down that way. Maybe taste a bit of home." He smiled broadly; my charms were working. "It will be nice not to be the second strangest person around anymore. Your hair beats my skin, I think." Not to mention my skin. It was a good bit lighter than Boreo's, but it had a red tone that made me look a bit like I was blushing all the time. Most people just thought I had a bit of the sunburn I never suffered from when they first met me, so that never got as much attention, even if it was just as rare.

"People 'round here inland aren't used to your skin, huh? We see people like you all the time on the coast, trading and such. The sea isn't so wide. Oh, but if you think my hair is strange, look at my eyes!" I pulled down my cheek for effect. Zeno whistled, and everyone crowded in for a closer look.

"They're green, like the sky!"

"Or the shallow water, out by the sea. "

"So pretty." It was a chorus I was tired of, but in this circumstance it was a welcome song. I was almost certainly not gonna get a thrashing, regardless of whether I deserved it.

At that moment, I heard an odd whistle behind me, and the gang snapped to attention. I surmised that our teacher had returned, so I turned around and imitated their respect, though he had hardly earned it yet.

Chiron was an intimidating figure. As the years of my schooling wore on I would come to understand that his demeanor sprang forth from his endless suffering, but at this point I was just afraid of him. He towered over all of us, and his torso was also proportional to his lower frame, which made him frighteningly huge as he stood before me. His beard and hair were long like a wild man, but very well kept. Many tiny flowers were tied in his hair, and it was all bundled into neat tails, probably to keep it out of his face in the wind. He was also naked, save for a leather bag he carried, secured around his waist and shoulder to keep it from shifting. Not that it mattered, as he had no interesting bits on display; the place where most men would show

24

proud was just a smooth panel of muscle. This was, mercifully, covered in the jet black fur that began about where his navel would be, if he had one. Even so, the sight was unnatural, mildly nauseating.

"Stop looking at where my rope should be, boy."

"Sorry, I... uh... "

Chiron burst out laughing, a clap and roll of thunder that bounced off the trees in the clearing. "Men are all the same, you can't help but look. I know, it makes ya feel ill, huh? That's not at all what I am for. Now, let's take a look at you." He pulled a strange metal rod from his bag and knelt down before me. "Just a few things, same look over every little hero gets. Now, open your eyes and look at me." I looked down the length of the rod. Inside of it was a very distant eye, in various lovely shades of red, like the leaves of the trees in Autumn. Not unlike Chiron's, but upside down. Years later my teacher would use the same instrument to teach me about light, and how it can be bent if you have the right means. "Ah, fascinating, so long since I've seen eyes like these." He directed the rod toward my cheeks, which were probably extra red with the attention. "And your skin, such an intriguing color. In that combination... I could swear I was looking at someone from another time. You are... Athenian? The fishing people by the coast?"

"People... say I've been touched by the gods."

"More likely your mother was touched by someone. Possibly a god."

"She wouldn't, she said... "

"It's not my concern. But, you were always an oddity, yes?"

I wasn't at all liking this, but my ride was already too far away to catch. "Yes... I got attention. Didn't always like it."

"Good! Can't have a 'hero' getting along too easily with everyone. You might just go along with some bad notion to make people happy. Then you'd not be a very good hero. I noticed you managed to calm the storm around here in my absence. Well done, I expected I would have to treat your injuries when I returned. Might still have to, after this." He returned to his full height, and addressed

the small crowd, "All the ladies homes? We gotta move them, I have
selected another spot. They're gonna learn there and you're gonna
learn here. They'll have a cart or two up here before sundown so get
to work."

"We are just gonna… move the homes?" This was a new concept
to me.

"We don't set our posts in the stone here, like you do in Athens."
Pythius spoke, his voice smooth and sweet. I rather wanted to hear
him sing. "You'll see, it's easier to break them down than you think.
The thatching on the roof comes off in rolls, like blankets. Just watch
the first one." The four of them grabbed long rods, each about twice
the length of a tall man, from brackets on the side of one of the homes,
and got to work. First they untied a series of knots from one side of
the roof, and then placed one of the rods against the edge of the roof.

"We put tools on these and use them to tend to our trees, but this
is why they are all the same length." Hillian said this without looking
at me, as he tied the edge of the thatching to the rod. They then rolled
the thatching up. The other two were already bringing up benches,
which they stepped up on as they moved over the crest of the
triangular structure. Within minutes the roof was off and bundled on
the ground. At this point, it was clear that the whole structure was
held together with rope and knots, which were strung through a
series of rods. The only solid bits were the front and the back, which
were made of boards which were slotted into the corner frames. The
boards themselves then had grooves in them, top and bottom. The
whole kit came apart in less time that it would take to make a light
meal in a well kept kitchen.

"This is amazing work." I said, examining the grooving on the
boards. Each one interlocked with the one above and below it, and
was better made than anything I had seen back home. The front set
made room for the door, which also broke down into panels after the
knots which held together its frame were removed. I couldn't believe
how flat the boards were, and how perfectly they mated with each
other.

26

"You think the Lapiths are primitive because they like their skins and their bare feet?" My teacher was smiling at me, he must have known most of the people of Hellea had this opinion of them. "They remember enough to know how much they have forgotten. It's why I choose to live here. Now, your turn. Hillian, you've been doing this your whole life, time to take a break. If the fish prince starts to mess it up yell at him. I've got to go take a shit." And he trotted off.

Besides nearly stabbing Zeno in the face with the rod on the way over the peak, my first roof removal went without incident. The two of us then took our place steadying the frame, while the other two worked on the knots on the inside.

"Not sure why he needs to run off like that. Horses don't smell that bad."

"Oh, gods!" Zeno burst out, "No, it's not like a horse. It's like a horse, and a man, and death itself. It's... "

"It's the worst smell." Pythius had a sparkle in his right eye, and a knowing grin on his face. His left eye was a hollow socket, which, to my eyes, only slightly marred his face. "If he gets his tummy upset at night and doesn't make it way away from camp, whooeeeee! It makes fish tails smell like fresh bread."

"Yes, none of us get a wink of rest." Boreo had just finished untying his side, and he spoke as the rest of us lowered the front of the structure to the ground; he door made this side a bit heavier. "We only lie there in misery and pray to the winds above to turn it away from us. It's just terrible. Really, though, it's the only bad thing about him. If he seems grumpy, it's his stomach that's doing it to him. He never gets mad at us."

Before long, we had a second structure bundled up and ready to go. I felt pretty accomplished, and kinda tired, as I leaned against a rod. Hillian clapped me on the back, "Well done, you learn fast. Only six more to go! Hades, I might even help if Chiron takes his time coming back."

Chiron did take his time coming back, but Hillian ended up pitching in after a while. Before the sun had touched the tree-line we had the buildings torn down and sorted into neat piles. Even so, I was more tired than I had ever been when our teacher and a few of the ladies in his tutelage arrived, driving two carts and horses.

"Ah, is the fish prince tired? Good, less risk of you ruining everything with one of my young women."

"I'm twelve." I didn't even sit up, "And I'm smart. I watch the older men making fools of themselves. When I turn into a fool, tie me down or something, gods!"

"I'm simply acting under the orders of your father, who thinks he can order me around. You are to have no contact with women. That's what he says."

"I'm not gonna... "

"Have an urge you can't stop? I'm not inclined to bet. In a more elevated age, I might expect more of you. But most men are like pigs. They lack self control if anything they want is before them. I expect no more of my students then I expect of any other man, in that respect. I'm not here to reform those urges, just bring some civilization to you lot of savages. But besides that," Now, he loomed over me, blocking the Sun. How could he move so quietly? I rose to my feet, every muscle in my body complaining. Before I could fully regain my balance he had taken me by the shoulder, locking my eyes in his gaze, "What about your self, your very life? Are you enough of a hero that you wouldn't dodge certain death if all you need to do is lay down one night and tell everyone?"

"Then Minos comes and burns us agai… "

"Your father can find another man who hasn't touched a woman, they aren't that rare. Just lie about the age if need be. "

"And if he does that then Athens will... They'll just murder him. If the rules don't apply to me like they did to the other kids… "

"All of this is about your father, what about you?"

"I... " I had been trying not to think about me. "I try not to think about me." My teacher, who still had a firm grip on my shoulder, appraised me.

28

"You're not telling me lies. Interesting... Yes, it will be fun making a hero of you, even if it is only to cast you away." He released me from his grip, and returned again to his full height. "All the stuff goes in the carts. Get to work, the men can take the nearest cart. Boreo, go cook some of my gruel, there won't be time for much else so we all get to enjoy it tonight." A few of the young men groaned at this, and the ladies catcalled from the other side of the carts, which was apparently far enough from my soft bits for safety.

"We're eating at big camp tonight."

"Not even cooking!"

"So nice, huh."

After doing more work than I had ever done in a day, once again, my hosts graciously let me retire to a cot made of rope, sticks and stretched skins while they cleaned up and finished dinner. I was a bit ashamed of myself. I didn't think myself so coddled, and I could easily run circles around the youths back in Athens. But every one of Chiron's student's surpassed me physically. The best I could manage as the ladies departed was a half-hearted wave, while prone on my back. They responded to that with an entirely deserved chorus of insults. I didn't even have my age as an excuse; one of the girls was younger than I, but she wasn't collapsed on the ground by the end of it.

The other side of this agony was the delight of the cot itself. The leather surface was supported by a clever web of ropes, which linked together with the legs and supported the whole thing. I'd never rested on such a comfortable surface before. It made the wool batting I'd used all my life seem crude and lumpy, almost a punishment by comparison. I resolved to get one of these for myself when I made it back home.

The realization that I would probably never again have the opportunity to sleep a night in Athens brought me back to my waking state just in time to eat a filling, but immensely boring meal.

It all went by so fast. Chiron was so expert at the art of teaching, at making every day an exciting adventure, that you hardly noticed the days bleeding into weeks, the weeks into seasons, the seasons into years. The difficulty with dealing with two camps was quickly resolved by a bit of creative scheduling and fast hoof work. Chiron was an expert at both of these things, and the boys camp made up for it by tirelessly providing their teacher with his stew to eat. His plain food was the only thing he didn't savor the flavor of, every other aspect of nature had unveiled its secrets to him by his endless, patient observation. The woods was his preferred classroom, and every leaf and insect provided him with his lessons. The depth of his knowledge about all things above and below the earth never ceased to amaze me. And though we would occasionally cross paths with the other camp, it was always under his watchful eye. This inconvenient arrangement was on my behalf, but Chiron eventually warmed up to me. My charms never ceasing, after all.

The fact that I showed little interest in sneaking over to the girls' side, unlike most of my classmates, did bring my teacher some comfort. I thought I was being dutiful, but I suppose my teacher had known enough men to know better. Three years after my arrival, after several younger students had joined our school, Zeno and Boreo made their way over to the other camp, and stayed there. Boreo made sure Pythius and I had a good handle on the cooking first, of course. On the occasion of this arrangement being formalized, my teacher and I had a notable, but typically brief, conversation on the topic.

"This arrangement is more typical, isn't it?" I said, as I unloaded the last of Zeno's things from the cart. One of our little homes had come along for the ride as well. At this point, my teacher was no longer concealing the location of the ladies camp from me, so I had come along for the ride. "You know, for the school. How does that... work?"

"The same way it always works. I'm here to turn your mud into a heroic vase, not change it into some other material entirely. By the time they leave, they are adults, what do you expect they should do?"

He turned and smiled at me through his braided beard. That was my cue to answer, but how?

"Well... I don't know, back home most men prefer their women to come without the attachment of children, so... "

"Men often get some silly notion of ownership over women. Regardless, the silverseed fixes that. My wealth is such that it is easy to provide, if only to save myself the headache." He must have seen the look on my face, as his own face practically split with a smile. "Now child, you know I have resources, why so surprised?"

"It's such a valued thing! The adults back in Athens would practically break out in fights over the shipments of silverseed that would come in."

"There are few things more valuable than joy without worry. Children are a joy, but... they are all the worries in the world, are they not?"

"So you just let them," I waved my hands at the school, "Get down, have fun?"

"It is less of a distraction on their studies than if I do not. My personal quest is not to change what you are." He laughed once, like the strike of a bell, and continued. "I would be a worse fool than I am. I would be frustrated endlessly. Even more so than I am. I just seek to elevate you, as best as I can." But now, he moved in for the kill. "Besides, it seems to me that you and Pythius have been keeping each other warm at night quite a bit of late. Is there no joy to be found in that bed?" I stammered, and tried to reply. "Speak not of it. It is better that youth should explore such things with youth. I have seen such fragile experiences bartered off to the highest bidder far too often in my time. Men have this disgusting tendency to grasp at their own youth, by depriving those that follow them of their innocence. If I send fewer innocent people into this world to be taken advantage of, and so wounded, then I am making stronger people for it. And that is all I have to say on the matter." And, indeed it was, he never spoke of it again.

He wasn't wrong, of course. Pythius and I had become very fond of each other. And he wasn't wrong in the other sense, as well. It was a blessing to explore such things with another youth, rather than having them forced upon me through some more businesslike arrangement. Such things fell into the same category of behaviors as selling off your daughters marriage rights before they can walk, or looking the other way while someone trading in lives makes their way through your patch of sea. Which is to say, it was frowned upon, but common regardless.

Before long, I had no trouble keeping up with the other students, physically or mentally. My own natural gifts showed themselves in the light of my training, too. Everyone came to trust my sharp hearing, and I could easily trace most anyone moving through the forest by sound alone. Only Chiron never ceased to be able to sneak up on me. His body was clumsy, and his lower half sometimes seemed to have a mind of its own, but he never struck a stick or a dry leaf as he walked. It was like magic, but I knew it was practiced skill.

Eventually, my teacher came to value my questions. Not that I understood everything he said, of course, but I knew how to organize my thoughts a bit so that I could ask a good, deep question, instead of an endless series of shallow ones. He loved that, and allowed me a few probing questions I'm sure other students wouldn't have gotten an answer for.

Besides that clear appreciation for my patient curiosity, and those accommodations that were needed to preserve me for my fate, he never treated me any differently from any of the other students. When some wondrous being came to visit, there were no favorites. Satyrs and Dryads would often drop by, for a dance and a song with Chiron. We all got a chance to greet them, and learn from them whatever mad thing they cared to impart that day. Even the other centaurs, despite their general distaste for humanity, would bear our presence to sit and smoke with their friend for a while. So I knew something extraordinary was happening when he burst into my little home one night, and called for me, and me alone to accompany him. Even more strangely, Pythius seemed taken by a stupor, and would not awaken when I attempted to excuse my absence. So I arose, and dressed, following him into a clearing deep in the forest. I was still half asleep. As I wiped the sand from my eyes, I broke the silence.

"Why have you brought me out to the woods, teacher? I'm a bit cold, but mostly confused."

"Shh, do you hear it?" I closed my eyes, and listened. Nothing. No insects, no wind. Even the birds were silent.

"What is happening? It's so eerie."

"Everything is in quietude, before her etheric energies. Be at peace, your Pallas comes. Watch: there!" He pointed to the sky, and there I saw the manifesting of my goddess.

First there were lines in the darkness, somehow more dark than the night, crisscrossing the patch of sky before us. They drew together into a great weave, and this weave closed, and folded. Seeing this thing, without form or depth, making itself before me nearly tossed me from my feet, and I had to steady myself on my teacher's flank as I conquered that moment of vertigo. By the time I had regained my composure, the black form had taken the shape of a cushion, taller than a man, which landed upright before us. The moment this envelope touched the ground it unfolded, like a flower in the morning light, and came to rest upon the armor on her shoulders as a cloak of perfect darkness. Her eyes, grey and glowing with their own light, pinned me to the spot. They shone forth from a face so perfect[2] I could not bear it if I was not so transfixed. It was cast from perfect bronze, but alive, and so terribly aware. She was wearing armor, in much the same fashion I'd always seen her depicted, though perhaps more practical in form, and less ornate. There was an easy casualness to her stance, as if it weighed nothing at all, though there was hardly an inch of her above the wrist that wasn't covered in shining metal. She

---

2 Only in regard to the gods does Thesius mean perfect in the modern sense, which is to say, to be without flaw. There are translation problems involved.

appraised me, for what seemed like an eternity, before she broke her gaze and spoke to my teacher.

"You've done well. He has grown strong and wise in your teaching. Thank you, Chiron."

"I did nothing different by him than any of my other students. I deserve no more credit than that."

She smiled at this, wryly, before she turned and addressed me. "Thesius, son of Aegeus, I have seen fit to equip you for your labors, and I have found a method to provide for you once you have entered the land of our enemy. I have come here tonight to see you for myself, to tell you what you must do, and give you what you need. Do you understand?" I nodded respectfully, though I honestly didn't understand anything that was happening at that moment. "Good. I feel you are fit for our purpose. You have two objectives in the land of our enemy." Two?! "First, you must shut the mouth of death that is swallowing up the people of Athens, by killing the godling of Minos in their temple of blood. Then, if you succeed in this, there is another matter to attend to. High in their tower is a sphere, composed of silver and gold, about so large." She held her hands out, to a width that was about two of my feet. "It will be humming, as if it is full of bees. You must take this thing and smash it upon the ground."

"I take it this machine is the reason you are sending a child to do this work." Chiron did not seem as awed by the presence as I was. I could hardly imagine speaking, let alone questioning her.

"Yes, it has prevented us from so much as looking over their workings. A source of endless frustration." Her face softened with concern, almost as if she were a brilliant woman instead of a brilliant impression of one. With the perfect hardness of her face, the growing terror within me also fell away, and I felt far more at peace. "I know I ask so much of you. I do not share the opinion of so many of my fellow gods, regarding the value of a man's life. If you manage your first task, you will have the advantage of a backdoor entrance, and surprise. These things are not to be taken lightly. If you manage your second task, we may be able to arrange a quick escape for you."

34

"May?" I was very glad Chiron was there to ask these questions for me, I was speechless.

"I cannot say how long the effect will persist after its destruction. I have experience with but one, and what kind of wisdom bases a firm answer off of one example?"

"None at all, of course. I might have taught you that myself, if you weren't just so perfectly wise. That was for our hero's benefit; he deserves to know the risks."

"Indeed, but enough of the dangers you face. I come with gifts." She lifted her right hand with endless grace, and beckoned with her open palm, and then I noticed the tree stump she was standing next to. Was it her brilliance that hid it from me, or some other trick? It was so large, like a table, how could I have missed that? Her gifts were arrayed on a folded piece of fine fabric, which was the most true red I had ever seen, like fresh blood. There were three objects, two of which seemed somewhat familiar. The sword, resting in a simple sheath, showed a familiar shape through its leather home, but the handle betrayed a wholly different construction. Strange holes were placed along its back length in a way that I had to assume had a purpose, piercing the pommel and the handle all the way through. The knife that sat next to it was of similar construction, but had some complication to it around the middle I didn't understand. It was unsheathed, and the blade itself seemed to be made of silver, or some other shiny metal. It was most unlike the bronze I was used to. The only ornamentation they wore was their shape, and it was beautiful, purposeful. In the glint of their forms I noticed that the third object, a small thing placed at the corner of the cloth, was giving off light. The lamp was about the size and shape of a large pine cone, with the ends removed. The light it shed was novel to me; green, like the moonlight, it cast a sharp, unwavering glare across the tabletop in a tight band. I cleared my throat, and steadied my nerves.

"May I?"

"I brought them so you might familiarize yourself with them. Of course." I stepped forward, and took the lamp from the cloth. "He took the eternal flame first. Under any normal circumstance I would be very impressed." This was clearly addressed to my teacher.

"How will he know where to stick his sword in that dark place, without a light?" Chiron asked, rhetorically. Wisdom didn't bother to answer. The lamp was smooth on all sides, like an eggshell, but had a pair of seams down the middle you could just feel with your fingertips. These divided the thing into two parts with a band in the middle.

"Yes, you are so close!" Athena said, with surprising enthusiasm, "Twist it. The top and the bottom do different things." Ah, that was the key! I gently played with it. At one extreme the marvelous thing was painfully bright, far too bright to look at. But at the other extreme, before it stopped producing light at all, it barely rivaled the sliver of a moon we stood under. With a twist on the other side it would open from a thin beam to a circle of light, casting forth from every angle. And every change came with a satisfying little click, like a beetle playing in my hand, and stayed firmly in place until I changed it again. It was by far the most amazing thing I had ever held. I could have played with it all night.

"Now, the sword." Athena smiled down upon me. At least she appreciated my own enthusiasm. "I favor a spear, myself, but the lair of the beast has many twisting passages, so it wouldn't be a wise choice." I picked the sword up, and stepped back a few steps so I could safely appraise it. I was very pleased to see that my initial assessment was correct; it resembled the single edged chopping swords that the Lapiths preferred. "Not a Xiphos; we have been watching you, and your preferences." The purpose of the many holes was clear as soon as I held it; even sheathed, it was amazingly light. I unsheathed it, to reveal a blade of the same silvery metal as the knife, with a continuation of the rounded triangular holes all along the back spine. I brought it to bear, and swung it around a few times, in the same manner I had slain so many reeds before, but had to check myself. It was so light I was putting too much muscle into it. I adjusted, and before long I was swinging it as if it was an extension of

36

my hand. This may have only been the second most amazing thing I had ever held, but I still could have played with it all night.

"Now, this last boon is less a gift from me than from the smith. I only ordered a sword, and he delivered a sword and a knife. I asked him why, and he said 'A sword has but one use. A knife has many uses.'" She related his words in an alarming monotone, before returning to her own voice. "I can see the wisdom in that, so you are also getting a knife." She lifted it from the table swiftly, and indexed it back and forth from one position to another with immense grace, like the warrior she is. "Look, press here, near the middle. It folds! No need to even have a sheath for it. Now, take it." We briefly touched as she passed it to me. I was expecting the cold rigidity of marble, but she was warm and soft.

The knife did, indeed, fold. It unfolded too, and would no doubt do the countless things you can do with a knife besides that. I couldn't deny the utility of the gift. I played with the mechanism a few times to make sure I knew it. When extended, it didn't seem any less solid than any other knife I had ever held, though it was hard to judge because it was also very light. My capability for amazement was reaching a point of exhaustion. I placed the knife back upon the cloth, and stepped back to the safety of my teacher's side. The heat radiating from his flank was immensely comforting, and familiar.

"Good, and now I must spirit these away to Crete."

"No. He is not done." Somehow, this was the most astonishing thing yet. Chiron was talking to her like she was a student, just flatly denying her! "He must familiarize himself with the sword. Carry it. Get used to its rigging, and how it rides. I am not pleased to send one of my heroes into battle with equipment he is not sufficiently familiar with."

"Time is of the essence, and... "

"There are months to spare, I know how fast you people can walk. Is this so you can keep this whole affair a secret from your father?" Chiron pitched his head a bit to the side, an exaggerated motion not unlike a curious dog. At this point I had to consciously close my mouth, so that I wouldn't attract flies; he was straight up arguing with her! Athena scowled, but her face quickly returned to statuesque placidity.

"Must we talk about this here, before the youth?"

"As you have a repeated tendency to vanish as soon as *you* think the conversation is over, I see no alternative." He crossed his arms. How was he still alive? How did he have such sway over a god? Wisdom considered her words, and spoke.

"My father favors a winner. And Minos has been achieving an endless series of victories; I cannot deny that. I have counseled him that allowing a new god to arise in this way mirrors the way we rose up, and came to overthrow our parents. But... "

"But he has little mind for words of Wisdom, eh?" Chiron was smiling broadly, in the way he did when he had one of us pinned on a point of ill logic.

"No." She shifted her weight to her other foot. This whole line of inquiry was not at all to her liking. "But I must act as my own wisdom demands. I am not without allies; Hephaestus had no reservation in arming you. Hermes pledges his assistance, if he can provide it. And my father... isn't invested. If Minos fell, he would find another entertaining empire-in-wanting to dote upon. I am not concerned about his wrath."

"It must be a comfort, to be so unconcerned. You're unlikely to get hit the next time he feels like swinging his rope around. I care not whether I live or die, and yet I am not care free, for their sake. No one truly deserves such wrath. Do you not see the wisdom in that?" She did not reply, for a long moment. The air quivered with anticipation. Wisdom simply nodded. "So, he will have no more time to train with his tools?"

"No."

"Then at least the boy knows why he is taking such a risk. I concede the necessity of it." Athena waved her hand dismissively, and in a moment, the cloth folded carefully around the gifts, lifted a few inches from the stump, and flew away like a frightened bird. The stump remained; I must have simply missed it before. Before I could think about it too long, my teacher gently thumped me on the back of the head with his large, open hand. "Say something, it is your right."

"I... " What could I say? "Thank you for your blessings. Thank Hephaestus for me. For the tools. And the other gods, for their assistance."

"I will pass along your thanks, but I must speak truthfully. The eternal flame was something I picked out from our pile of treasures. I suppose the smith could make such a thing, but he would have to make many other things first, in order to use those things to make that thing. I would take... decades. Too long." She smiled, "It is wise to use what you can make, what you can find, and what you are given. To forgo a tool is to cut yourself off from the possibilities that tool gives you. Remember that, and what Chiron has taught you, and you may yet survive." And with those closing words, her cloak closed around her once more, and she was gone.

"The very moment she thinks the conversation is over." My teacher turned, and looked me over. "What are you so afraid of?"

"I don't... You! I'm afraid of you! How are you still standing?" The muscles in my chest were quivering. My legs were like jellyfish underneath me.

"Now Thesius, sit down." Chiron reclined. I'd so rarely seen him off his feet, and I didn't understand. "Please, I insist." He grabbed me by the shoulder, and gently pulled me down against his side. "That was an awful lot to experience, and the night air is cold. It could do you harm. Practice your breathing, and lean against my flank. I'll try to explain a bit. But my words about this do not leave this glade, understand." I nodded, and huddled against him. I was shivering now. "Think about the stories. You all know them, they wouldn't work if you didn't. Athena's father, speak not his name, but tell me what his role is."

"He is the heart of all storms, the all father."

"Yes, storms and father of all things. Great power, in that. But tell me, in the stories, did he himself have a father?" I considered this question for a moment. Was this some point of philosophy I had forgotten, a little rhetorical trap?

"Yeah... he tried to eat them." Why was I so cold? I huddled against my teacher, even closer.

"So, the all father... has a father? The storms, they raise all that is green from the earth. You have learned the whole journey, from the rise of the water into the clouds, the fall, and the slow return to the ocean. Do you suppose that precious fall of water, the crack and bolt of new life, only began with him? What of the trees?"

"I... " How could they have? "I suppose not."

"The gods, all of them, represent a thing. They can not precede the thing they represent. It is man's regard for that thing which gives it power, and no power can spring from nothing. It's a terrible power, but it also binds them. He once embodied wisdom as well. He did not care to do wisdom's bidding, and be bound by it, so he threw it away. That those two find themselves in conflict is no surprise." He looked down at me, some genuine concern in his ancient golden eyes, "Are you steady again?" I was not, and I shook my head. "A few more minutes, then. But you'd be best back in your warm bed, it would do you good now." I leaned back, for warmth, but also to pin him down.

"You didn't answer my question, though. No one defies them like you just did. How?"

"Hah, you insist? Tell me, how old do you think your goddess is?" He waited a long moment before answering, "I'd say she was about 500 years old. Her father is a bit older, of course." That span of time, ten good long lifetimes or more, was tremendous. I could hardly comprehend it. "Now, how old do you think I am?"

"Older?" It was the obvious answer, but also a difficult choice.

"I stopped counting, but I would bet I've been on this world for more than 9000 years." He paused, and let me catch my breath, "I've seen gods and goddesses come and go, as their empires of men rose and fell. When I was made, ice gripped this world, now it's nothing but this blasted heat. The men who made us, made us for their amusement. It wasn't convenient for them, that we should die, except at a time of their choosing. But they are gone, and we are still here. We cannot even choose to die... That choice was taken from us." I gazed up, and I'd never seen such a sad face; I felt a tiny bit of his pain, and it was more than I could bear. "We once made a sport of spitting in gods faces, in hope they would end our suffering. But they won't. Maybe they can't. We didn't make them. Perhaps because we are blameless in their creation, we are immune. I don't know."

"Then... that's why there are no women centaurs? You were made, not born?"

"Yes, think of our shape. To give birth to this," he motioned over his form, "would be inevitably fatal. We were grown in vessels of obsidian, with techniques long lost. Showpieces, to demonstrate the improbable skill of our creators. Objects of entertainment. We are not their only orphans, either. I pray you will never meet my sisters, who were made with a purpose in mind."

"A purpose?"

"To kill." He frowned, "My creators were men. More clever, perhaps, but not different from men now. They could have joined the travelers in the stars... But they chose instead to kill. I pray I can make better men, then the men who made me." He paused, for a long time. The night bird sang, and it was a comfort to us both. "You remind me of them, more than I care to admit. But it always felt like you were the better man. Now I am sending you to die." He wrapped his arm around me. I wasn't used to this much warmth from my teacher, but I needed it. "Tell me I haven't failed you... You can lie, if you wish."

"Chiron... I am a far better person than I was when I met you. Far more capable, and wise. If I am to have any chance, that chance is one you gave me. The finest sword in the world wouldn't do me any good if I didn't know where to stick it, and why." Before I knew it, the side arm was a full hug. He ended it by lifting me, bodily, to my feet.

"Good, now let's get you back to that warm bed. If you can't walk, I'll do the indignity of carrying you."

I didn't need Chiron to carry me, not any more than he already had, through all those years of teaching. The walk back with him, in the glimmer of the moonlight, seemed more like a dream than the actual dream that followed, as I reclined in Pythius' strong arms. I wouldn't leave for months yet, but that night felt like my graduation. My teacher had become my friend.

By our fourth day on deck, we had all run out of jokes and mirth. Athenian ships were well shielded from the relentless early summer light, partially by a solid wood railing that rose to waist height, and partially by movable woolen panels which shielded us from the direct gaze of Apollo. There was ample room around the edges, in this shadow, where we could comfortably recline and rest. But the salt spray was biting at us, relentlessly, and (it turned out) most of us had lost our sea legs in our years of isolation. The food we had was good, the best Athens had to offer to their poor doomed children, but between the salt in our eyes, the frogs in our stomachs, and that doom hanging over all of our heads, no one had an appetite.

I looked down at my knot, on the cushion next to me. It was carefully hewn from a single piece of burled oak, with a skin over the bowl. The neck was lopsided, but fit very nicely against my arm. I suppose because it was made for me. A Lapith family had given it to me several months after I had saved a few of their goats from the mire. I heard them bleating in the woods one evening; Chiron thought it would ingratiate ourselves with our hosts if we helped, and he was right.

"If you find yourself in a new place, find something that needs doing, and do it faithfully. Before long, you will be indispensable, not a stranger." He did practice what he preached, but it seemed like we always reaped the rewards. But then again, what did Chiron need that he didn't have?

I turned the pegs, and tested the tone. The salt air had done a number on my strings, and no amount of oil was going to keep them from drying a bit, so I had taken to loosening them when I set it down. I turned each of the three, in turn, to about the right tightness, and strummed them once to make sure they were in tune, at least in relation to one another. Estius looked up, and followed my lead, quickly tuning his own instrument; I set a rhythm, and he picked up the melody. Ah yes, that's a good one, the sailors used to sing that one… I dropped rhythm and picked up harmony when a few people on deck started slapping their palms against the railing in time. And before I knew it, there were pipes and horns! Helea and Miletta had produced simple flutes, but Neame had evidently been hiding an aulos in her bag! She was manipulating it expertly, filling the air with it's quivering note. Kato had also given into the music, and was using the ship's horn in accompaniment. And then, the sailors broke out, their solemnity dashed, as their words rang out across the sea.

> Where do the fishes wait,
> When I go out to search the sea?
> How can I know what bait,
> Is their salt, and their envy?
>
> In mind the time they show,
> Brings the net heavy sown.
> In heart what prey they know,
> Draws them in to the line you tow.
>
> Poseidon waits in the greatest deep,
> To take our lives as we earn our keep.
> Sail by day, and oar by night,
> We fight the waves to earn our bite.

And so, in what seemed like but a moment and also a glorious eternity, we all made merry music as we slipped every closer to our fates. By the end of it, we were blessed with a fine appetite, and I slept soundly that night, for the first time since I had come aboard.

Four

Another day closer to the new sacrifice, and my body was nothing but nervous energy. I paced my cell, and cursed my inability to sleep for as long as I might care, like the bears in the hills. Even my lamp was denied me; there were sure to be a few visitors in and out over the next few days, as they conducted some semblance of ritual in the central chambers. I dare not betray my tricks.

I might not be able to run away, but these halls are still long, and I know them well. And so I ran. I was as blessed for throwing myself forward as I was cursed at standing still; my strange legs and feet made it so joyfully easy to move, but I needed something to lean on if I were to stand. Even my brother, skilled as he was, never beat me in a race once I got the knack of it.

I turned away from the twists, tossing myself off the wall with a practiced bounce, and entered the main chamber. This long colonnade stood in the same place as the grand chamber at the center of most temples. An empty platform stood where the god would normally recline. But for now, it was my gymnasium. I changed direction again, kicking off the platform at this end, and peeling down the center of the chamber. Each time my feet would strike the floor with a hard rap, I would bound one twelfth the length of the room. I counted my foot strikes, and stopped just in time to slide to a stop against the far wall with some force.

"I'm getting better at that. It'll be eleven strides before long." I said, to the darkness. But there was no reply, though countless empty sockets stared down at me. It was easy for me to see, in my mind's eye, those red columns, topped in black marble. The many grinning faces of death, carved into each finial. It was hard to feel joy, in such a dark place. Even the joy of my own body seemed like a cold comfort, under their steady gaze. I sat, my back against one of those columns, fully deprived of the energy that had possessed me moments before.

Death is all about this place, my home. Death is its reason and purpose, and death dictated its very design. It was death that delivered me to this place, and most likely, death that would deliver me from it. And so I sat there, and wept, and thought about death.

Grandfather's death was sudden, as these things often are. He was white around the brow, but spry and fit. Then, one hot day, he was found by a servant, collapsed in the olive grove. He barely got out a few words to his daughter before he said no more.

The funeral was three days later, as is the custom. Everyone on Crete sent their representative with offerings. By choice, or obligation, it hardly mattered. The festivity was on such a scale it seemed more like a gaudy imitation of the Cretan tradition than a proper honoring of it. As was appropriate, I suppose. The family of Minos intended to rule not just this little island, but the whole of the world! I was dressed up like one of the crown jewels for the ceremony, and was then paraded across the square along with those jewels for my father's coronation. I barely remember it. I was unaccustomed to such crowds, and mother gave me some sort of bitter, herbal drink beforehand to calm my nerves. Well, I guess I looked the part; like a regal little puppet. An object of wonderment. As I am.

I wished it could have been more like the funerals of the common people, where they come together to feast with the family of the departed and provide for them. They create clever works of art, representations of the goods of life, to be interred with the deceased as a symbol of love. But Grandfather got no such representations; he was interred with the real thing. The thought of that great heap of treasure and food rotting around him in his stone crypt turned my stomach. Father, likewise, got no feast; he received an endless stream of wealth and excess, as is befitting the future King of the World. So much wine flowed over that week that a number of people breathed their last from drinking too deeply of it. I spent most of it in my room, reading, and praying that the party downstairs wouldn't end up burning down the palace. In retrospect, it would have been better had we all gone up in a great gout of flame. I didn't know my father well enough to know how bad it would get.

Hark! A distant, pleasant sound broke my trance. My ears, prominent by any standard, had grown so sharp down here, barely a whisper would miss them. As they should; I should bear in mind every footstep, if I am to play my part. I made haste; it would do no good to be late. Back, through the twisting passages, along the outer wall toward the latrine. The royal chambers shared some plumbing with my own facility, and this concealed one of the gifts Ma'aht had left for me.

The sweet sound of my mother's playing did call me to it; an alcove in the wall that cleverly concealed a shaft upward. Even on close examination, it might seem to be little more than a ventilation shaft, until the queen did part a certain curtain in her chambers, which would let through a bit of light, and a bit of music. I rapped thrice on the wall of the alcove with the ring on my hand, as was our custom.

"How fares you, my darling child?" My mother's welcome voice pierced the gloom of my temple far better than the trickle of light she was letting in.

"I yet live." I paused for a moment, expecting a reply, but perhaps that answer cut too deep. "Your gifts do always help."

"I have more. The nut cakes you always like; a good package of them. Ariadne told the mess I wanted a plate of them always available in my room; sweet thing, she still thinks of you sometimes. More scrolls, no one seems to miss them. And some lamp oil."

"I live in gratitude." Though, part of me wanted to grouse. Did she think I lived on cakes and sweets? No... I knew what she thought. It was best not to think of it, and best not to give her cause to think of it either. The less my mother and my sister knew, the better off they were. "Three loads then?"

"Yes, no more scrolls and oil together." We shared a little chuckle, in the dark, recalling that disaster. First came down the cakes, wrapped in a clean cloth. I untied the bundle, instinctually, and set it aside. The trickle of light from above wasn't enough to clearly see. It was only a hint of the thing I had lost. I gave the rope a gentle tug, our only handshake, and she drew the rope back for the next trip. Next, the scrolls, also wrapped in a linen. And then finally, gingerly, an amphora of oil, tied around both loops for stability. I prepared my own bundle; a few squares of cloth wrapping from past shipments, and an empty amphora. It wouldn't do to have too many things go missing. I tied it on, and tugged, but... nothing. I looked, but saw no light. Had she been interrupted? I waited, with my heart in my mouth. It didn't ease my concern when an unfamiliar voice called down.

"Asterius?" I paused for a long moment; this was a young woman's voice. Not too likely to be a guard...

"Yes?"

"Oh, it's Ariadne!" She was doing her best to not be too loud in her excitement; it had been a long time since we had last spoken. She quickly drew up my bundle, then returned to the aperture. "Mom got interrupted. Called down for some dreadful court thing." Ariadne never did care much for the messy workings of the state. And she was right, it was all dreadfully boring, if only because my father never trusted anyone enough to do anything independent, or interesting.

"It's been so long, I didn't recognize your voice, my dear sister. How goes things?"

"It's terrible. Father's been in the worst mood since Taitale escaped with his son." This was news to me, but I didn't have time to inquire further before she went on, "Dad thought I had something to do with it just because I fancied his son a bit. I didn't do anything but make sure they had fresh bedding, so they weren't sleeping on the stone! But now I can't see any men at all! Dad says I am to be queen of the world, and I have terrible taste, and no one I like is good enough for me. All of my maids have been betrothed, and here I am, alone." This was the worst thing happening in her life? I was of mixed mind; I wanted to rage, to bellow my agonies. But also, I deeply ached to laugh out loud, and inquire, with my tongue firmly planted in my cheek, how Taitale and his son made it down from the tower. Did they sprout wings and fly? I checked myself. Raging at her would only hurt me, and possibly expose my secret. And she clearly didn't want to talk about Taitale's escape, let alone in a mirthful tone. Love did call to me down this shaft, and I would do my best to send up my love.

"Worry not, my sister, you are but 16 years of age... "

"17 next month!"

"... and, I'm sure your maids aren't that far ahead of you, unless time is going much faster up there in the light than it used to." I smiled. It was easy to imagine us having this sort of light conversation together, up there.

She protested, "Three of them are betrothed! And one has married and left to start her own house."

"And you have a dozen maids at your service. If you lose all of your maids before you lose your maidenhood, then father's court would do something about that, it would be an embarrassment. Besides, what are we to do if you fail to rise as Queen and bear an heir? Select someone like the people on the peninsulas do, by a popularity contest? Can you imagine?" There was a long silence. That had clearly made her think.

"You should be king. You're the eldest."

"Come now, sister, am I being raised up as a king? Here, in this hole?"

"But, grandpa thought you were... "

"Auro's dead. And you never knew him. And none of this is what he would have wanted, no matter what nonsense dad is filling your ears with." I was getting angry, I needed to control my tone. "Grandpa thought I was a herald of the gods, not actually a god." I hissed it through my teeth. Quiet, but it got my point across.

"I... I am sorry brother... The next group from Athens is set to arrive soon. They have been setting up the festival to greet them for a few days now."

"No doubt they will have a wonderful party. You should go dance with them, I'm sure you'll find a lovely suitor."

"Don't be horrible, brother." She was on the verge of tears.

"Why not? Is that not what Father wants me to be? Horrible? A terror to bring the gods themselves down to their knees? What do you think they are casting those people down here into the darkness for?"

"Stop it... "

"Do you think I'm living on the cakes and sweets you throw down this toilet?" This was, truly, unkind. Very nearly a lie.

"No... I'm sorry, I... " She *was* crying now. I felt like there was something else bothering her, but I had already hurt her enough with this conversation.

"Close the curtain, and pretend I'm not down here. Pretend none of this is happening and try... just try to be happy. Just do that for me." And the light was snuffed out, in an instant. I sat down on the hard stone, into an old mark, now too small for my rear. I tried to breath, and pressed my back against the wall. But the darkness pressed in on me, a world without depth or form. I leaned my head back, until my own bones were resting on the limestone, the chill of it instantly penetrating my skull. I let go, and sobbed quietly, as my own tears did flow.

If only things could have stayed the way they were just after Auro left us. Things had not changed much in that time; father was still focussed upon our borders, my brother was still mostly busy with trade and sport. I was stuck in the garden, as usual, but I was happy enough. My mother kept me company; she really was my world at that moment. But still, she was queen with an absent king, and she had a lot to do. Without Auro goading me on, I found myself without a tutor or a guide. I ran wild in the garden for an entire year, but never once did I think to run out the gate. My empty stomach and the promise of a full bowl always kept me there.

Androgeos was fully a young adult now, 19 years on this world, and with a full plate of responsibilities and accomplishments. He was afield so often, on some conquest of trade or sport, that I rarely saw him. I think he was warming to me though. I had taken a minor interest in sport; perhaps it was just to win his heart a bit, perhaps I was just bored. I was large and strong for my age, so I at least gave him some challenge. I was just beginning to love him as a brother. Things seemed as if they had reached a comfortable balance.

He wouldn't make full adulthood, of course. Many men die before they reach maturity. Most raise their families most of the way to young adulthood themselves before their beards go a touch grey, and they earn the distinction of full adulthood. That, unto itself, is not a tragedy. But we all chose how we deal with our losses. Father did not deal with his loss well.

I sometimes wonder if our wrestling in the garden led him to challenge that bull in Athens. It wasn't his usual choice of contest; he preferred to stand toe to toe with other men, and best them personally in some feat of strength or skill. Arbias preferred a version of the story in which all of the men of Hellea he had bested in sport somehow arranged for him to be trampled to death, perhaps by drugging him. This has always seemed convoluted to me: a grand conspiracy would not have been necessary to goad him into doing something foolish to prove his might. A sharp word from a young woman he fancied would have been enough. But whatever the cause, he was gone, and with him went my life.

Any little remnant of kindness that had been left within my father, after a lifetime bathing in the blood of other men, left him with his beautiful, beloved son. His endless ambition, and Auro's vision of the rebirth of the Heaven's Gate, came together into a plan. He had his chosen location, his given godling, and now he had an appropriate source for his human sacrifices. He just needed a man with the sort of vision to make it real; the great inventor who lived on the isle to the west would be ideal.

So he stole him. From my perspective we had just taken down the black banners of mourning, and put out the fires of our offerings to the gods of the sea and the winds, when this new man was in the

50

court, arguing through an interpreter[3] with my father at all hours of day and night. For some reason, I ended up taking care of his son several times. Ithicus, I think? Sweet kid, I think I taught him a few words. But then, the plans were set, the first stones were cut, and it was time to spring his trap. He arranged for a dozen ships to take his revenge; small for an invasion force, but sufficient to commit a great act of murder. A year to a day after my brother's death, they sailed for Athens, armed with one of Auro's greatest discoveries: a weapon.

Such a beautiful, dreadful thing. Auro made sure I was familiar with it; its power was to be mine, in due time. He called it the Sun Eye, or the Fire Eye, or just the Eye, whatever his mood when he spoke of it. And, at least within the court, he did speak of it a lot. It was, perhaps, his favorite discovery. His speculation was that it was created by an even older civilization, the one the people of the Nile still speak of in hushed tones, for fear it might hear them and return; the great lost empire of the Atlantic, that ruled this world when it was still bound by ice and snow.

There have been so many empires of men, and all of them have picked up pieces from the ones that preceded them, and called them their own. The Heaven's Gate was no different. Some of the wonders Auro found were of their creation. Some were taken in trade, from the travelers who came through the gate to buy and sell. And some were recovered from the past. That this great empire would use these same methods Auro had adopted to gather power unto themselves, served as a validation of his own actions, so it might be why he favored that theory. But the Eye was also so different from most of the other objects of power that he recovered, in ways that were plain to see in comparison.

I hadn't seen any of these wonders in years, of course, but I remembered the Eye well. The whole of it was no larger than a bundle of wheat, and roughly the same shape. Composed of a hard reddish orange metal none of our metallurgists could identify, its creators saw

---

3 Languages, and dialects, exist.

fit to decorate it finely with vines and flowers, cut delicately into the dome and along the sides of the cylinder. How that was done wasn't clear, as we couldn't touch it with our best bronze chisels. I was made familiar with most of my grandfather's discoveries, and the machines crafted by the Heaven's Gate were clad in silver and gold, and lacked ornamentation beyond the purely descriptive. Auro saw no evidence they had any capability of working in this material at all. The silver tools grandfather had made for his workings could only leave a thin line on the material before they would dull, so any thought of opening the thing and seeing how it worked was swiftly abandoned. This was fine by Auro; even if they discovered how it worked, could they then reassemble it? Or make a new one? Probably not! He thought it is best to keep such a terrible treasure intact and usable, for as long as possible.

The function of the Eye was much more simple to comprehend than its workings. Any fool of a man could operate it, with a few minutes practice. The whole of it rests upon a rod which is fused to a plate of the same hard orange metal. That rod ends in a sturdy mechanism, under the metal skirt of the machine, which allows it to be easily rotated, and pivoted back and forth. This whole contrivance is necessary as the eye is terrifically heavy, and must be aimed at its target. Brackets had been attached to the sides of the cylinder at some later point to aid in carrying it, by threading rods through and thus distributing the weight outwards. Auro always had four strong men carry it, one on each corner. There was no sense in dropping his prize and ruining it.

Above all of these mechanisms, well crafted but conceivable, is the true wonder of the device. On one side of the dome is a great circle of inky, glossy blackness, and another smaller one below it. On the opposite side is a square of the same material. Until you depress a small button below it, between the two vertical grips, it also looks like a pool of perfect obsidian, but afterwards it shows a glowing vision of what the smaller 'eye' on the front sees. Then it is a simple matter of lining up your target by taking hold of those grips, and squeezing the grips together when the target is shown in the center of this vision. The Eye would then emit a single note song, quickly rising up from a low murmur to a shrill scream as it gathered energy. Moments later whatever it gazed upon would first be lit, as if by the sun, and then would burst into all consuming flames, before being swiftly reduced to ashes. Auro knew enough of how it worked to demonstrate a few things to me. The first light is just a warning, to ensure the weapon is on target. The actual burst of heat comes invisibly moments later, just after the light ceases. On a few occasions before his death, Grandpa would take me up into the tower in the evening, and we would set alight straw targets which had been set up on the ridge far beyond the palace walls. More often, we just practiced from the wall itself. I confess that it was immensely fun. Though it didn't strike me, until we attacked Athens, that those were straw *men* we were setting alight with such glee.

The construction of my new home took three years. I practically lived in the temple while the work was in progress, but the purpose and function of this place was carefully kept from me. It wasn't until just before the door slammed shut that I came to understand my fate. Ma'aht was the first to tell me; though he did not have that right, he took liberties. He took so many liberties. May he be blessed for it.

Well lit, these twisting passages are not so threatening; there are many times, as I walk these paths, that I simply close my eyes and imagine it as it was, illuminated by lamplight. In this way, I can see the red sandstone walls and the stately ochre columns, topped with black marble imported from the great continent to the south; beautiful touches, lost in the darkness. I try not to think of how those finials are carved, but sometimes I slip.

Sometimes, when I close my eyes like this, I can almost hear Ma'aht's quiet footsteps, as he leads the way. It was not in these twisting passages that I first met my teacher, but it was here that he became my teacher. He quickly appraised me on our first day together in the temple, with endless questions about how I felt about various things. I'd never had someone so interested in my own perspective. I honestly had some trouble sharing it, at first, but he overcame my shyness with a quietly powerful generosity of spirit. Even though he was far from home, and even though this life was one that chose him, rather than one he chose, he carried on, helping and giving however he could within the context of his imprisonment. As these walls rose up within this vast cavern, he taught me the twists and turns within them, but also the twists and turns within the human spirit. His whispered lectures about the inherent value of humanity, and man's capability of debasement or enlightenment, will follow me forth no matter how many steps I take, here in this darkness. Whenever I start to mourn for myself, and my lot, I think of him, his bravery, and his kindness, and I am inspired. Even when he understood his fate, he never wavered, and saw his plan through to the end. I must do the same, in his honor.

My sister came into the family a year after the door closed on me, and six months after Athens sent their first sacrifice. They were too young; the king wanted adults, and these were adults by Athens' way of thinking, not ours. Not that it saved them from their fate, of course. Taking care of that mess was an immense distraction for me, and my mother was very heavy with child before I was even aware. There was some concern around the pregnancy; Elaía was not a young woman, and she took to a series of fainting spells during the last several months of her ordeal. Once, she fainted while in her chambers, shortly after one of our conversations. I could do nothing to help, not even make a sound, lest it betray our secret. The few seconds before her attendant stepped in and found her were the longest moments of my life.

I never got to hold Ariadne in my arms, but I did grow up with her. I heard her cry and fuss, I listened to my mother's jubilation over her first steps, I even taught her a few of her first words. All ringing down the hidden shaft in the queen's chambers. I actually wore a divot in the stone floor next to that portal, from sitting there for so long, as I listened to the normal life up above. After I realized I was leaving a mark, I took to leaning against the walls; I couldn't bear the thought of our secret being discovered. I mourned bitterly the day my sister moved out of the queen's room into her own chambers, but soon thereafter I had a second group of sacrifices to deal with. After that, it was never convenient to have her in my mother's chambers unattended. Years would pass between our conversations; I wish it could have been different. I wish so many things could have been different. But... I do my best.

Another familiar sound, this one less welcome; those horns meant I would have visitors soon. I leapt to my feet; I had to don my costume in time to take the stage, and play my part. I had to give my audience what they expected, and it was gonna be quite a show.

Five

We couldn't fault our navigator for a lack of precision; on the morning of our fifth day, we sighted the cliffs of Kokino. We set the coast to our steering side, and followed it towards Minos. The wind was kind, or perhaps unkind, and we heard the horns of Minos as Apollo reached his apex. Before long, the fires of the city showed themselves by their trails in the sky, and we passed a few fishing vessels. They maintained a respectful distance. Soon the number of vessels increased, until we were surrounded by a great crowd of ships, far more than I had ever seen at once. Kato blew his horn, and cried out.

"Port in sight! Draw down the sails, and man the oars. Relations, best to say your farewells. Remember, they don't let us off the ship." A number of people got to their feet, and began exchanging hugs and farewells. More than half of the oarsmen came up; we were a small community, and everyone knew everyone. A good number of people wanted to hug me too; I was everyone's little hero before I went off to become one, I guess. Or perhaps they wanted to give me some comfort, as I had no relation aboard. I appreciated it, regardless.

That disruption behind us, we began rowing towards the port. Once we crossed the threshold of the breakwater, the horns blew once again, to herald our arrival. As we neared, two Minoan warships approached us, their black sails drawn up tightly against the mast, and all oars out. These ships had two decks, to our one, and as they drew up beside us a crowd gazed silently down upon us. There were archers, but no one had their weapons in hand. The advantage was too great to even consider violence.

"They will escort us in. Then they will take you aboard a skiff, and then to shore. Take your things, they will demand them if you don't take them. They're gonna give you the silent treatment until you get well ashore, and then they are gonna shout at you. Brace yourselves, and gods be with you." Kato had been through this before, and he meant well, but I twisted inside. I knew the gods would not be with us. I kept that to myself.

I tried not to be too distracted by the ships, with their glaring warriors in black and red, and carefully observed the port as we entered it. It was vast, compared to the port of Athens. Dozens of vessels were anchored within it, and on either side a great breakwater of stone had been constructed. Atop each of these a bronze bull and a great brazier of fire had been placed. Each of these statues was far larger than the house I grew up in. But most impressive to me was the fact that half a dozen large ships were moored directly to the stone pier. This harbor must be deep!

The city itself rose from the ocean before us: a hundred stone structures, and countless wooden ones between them. Tiny wisps of smoke from a multitude of fires, each representing a warm meal, a hot kiln or a roiling forge, evaporated gently into the clear green sky. The central part of Minos seemed so dense with stone that it was akin to one great building, rising up in steps to meet the ridge, beyond which we could not see. It was the greatest city I had ever seen. I would have been overcome by the beauty of the place, had I been here for any other purpose.

It all happened just as Kato said. As we approached the shore, a skiff approached us. At this point, the archers brought their weapons to bear, to make our choice more clear. The fourteen of us climbed down our rope ladder, off the side of our vessel and into the flat end of the Minoan skiff, clutching our finery and our things. They were a part of the ransom we represented. We were directed, silently, to take a seat straddling the center bench, in a line. There was one warrior at the head of the skiff; all of the archers who had their weapons trained on us made his role more or less ceremonial. The rowers were all women, and while I was sure there was a fascinating ritual reason for that, I didn't care. They seemed strangely distant. Estius was seated ahead of me, and I gripped his shoulder to try and comfort him; he squeezed my hand in response. Not a word was said as we rowed alongside the waterline, and a plank was dropped onto the vessel.

The warrior motioned with his weapon, a double headed axe, that we were to go.

Once we were all ashore we weren't given a chance to regroup before we were driven on by that warrior. He walked behind us, his axe to bear. Not that we had any choice to run, or even to turn aside, as our route was lined with a vast, silent crowd. It was obviously an intimidation tactic; I did my best not to look at their angry faces, and focussed upon the city itself. The street was paved with stones, rather than compacted soil, and they had solved the cart problem with bronze lined channels cut into it. Does that mean all of their carts are the same width? How do their horses' hooves not split? It was also very clean; there was no channel for offal, no piles of garbage. The second mystery was solved when I observed a child throwing a handful of shells into a large open basket, almost taller than she was, and I noticed that these baskets were regularly placed. So, they collected their trash. But I still couldn't understand the absence of a channel. Do all of these people leave the city to answer the call of nature? Mother Gaia can be an insistent master, and if you race her you are bound to lose, and yet I could smell no hint of a mistake. Other than the smell of fires, most of the customary odors of settlement was absent, replaced with a low spicy aroma. It gave the place a feeling of unreality, as if we had stepped out of the realm of men and into some abode of minor deities.

We were climbing now, up a steady incline, into the city center. The buildings here seemed built on top of one another. The Minoans must have decided that one stone building wasn't enough, and so they had just started stacking them. They were composed of a light red stone, accented with black and white marble for decorative or structural purposes. The stones themselves were massive, much like the stones that made up many of the temples I saw as a child. To build an entire city as one builds a temple would require so many people, or so much time. Minos had risen up so quickly, how did they manage it?

Wooden balconies and porches hung off the sides of these buildings, and layers of people were staring down on us. We stopped in the square, and my Athenian brethren gathered into a circle. A low murmur moved through the crowd, which was quickly quieted. It seemed as if the whole city had turned out to see us, and it was impossible to not look at the people now, so I tried to focus on their clothing.

Whereas most Athenians, male and female, would spend most of their lives in a wrap of cloth and cord, twisted in whatever way would be best for the situation, the people of Minos had much more varied and elaborate outfits. The only commonalities seemed to be a broad metal belt, extending from the waist to just below the chest, which Minoan men, women and children all wore with some minor variations, and a general preference for shades of red, brown and black. The children were dressed uniformly, in a tube shaped piece of cloth with holes for the arms, bound around the waist by that belt. Some of them wore little square hats. The men almost appeared to be dressed for combat. They wore pleated skirts to knee length, with alternating colors in the pleats, and high sandals that were bound about their calves. The triangular serration at the end of each of those pleats gave the impression of a toothy maw. Above the belt most of them were bare, though I noticed that the actual soldiers seemed to distinguish themselves with a bronze bowl shaped hat and a circular shield strapped to their right shoulder. The women had a longer, wider skirt that ended above the calf, which seemed to be filled with layers of more skirts. Some wore pleats, some did not. There was more variety in pattern and color amongst the women; a few of them were in bright shades I was unfamiliar with. Rather than covering the top of their chest from the sun, their outfits seemed designed to thrust it into the air, and their belts were constructed so as to support their chest in that unnatural position. It looked uncomfortable.

My moment of sympathy was broken when the horns, those same horns we had heard earlier heralding our arrival, blew. Moments later, on that cue, every assembled person broke out in a horrible, wordless scream. Dust peeled down off the rooftops, as this howl of beastly thunder shook us from our skin to our bones. By the time this cruel roar had transitioned to a peal of mocking laughter, twelve of my fellow Athenians were cowering on the ground around me. Only Miletta and I kept to our feet. My estimation of her rose like the terrified birds of Minos, in that moment.

It was then I noticed a man who was distinct from the rest. He was wearing a robe under his belt, and he had a ridiculous hat, which looked like the front half of a fish with its mouth agape. Two younger men in similar attire, but without the hat, flanked him. They had bundles of cloth under their arms. They advanced and laid out their burdens before us; white tubes of linen, sewn down the back, with arm holes. Not unlike the outfits the children were wearing.

"Change." The man in the funny hat, who I had now concluded was some sort of priest, spoke one of the many words our tongues had in common.

"In front of the whole world?" Miletta, who still had hold of her words, said this loud enough to ring off the stone walls, and with a sharp edge of indignity.

The assembled crowd answered with a brief cry, and by stomping their feet, once, twice, and then again. We began changing. It was deeply humiliating, but that was the point. I focussed on the stones beneath my feet and pulled the thing over my head as quickly as possible. When I looked up, the priest was before me.

"You are the prince?" How did he know? Oh yeah, they had years to find out, and I could hardly hide in a crowd. He then said a few words I didn't recognize. Chiron had done his best to familiarize me with the Minoan dialect, but he hadn't been to Crete in many years. He read my face, and tried again. "Your music thing. Take it. You perform for the King tonight, after they go in."

"No. I am done with being treated differently." The thought of being separated from my companions, once again, and for the same reason? I was furious.

"Hah, you choose now?" He laughed out a series of words, perhaps profanity. "You are a prince, I can see. No choice now." One of his assistants grabbed my knot from my pile of effects, and two soldiers advanced to seize me. I pulled back, into a fighting stance, but the third soldier I hadn't seen struck me on the back of the head. I staggered, and barely stayed on my feet. In that moment, the other two grabbed me by the arms.

"Fool!" The priest struck the unseen soldier with his rod, hard. The horns of the adornment, a bull's head, left a nasty wound on the man's face, but he made no effort to defend himself. "If he is bruised it will be your scalp, not just your cheek." And then he spat on his sandal for emphasis. It was clear who was in charge here. As I was being lead away, I looked back on my fellows, a scared cluster of white in a sea of red and black, like sheep cast into the mouths of countless wolves.

I couldn't say any empty words about the gods and the mercy they weren't here to give, so I called out: "Love and courage, to the people of Athens!" And then, I was pulled around the corner, and I saw them no more.

"Worry not, prince, they will be well fed, before they are fed well." The priest evidently thought this was a tremendous joke, as he broke into laughter. His assistants took the cue, and laughed politely with him. I was in no mood for humor, so I walked on in silence. We left the city center, and crested the ridge. Before long even the wooden buildings ceased when we hit a boundary line of fencing, beyond which there were groves and fields. The stone road continued, though, and we followed it for half an hour or so, before I saw the palace rising before me on the mount above the city. Even then, it took another quarter hour for us to arrive there at the pace of a forced march.

The glory of the palace made the city seem like an afterthought. Great columns held up the front of the building, larger than I had ever seen, even in the temples back home. The facade extended beyond these columns to my left, and there were several levels of patios hanging above the earth, each with their own gardens and seating areas. I could see in the distance two round towers of stone, one taller than the other, and each topped with an onion-like roof. Between those columns before me, but below the roofline, on shelves placed high above the ground, stood statuary of great people and gods. I picked out Zeus and Poseidon amongst the crowd, though there were some unfamiliar figures there as well. The thought of putting a representation of the gods upon the outside of a person's home, even a king, seemed unspeakably arrogant to me, but perhaps that was the fashion here. At the center of each column hung the two primary symbols of Minos: the bull's head, in bronze, and the double headed axe. The axes did not appear to be purely decorative.

"The others are just behind us." The priest knew exactly what was on my mind. "They will take the side door, the prince takes the front. But don't worry, you will get the same treatment, after Arbias has had his amusement with you." We scaled the steps of the palace, and entered between the columns. This central space was lit with an oculus, and had marble flooring in an alternating pattern of diamond shaped black and white tiles. Countless arches and doors led out of this central chamber, and a staircase here led to the second floor. Each door had two guards around them, and was outlined in ornamental stonework of black marble. Between the doors there were more columns, or half columns against the wall, and every one bore the twin symbols of Minos. The palace guard wore the same uniform as the other soldiers we had seen in the city, but had a red tassel on top of their bronze hats to show their rank.

I was escorted up some stairs, around a bend, and down a hallway. I'd never been in so large a building. The priest turned to his left with a practiced turn, and did so with such speed I nearly ran right into him. He grasped the ring shaped handle on the finely crafted wooden door, and slid it to the right, where it smoothly mated with the frame with barely a sound. He then walked in to a sun lit room beyond. A jab in the back confirmed I was supposed to follow, so I did.

"You will stay here until our feast this evening, to celebrate our continuing victory over you lot of savages. I don't want the floor to have to be cleaned again. So, I will show you some things. Try to pay attention." This first room was a sunny looking home. There were ample cushions to recline upon, and large openings to let in air and light. I noted that these openings were covered with bars, but I had a nice view. The Minoans must have made a habit of keeping prisoners comfortably available in the palace. "Now! I don't have all day to explain baby things to you." The priest had already moved on to a side room. I followed, and found myself in a mystery.

I had no idea what this room was for. It was smaller than the living space, but ample. To one side was a raised lip in the floor, setting aside a space with a strange metal thing hanging over it. More machinery jutted out of the wall below it. On the other side of the room were two bowls, made of bronze and copper. Both were attached to the wall; one low, at about knee height, and the other, on the opposite wall, was about the height of my waist. The higher bowl had some similar machinery at the top; I recognized them now as levers, not unlike the ones we would use to make fine adjustments on the rigging of our ships, or the tension of our strings. The lower bowl had a bronze box hanging over it, mounted high on the wall, and out of this a chain dangled. Between them were two buckets and a pile of rags.

"This bowl. You sit on it and do what you need to do. Then... " He pulled on the chain, and the water in the bowl was swept away in a mildly terrifying whirlpool. "... it all goes away. Clean yourself with the rag and the salty water. Put dirty rags in the empty bucket, no one likes it if you put them in the water." He then walked over to the other bowl, turned one of the levers, and washed his hands in the sink. "Don't spread shit all over, pretend you aren't an animal while you are here." He dashed off the extra water, and wiped his hands on his robe as he walked out. "It will take a few hours, before he comes back out. Then we feast. You perform." I was really sick of this mocking child talk.

"And if I choose to not be a gaudy spectacle for your carnival of blood, do you intend upon extinguishing my life a second time as punishment for my terrible misdeeds against you and your house? Do enlighten me as to how I can be harmed more than you intend upon harming me."

"Oh look, the golden ape has some words!" His assistants didn't need a beat to laugh at this jab. "We might **word** (sounded like murder?) you twice, if you don't wipe your ass. If you don't perform, we'll just **word word word** your little fish gut town. Again." Was it just profanity that I was missing? How much do they curse around here? Can they really kill me twice? No... that was just a flourish, no matter what wonders they have here, I don't think they can do that.

In regard to the other threat, he had a point. I was not in any place to negotiate, not if I cared about anyone else. They waited for a reply, and when they saw I did not intend upon giving them the satisfaction, they simply left and slid the door closed behind them. I could hear the guards taking their position after they left, so I didn't even try the door. My knot had been left on one of the cushions; did they intend that I should practice? I laid down, and tried not to think of the other Athenians. When I failed, I just cried myself to sleep.

I was awoken with a kick. Not one vicious enough to pull me fully from slumber, but it was enough. I wiped the sand from my eyes, and noted that the day had nearly gone by. One of the priest's assistants was in the room; he was about my height, but more sleight, and had the sharp nose so many men seemed to have around here. No hair on his cheeks, of course, he was a cleric. Under another circumstance I might have found him handsome.

"You have a short time, before you must go." I got up to my feet, but he grabbed me by the shoulder, and moved in with an unwelcome embrace. I stepped under his arm and away; the wrestling move came naturally out of my body and it caught him by surprise.

"That seems excessively familiar." Overuse of words was evidently a reflex as well.

"Oh, you have no room for joy or comfort before you go? You go right to your fate after the show. And you are striking. Beautiful. It would be a shame; I saw where your eyes went, back in the square." I died a little death right then; was I so obvious, even when it was the last thing on my mind?

"Did I not gaze upon your women? I seem to recall differently."

"You gazed upon their clothing. Every other man amongst you was gazing upon their **word**."

"Their chests?" I took a guess.

"Yeah." He took another step towards me, but I sidestepped several feet away. "This is not the dance I had in mind."

"I would rather make love with a burning ingot, pulled straight from the fire." I gathered up to my full size. There was no chance of him overpowering me.

"That might be arranged, but I think what we have planned for you is better." And he spat on the floor, before wheeling around and heading towards the door. Does everyone spit here to show disdain? That seems only slightly less gross than what his boss was so worried about. He stopped in his tracks; there was some official business to take care of. "When the horn sounds you will gather your **word** and come. Put some water in your hair or something before you go before the king." And he left, slamming the door behind him. At least he left me with the gift of knowing what the locals call my knot.

I followed his advice, and cleaned myself up. Not with any Hope of saving myself, any such whisperings could only be an impossible lie, but perhaps I could shame the court with my beauty. It would be nice to actually make use of the accursed thing, for once. I noted that above the sink was a burnished piece of bronze that worked much the same as the sacred psychomanteum mirror did back in Athens, though more dull due to its less precious construction. In that eerie reflection I made myself pretty. I rinsed my hair, and made sure my curls were laid well. There was a shell on the shelf next to the sink, and I trimmed up the edges of my beard. I smiled at my own reflection, and it smiled back. I'd never get used to that.

I then realized I needed to make use of this room for its primary purpose, so I sat down. It was cold, and a bit higher than the slanted board most of our outhouses had to help support you. It took me a moment to trust it enough to shift my weight back upon it, but it was sturdy. Once I finished I cleansed myself as directed, and washed my hands. I had to satisfy my curiosity, so I examined the area in the corner. As I suspected, the levers had the same purpose as the ones on the cleaning bowl, and a torrent of water fell down from above. Initially it was intolerably hot, but after fiddling with the other lever I was able to cool it down. These people don't even need to carry water to wash themselves!

I shut it down and left, shocked at the primitive existence the people of Hellea, everyone I had every known, lived with, compared to this. I had only taken my seat back in the other room for long enough to tune my instrument when I heard the horn. I took my knot in hand and walked right out the door as it opened. They didn't expect me to be quite that ready, and I did look striking, so it took a moment to get their line in order. As soon as they were ready we marched deeper into the building. We walked up more stairs, around another corner, and down a long hallway. Oil lamps had been placed in alcoves well above head height, and we passed a servant who was lighting them, one by one, with a hot wick on a long stick. We took one more turn, through a black marble door with a peaked arch, into the king's court.

I didn't know what to expect. Certainly not anything like my father's court, held as it was in a building of wood. Within the room was a flurry of activity, as if the king had taken a festival inside for his convenience. I held true to my training, and tried to focus upon my environment.

The only resemblance I could find was that the tables were arranged in a roughly circular pattern, and there was an oculus in the wooden ceiling. Everything else differed. The walls, and floor were made of fine masonry, not wood and dirt, and the room itself was vast, so much larger and more airy than the court of Athens. The lamps were plentiful, and very bright. I could not gaze upon them. They were inset high in the wall, and I couldn't understand how they had been lit. Certainly not with a hot wick on a long stick. Set into those walls with careful precision were a rainbow of precious stones, depicting various scenes of heroic conquest, gilded in gold wherever there was skin, and brilliant sienna and ochre wherever there was blood. There was a lot of blood.

The tables and chairs were all cast in bronze, with wooden pieces on the seating surfaces and the tabletops. The finest chairs at the head of the room, including the throne reserved for the king, were further decorated with gold and jewels. On either side of the throne were golden bull's heads, their exaggerated horns reaching halfway to the ceiling from the wall on which they were mounted. If they were real bulls they could have swallowed a man. But if they were real bulls, they would probably prefer grass. Between them hanged a double headed axe, bedecked with finery. No man could have wielded it, it was like jewelry, for a room.

The head priest approached me, in his stupid fish hat, and grabbed my hand. He led me into the center of the room, and the dancing and the music stopped. The crowd of dancers, in their poofy wide skirts, parted before us, before taking a seat on a ring of cushions placed in front of the tables where the important people sat. I made a guess that this was so their view of the king would be unobstructed between performances. The priest held my hand up, and I noticed that in his other raised hand he held a small grey object, roughly the size and shape of a chicken egg, but flattened.

"Now, for the benefit of the court, the test." He held the object to his face, and squeezed it, before whispering a few words in a language that was unfamiliar to me. It let out a small burst of blood red light, and then he forced it into my hand. "Hold it." It had a similar feeling to the lamp I had examined under the eye of my goddess, smooth and grabby like a river stone, but oddly light. Three seconds later, it flashed green like the trees, so brightly I turned away.

"Never has he laid with a woman, the prince of Athens is a virgin!" The priest announced, triumphantly. And the court erupted in jeers and laughter. I wondered what the priest thought of this; no doubt, he was a virgin by this standard as well. He took back his precious object, and grabbed me tightly by the shoulder. I was to speak with the king. As we approached, a horn sounded, and a crier announced:

"Arbias Minos, King of Crete! He blesses you with his words. First in War, may his days be long and his conquests many!" I scarcely saw the point of this, couldn't he just... start talking? But then... he didn't. He just stared at me for half a minute. It gave me a chance to look him over. He was more broad than my father, and taller; at least as tall as I, but it was hard to judge with him seated. A bit of grey shot through his oiled black beard and the lighter hair at his temples, but he somehow looked younger than Aegeus did the last time I saw him. I knew this not to be true. Perhaps he spent less time on the sea as a youth, or perhaps the conveniences of this place kept you young. His dress was the same as any other man in this city, just more so. More pleats in his skirt, so many you couldn't count them, more gold and gems on his belt, more patterns and colors in the fabrics that made it all up. His chest was covered with a second wrap of fine cloth, in an unfamiliar hue somewhere between green and red, and this was fastened with a pin in the shape of a tiny golden axe. Most of the men here also had their chests covered. They were probably forced to adopt some element of winter dress to deal with this cold stone building. His eyes, cold and grey, met mine.

"How did you like that little toy? One of my favorite things we ever dug up. The former king thought it was a game. For parties. The game was; find out what experiences you don't have, and then the party would give them to you. It doesn't just find virgins, you see. I could have it tell me if you've ever gone swimming, with the right words. Isn't that a marvel?" I think he expected a reply, but I held my tongue. He pursed his lips, then continued, "You are just as striking as the stories said. When my spies told me that the king's own son had pulled the lot, I never thought I'd get to meet you. Surely the king could find some substitute for his only beloved son?"

"Had he done so, the grieving parents you have left behind would have taken his head." I didn't mention the topic of our conversation before my departure. His honor was the honor of Athens, after all.

"It is strange to me, for a king to be so afraid of his subjects."

"They respect each other. It's a better way of running things." The King of Minos forced out a laugh.

"And look at all the good that respect has done you! No better than a commoner, and I'm done treating you differently. Play for us, but do not sing. I've had enough of your words." He dismissed me with a wave of his hand. I turned on my heel and marched right to the center of the room, returned my gaze to the king, and began playing.

My first song was a furious one, the one they play when they are threshing the wheat. I struck my strings to set the rhythm, and before I knew it, I had the accompaniment of a few of the court musicians. This must be a tune they use around here as well. At the finale one of them let out the customary cry; the song would hardly be complete without it, and I was glad someone else took it on themselves. I followed up with a slower song, one I composed myself and used to play on hazy summer days, as we all took our leisure at the school. I'd never played that one as anything but a solo, but the aulos player managed to accompany it very well with his haunting, warbling note, given that he couldn't have known the song. I began to play a third song, but I was interrupted by the king's applause. The rest of the court followed suit.

"No, that's enough. If you play anymore I'll have to keep you, for my amusement. Go sit, and feast. We always give you Athenians a last meal, and the prince will be no different." The priest then advanced upon me, but I was done with being led. I walked ahead of him, towards the back corner of the room where two tables were piled high with food. Behind these tables attendants would keep the platters full and heavy, and they had their own entrance to the back so they could come and go without interrupting the activities of the court.

I had been told that the people in Crete eat a lot of meat, but I had no idea. In Athens, even fish is precious enough that it is like a spice on a meal, not the bulk of it. But here, they had several whole animals worth of meat laid out on each table. It was more meat than I remembered being served at the Festival of Athena, and that was for the whole city! It even looked like they had meat stuffed with more meat in several configurations. I didn't even know where to start, and I had no appetite, so I just took a plate and filled it with sides, and grabbed a cup. At least I understood the bread and carrots. I noted there were bronze chairs along the wall, so I went in that direction. On that same side of the room, the priest's assistant I had words with earlier was waiting for his orders. So I did a little turn, tossed my golden locks, and blew him a kiss. The look of abject horror on his face, at what he had missed out on, gave me the best feeling I'd had all day.

It turned out I didn't understand these simple foods as well as I thought. The bread was too sweet. I couldn't swallow my second bite of it, and almost choked before I washed it down with some weak beer that was also far too sweet. I was halfway through a carrot when I felt someone approaching. I looked up, to see a young woman walking towards me with a determined look on her face. She was dressed even more elaborately than the other women, even the dancers, and her outfit made great use of that weird color, like the hyacinth flower, that I found so hard to describe. I concluded, before she even opened her mouth, that she must be royalty.

"My father has ordered me to talk to you, so as to torture me. I am Ariadne."

"You are the princess? It would be a pleasure to meet you, under any other circumstance." She turned, and placed her back against the wall alongside me, before continuing in a whisper.

"Father doesn't know the favor he has done me, though. Your Lady of Wisdom sends her greetings." If I'd been eating I would have choked, and I just managed to keep my face straight. "I have delivered her gifts, and a gift of my own. The first room you enter is a long colonnade. At the end of that room is a raised platform. Behind that is an alcove, and to the right you will find it, hidden. You will have to find it in the dark, there is no other way. Use my gift to help find your way back out... when you are done." Her face contorted at this; she seemed conflicted. "If you make it, try to rescue me. Father would kill me if he found out what I have done. I have to go. Forgive me this." And she wheeled around and slapped me, before letting out a few of those now familiar curse words. The whole room laughed uproariously at my suffering. As she walked away, she loudly lied, "The men of Athens are worthless pigs!" It was a good act, and I was grateful.

Apparently this little show was what the king was waiting for as well. He pounded his hand once on the arm of his chair, and everyone fell silent. "I think it's time for our guest to enter the Labyrinth, and meet my other child, don't you think?" The court signaled their agreement with another peal of laughter. The Labyrinth; is that what they call it here? "He seemed a bit tired when he came out to thank us for your gift, and to bellow and scream. But I'm sure he can take care of you, little man. If he doesn't, the Labyrinth will, and his larder will suffer for it." I was taken away, leaving my knot behind. It was part of the ransom, after all. A part of me was deeply relieved, as I would rather die than spend one more minute in that accursed court. I walked ahead of my guards, head held high, as I went to meet my fate.

Six

"Lonely rolling star!" All I could see was haze, and light. I felt like I was a feather, aloft on a warm current, lost. "Come to me, lonely rolling star." It was such a kind, soft voice. Was that my name? No, I remember. It's my title, my role, and my task.

The light separated, and resolved. I could feel the cushion beneath me, my legs crossed, my tail curled comfortably within the space between my thighs. I looked down at my hands. They felt odd, as if I was unused to them. They looked a bit different. Was it the shade of the light? I looked up, but my vision was still hazy, and I had trouble focusing. How had I gotten here? I retraced my steps; I had finished my task, well, most of it. Father always found a way to complicate things. Then I reclined to rest, for just a moment, and... had I fallen asleep? I closed my eyes and rubbed them with my hands. When I looked up again, I could see.

Before me sat three other beings, each on a shiny blue cushion. It was like looking in the silver mirror they used to light the theater in the day, or in the still pond in the back garden. But no, the one before me, she was female. She had less hair on her face, and somehow I just knew. I looked to my left and right, in each of their faces. Another female, and a male, each bearing a slightly different shade of brown. They were naked save for what nature had given them, a simple gemstone pendant, and the fine woven blankets on their laps. I noticed that I had a blanket as well, and I ran my palm across its comforting, soft surface.

Behind them and around us were vast, smooth panels of gemstone, the one they call the blood of the earth. These extended upward far above our heads into a crown of crystal, and were illuminated from below by an amber light. The cushions were placed on grass, and I noticed there was greenery all about us. A purple sky shone down from above. It felt so achingly familiar.

"Welcome back. How goes your journey?" Yes! This had happened before, once when I was very young. How could I have forgotten that? But worse, how could I answer that?

"I, uh... " I coughed. My throat felt strange. Even my words did not seem my own. "Oh yes. Fine! Everything is fine."

The three of them gave me a profoundly skeptical look. The male to my left spoke, "He is lying. Why is he lying?" The one before me did not answer this, but looked me right in the eyes and spoke again, this time with more concern, and less softness.

"Tell me your situation. Now." She crossed her arms, and awaited my response. I tried not to speak, but it was like my mouth was full of honey, and it formed the words even as I tried to say or think of anything else. I was compelled.

"They are trying to turn me into a god. I am trapped in a temple of death and darkness." The three of them immediately began barking at one another in a cacophony, but after a moment the one before me extended her arms, and all were silent.

"We are pulling you out, this is unacceptable." I panicked. I somehow knew this was within her power. She didn't know!

"No, you can't... people need me!" I had to cough it out, around these foreign lips.

"I know enough." Her eyes were hard, but also seemed on the verge of tears. "No matter what has drawn you back there, this risk is too great." I felt love, distant but powerful, as if a great many people were calling my name. I had a thought. I started to force myself to wake up, in the way that you do when you are in a nightmare. It was hard, this place was the opposite of a nightmare. "Don't you pull back! You're risking everything, your eternal self... " It was working, that blessed place was fading, the sweet smell had diminished to the scent of nothing. Then, I could smell the stale stench of the pit. "No! Return... return to us... "

I awoke with a start, and sat up. My lamp was alight. I was such a fool, how much time had I lost? I looked down at my bloody hands, my stained and stinking costume. All the careful choreography had left me with no time to clean up. I dropped my belt, tossed the clothing aside, plunged my hands into my cleaning bowl and rubbed them vigorously. I wiped them off, and then used the moist rag to clean off the spots of blood that had spattered onto the circular links of my belt. Not a fine cleaning, but it would do. I looked down at the hateful costume. I couldn't bear to see it, so I crumpled it up and tossed it in a basket, which I slid under the stone platform I used as a bed. It disgusted me that it had touched my furs, what was I thinking? I donned my clothes, and dashed out into the temple. I might be too late for my final guest. I couldn't bear the thought.

Seven

As the stone door rolled into place behind me, I did my best to remember my last glimpse of light. This chamber, lined with columns, seemed to go off forever into the darkness, but I knew it had to come to an end, unless Ariadne was a liar. I stripped off my sandals, and tossed them aside; my years in Thessaly had left me with thick calluses on my feet, and I could move much more silently without them. I oriented myself to my memory of the columns, and crept forward. I had been taught how to judge the size and shape of a chamber by the sound in the air, in the caves during my schooling, so I wasn't truly walking blind. It would be easier if I could yell, but I dared not make a sound, here in the dark lair of my enemy.

After what seemed like an eternity of walking, I felt a certain closeness in the air, and I slowed my gate to a shuffle. My toes soon bumped into a barrier. I bent over, and felt the dias, just where it was supposed to be. Taking to my hands and knees, I tried to crawl before failing completely, as I was bound up in my garment. As I composed myself, I realized this thing must force the kids to walk instead of crawling. Clever, in a cruel kind of way, like everything in Minos.

I hitched it up around my chest, allowing my exposed rear to moon the darkness, and tried again. This time I made it to the far wall, and I began feeling towards the right, still on my hands and knees. Before long I reached another barrier. I felt around; there was a gap in the masonry here. I breathed for a moment, and found my peace. Reaching my hand into a dark hole, in a dark place, surrounded by death, took some courage. I reached in, and felt around. I had almost given up, when I felt the brush of cloth, so I shoved my arm all the way in, and soon had a package in hand.

I unwrapped it in the darkness, keeping careful hold of the round object I had felt through the cloth. I didn't want it to roll away into the void, that would be a nightmare. I turned one side, and nothing happened, so I turned it over and tried the other. One click in, and light filled the space. My memory of the lowest setting was that it was almost useless, but in this perfectly dark place it was almost enough. I trimmed the beam, and turned it up.

My view was a mirror image of the one I had seen at the other end, but I could see the details better in this light. The stones in the floor were of a single uniform size, which was very large, and I recognized the true ratio in their proportions, somewhat longer than they were wide. The same sized stones, perhaps identical, were positioned vertically to make up the walls. A tightly constructed wooden roof was held up by the colonnade, but no hint of light came through. The rumors of the Labyrinth being underground were true, as entering it required exiting from the back courtyard down a staircase, deep into the earth. The red columns were topped in a macabre decoration, that inspired feelings of dread in me. I tried not to look at them. At my end of the room, four doors led off into the darkness, two on each side of the dias.

I took a moment to examine my tools. I immediately noticed an addition to my rigging; a cloth pouch, tightly clasped, had been attached at the waist. I could feel my knife inside. Clever girl, she must have known this outfit has no pockets. This was not Ariadne's gift, though. That seemed to be a spool of thread. I pulled out a length of it; it sparkled in the pale green light, as if it were partially made of metal. I tried to break it, but couldn't; it was very strong. Was this the thread they used to embellish the edges of their dresses? It did seem like quite a length of it; the flattened oval of the spool was as thick as my wrist and as wide as my fist.

I got to my feet, and donned my rigging. It was designed to attach to my cord, but I didn't have one, so it was a bit sloppy, and I tightened it up a bit at the latch on my belly. There was a leather tab over the cross guard on the sword; I was torn, but decided upon leaving it unlatched. I might have to use it at any time. I made sure I could unsheathe it easily, and then returned it to its home.

Looking over my problem, I decided to go about it systematically. I tied my thread to the corner column, down low to the ground so that anyone walking through would hopefully miss it, and entered the first passage to my left. I thanked the gods that the spool itself was whisper quiet, as I was making every effort to create as little sound as possible. My only path to victory was through the narrow strait of surprise.

This passage was made of the same stones, and the air was less clean here. I made a left turn at a junction, but this ended in two blind ends, one just around a corner from the other. I retraced my steps and tried the other direction. I continued on, and came upon a four way junction. To my left was a stagnant passage, and ahead and to my right were fresher air. I continued on my left, to check on a hunch. As I suspected, this passage ended in a dead end, this time with small sharp blades cruelly placed on the walls to catch anyone who ran down here in a blind panic. I saw a crust of old blood on a group of them, about elbow height, and shuddered.

Knowing that I could follow my nose to avoid dead ends simplified my work considerably. After retracing my steps to the four way I crossed directly ahead, and after a turn I entered into the large central chamber once again, this time through the door just to the right of the dias. How had I missed the passage in between? I racked my mind; there was an incline, very slight, that first went up and back down. I retraced my steps again, rewinding as I went and confirmed that the upright stones in the passage I had just emerged from were not as square as it seemed. It was all to trick people who were feeling around in the dark. My own anger darkened, as I imagined my fellow Athenians stumbling around these horrible passages, in the blackness, fleeing some monster. What kind of mind would be inspired to build such a thing, as the Labyrinth? I didn't need to wonder at the owner of that mind, even if I couldn't fathom its character. I had just met the king, after all.

I continued retracing my steps, keeping mind of my thread, and took the last unexplored door at the intersection. Down this passage there were several points where I had to choose left or right, and I chose the fresher air each time. Finally there was another choice, between the familiar staleness and a rancid funk. I chose the funk, and what met my eyes was a horror.

Some semblance of a living space was before me. Torn and bloody rags, the tattered remnants of the white cloth I also wore, laid about, and were fashioned into a grisly cushion and bed. At the foot of that bed sat a great pile of treasures, more wealth than I had ever seen in one place. I bore it no mind. What possible use could it be to me? To one side, along the wall, were neatly laid a bundle of parcels, wrapped in the same cloth, all flat upon the cold floor. The blood that shone in my light, soaking through their wrappings, was fresh. I wretched. Was this the fate of my fellows? But I gathered myself, and examined the area further. It seemed musty, rarely used. I drew my sword, and gingerly opened one of the parcels. It contained the gore and meat I was expecting but... Why was it so well butchered? And how, here in this blackness?

Something else that had been bothering me forced its way to the front of my mind. I had imagined such violence, as my fellows were slaughtered by this beast, but where was the evidence of it? Other than the bit of blood on the trap, this was the first blood I'd seen. Surely my fellow Athenians put up some sort of fight? Even though they were lost and blind, they had the advantage of numbers. So many had been lost to this place, where were they? Was he so efficient a carnivore he would lick up the leftovers? It seemed unlikely.

This train of thought was interrupted by an unexpected sound; in some distant place, I could hear someone playing upon the strings of a lyre. Then, I could hear movement, in some other distant passage. There, that was the beast! I extinguished my lantern, and slowly sheathed my sword. If I needed to move fast, it would be better to have it out of the way until the moment I needed it, or it might bite me in these confines.

It moved so quickly! I was stunned when mere moments later it passed right in front of me, not twenty feet ahead, at an unexplored junction just beyond this charnel house. It ran down the other passage, and I grabbed my spool from the ground and crept behind.

At the junction, I turned the other way and walked as quickly as I could, while still being silent, in the direction from which it had come. I hadn't made it thirty steps when the spool tugged itself out of my hand. It fell with a minor clatter, but it sounded like a thunderclap to me. I risked a thin ray of light, and rolled it against the wall, before continuing on. I walked through what seemed like an endless series of passages, following my nose and that thin line of light, and I ended up emerging from the fourth door, to the far right of the dias where I had started. So much for following the thread out.

At this point, I could hear it moving again, moving so quickly, and heavily. It was not exactly the clatter of hooves I was expecting. I did a quick calculation, based upon what I knew about the layout of this maze, and I took off down the unexplored second hallway, the one that went underneath. The air was very fresh down this way, and that felt good. I quickened my pace, with my thin bobbing ray of light penetrating the gloom only a few paces ahead.

I ran through an arch into a large space beyond. Had I been looking up rather than down, I would have surely missed the point at which the finely hewn blocks of the floor simply ceased to continue. I struggled to stop, but the floor was slippery, and I fell on my rear, sliding to within inches of the precipice. I held tight to my lantern, and upon taking a seat I turned it up. Before me was a grand gallery of stone, a cave of such height and volume it must have awed everyone who had seen it, before they built this thing here.

I was unaware of the catastrophe that had just occurred, even at this point. That is, until I heard a distant clang of metal against stone. I turned my light down into the impossible abyss, and saw no bottom. I reached up with my free hand, and felt the empty aperture of my sheath.

Gods damn me! The priest was right, I'm no better than a golden ape. As if in answer to this thought, more loud clanging noises rang out from the pit. How deep was that thing? Worse, there was no way the monster had not heard that. So much for stealth.

I jumped to my feet and looked around. There was another passage, and I could hear something approaching from where I came. I still have the light and my knife, maybe I can recover this somehow. I wouldn't give up, for Athens! I ran into the unknown, and followed my nose; if this is where the air was coming in, then it had to go out somewhere. It might only be pooling in the big room, but even ending up there would be a better place for a fight. I moved, as quickly as my feet could carry me, until I passed a door to my left with a rank, but somewhat fresh, smell. I turned my lamp into the space to see a bathing room, not unlike the one I had experienced upstairs. I curled my lip; my mother died shitting into a hole and this monster has a pool of water to do his business in. But still, it felt strange that this room was the first one I had seen that really felt used. Once again, my thoughts were interrupted by an unexpected noise.

A horrible cry rang through the halls. I ended in a croak, and a sob. It was not a war cry, or the howl of a rabid dog in the night. It tore my heart in two. What was going on? I resolved that my mind should not stop my feet, so I continued following my nose.

I almost missed it. If I had not had both my lantern and my nose, I almost surely would have. First there was a side passage that had a raised entrance, just below waist height. Stumbling along in the dark, there is no way I would have noticed it. I pulled myself up and in, and shone my lamp ahead. It appeared to end in a blind passage, but one of the stones seemed... wrong. My experience earlier had taught me there might be trickery in those stones, and a close examination showed that it was not truly square; it sloped, and tricked the eye. If you just glanced in here in the flickering light of an oil lamp, you would think it was a dead end.

I walked around this queer stone, and into the open air of the cavern. I could hear water running, far in the distance. I'd been in caves before, there is always water, and it is best to avoid it. But, there was a path. Had it been left after the construction? Having no better idea, I followed it.

As I approached the far wall, I saw there a patch of gravel, about twenty feet across. I stood there for a moment, surrounded by a gallery of cruel stone teeth deep beneath the earth, and caught my breath. Where now? I held my arm up, and by the tingle of my many fine hairs I could feel air movement. There was an opening in the cave wall, but it looked rough and unhewn. The bottom met in a crude V, and it seemed awkward and uninviting. I walked forward to examine it, and when I did I could feel the air. I risked turning up my lamp again, and beyond I could see masonry. Having no reasonable alternative, I stepped through the strange portal.

The stones in here were smaller, and of varied sizes. Still finely hewn, still intricately placed together, but... clearly different. Had I stumbled into something else entirely? It couldn't be worse than the place I had come from; I pressed on, towards the air. I turned the bend, and entered a cozy home.

I almost dropped my lamp; I could scarcely believe my eyes. It certainly had all the comforts of a home. To one side, there was a wooden desk, with many scrolls stacked underneath and atop it. Before it sat a sturdy wooden bench. To the other side, there was a large slab mounted in the wall that seemed to be serving as a bed. It was piled high with furs and looked inviting. A large flask hung on the wall right next to the bed. Convenient, I get thirsty as I slumber too. Next to the bed was a small table and a well made stool fashioned from a single solid log. The third wall had a bowl, for washing, and even a bronze mirror, though this one seemed a bit damaged. Drawings on parchment were posted on the walls. Most of them looked... interesting, if a touch clumsy. A few showed centaurs at play, others natural scenes. They had a depth to them. It was hard to describe, even really see. Like they were sculptures rather than drawings.

One of them was stunning, though, and depicted in amazing detail what I could only assume was some sort of city. It rose into the sky from the waters of a lake, which was encircled by a ring of mountains, and was surrounded by a flock of great birds and strange clouds. The impossible city had so many towers, it seemed to be nothing but towers, and they were topped in sharp angular shapes, like they were a great crowd of swords. It felt real, like I was looking into the page, but I couldn't fathom why. It was just a sketch!

What was this place? I sat down on the stool, and placed my lamp and knife upon the table. As I tried to find my North Star in the dark, I noticed a harp was hiding in the shadow of the bed. I may never know why, but I reached out for it. Perhaps I just wanted to hold something familiar in this bewildering, alien place.

Once in my hands it did comfort me. The tuning gear was well made, and the arch had been bent expertly from a single piece of fine wood. I ran my hands over it; the surface was worn, and smooth with care and love. The strings seemed a bit widely spaced, as I began playing.

I played, and in that moment I was free, a student again in the fields of Thessaly, as I composed my own little tune to the hum of the cicadas. I might have grown to favor the knot, as every song needs a beat, but I am familiar with the sweet call of melody. My hands played out my leisurely song for hot summer days, or a version of it at least. Before I knew it I was a child again in Athens, and my hands worked out the song we would play as the storms gathered, and the refrain we would play as they blew out their energies and departed for another day. I was just finishing, with tears in my eyes, when my reverie was broken by applause.

I dropped the instrument with a sour note and jumped to my feet. Somehow, the knife was already in my hands, and to bear.

"Careful with that, it was a gift!" Said a voice in the darkness.

"Who are you?" I said it so fast it was almost one word.

"I should be asking you that. You're in my home, uninvited. Playing my instrument, too. You were doing so well, until you dropped it." It was a man's voice. Low, and sweet, like a singer who is face first in the fire through his working days but... different.

"Show yourself." My voice cracked with my nerves.

"Oh no, I won't be doing that, my uninvited guest. Living around here you get to be pretty cautious around strange light sources. No way I'm stepping in line with that thing." I realized this was probably wise. My own experience had taught me that light comes before power.

"Well, then... we are at an impasse." I straightened up out of my fighting stance, and held my knife to the side, "I don't care to turn off my lamp, because then I'd be in the dark and you could attack me."

"True, this is my home, and I know it well." There was mirth in his voice, as if he was actually happy to see me. I shuffled my feet, considered, and responded.

"Sorry about dropping the harp. It's nice."

"I forgive you. I did catch you by surprise." More mirth, as if he might break out in laughter. He could have killed me, but he applauded. He had every right to, I was in his home, uninvited. "How about this as a solution. You take your marvelous lamp, and hold it before you. I'll feel safe in the shade of your body. You can even keep your knife out, if you like. I'll stay a good few paces behind you, and you can walk ahead of me. If you trust me, I can get you out of here." Is he serious? No, of course he is, that air must go somewhere, and where else would he go? Across the span of the cave, into that blind house of horrors?

"Fine, I agree." A thousand thoughts were rushing through my mind. An image was forming, but it wasn't quite clear yet. I turned, held the lamp ahead of me, and my knife to the side, where he could see the blade in profile. And I began walking out the other door, towards the air. I had counted out fifty paces into the gloom when I almost stopped and turned. Was he still behind me? Even my sharp and honed ears couldn't tell, over the beating of my heart.

"Worry not, I follow. You are not far." It was such a fine voice, somehow both sad and happy, both smooth and gravely. Another fifty paces, and I emerged, into undergrowth. An arch of plants was woven overhead, and beyond the glare of my lamp there was only darkness. "Now we are out, but not out of it. Keep going." We walked on, in the cool grass, for two thousand paces or more. I wasn't tired, it felt like I was reborn. I never thought I would hear the night bird sing again. Ahead, I could see the moonlight, in a wooded clearing. I walked out, turned off my lamp, and turned to see the face of my savior.

Eight

He stayed on his feet. Most of them don't, when they first see me. Instead, he looked right at me, as if my face was a puzzle and he was trying to solve it.

"You can finish the job you came to do, if you like." I exposed my chest to him. "I won't stop you." I was only half joking. A part of me wouldn't mind if he stabbed me. But he fell into a relaxed stance, and looked around the clearing.

"The drawings were yours."

"All except the city."

"Yes. It was too good. Magical. Your teacher's work?"

"I suppose. Sort of?"

"Friend, then? Is he one of the two centaurs at the edge of the clearing, hiding in the shadows?" Had he heard them? I barely had; his hearing must be as fine as the rest of him.

"Yes, a dear friend." In response he closed his knife in a swift motion. It could fold!

"The centaurs have no love lost for man, but they wouldn't participate in a mass murder. Earlier tonight, I looked into the eyes of a monster. But... " He looked me right in the eyes, "I am not now... Where are they?" He had figured it out! I was overjoyed that I had no need to explain what had been done, yet again. It was such a tiresome speech, no matter how well practiced.

"Two hours hike from here, in a hidden basin. Most of them, anyways. I couldn't... I couldn't save them all."

"But you... " He was cracking, trying to speak between his tears. This was more like what I was used to. He coughed, and composed himself. "You saved them?"

"Yes. You're the first to figure it out."

"It solves a number of mysteries."

"Such as?"

"Such as, how you learned to do precision butchery, in the dark." Oh my, that was an oversight! "Show me."

"Well, yeah, where else would we put you." I raised an eyebrow. Some of my facial expressions were... difficult, but most everyone got that one. "There should be a canteen, in the weeds there. You might want some before we move on." He found it where I had pointed, and took a long drink. The Labyrinth is a very dry place. "I can lead the way."

"I would prefer to walk by your side. I have a few things to ask."

"As you wish." We walked, across the clearing, and into the woods. Chianten and Tileron had run ahead, to herald our coming to the Athenian camp. We walked in silence for half an hour, at least, before he spoke again.

"That was the strangest of introductions. Let's pretend this is a new start. My name is Thesius, I'm the prince of Athens. How goes the journey?"

"I'm Asterius, of the House of Minos. I'm... sort of a prince?" I quietly laughed, and risked a half grin. He didn't flinch at my teeth. His rhetorical question resonated with me in a strange way. Had I forgotten something? "My mother always claimed I was my father's son. I'm not sure I see the resemblance." Now it was Thesius' turn to laugh, which he quickly stifled.

"You know, I used to get that too." He turned and smiled. At this moment I realized that he already had a beard. Usually the Athenians only grow those out in their 'afterlife'. Odd. It was fetching. "You might have noticed why."

"How could I miss it? I know I've been... sheltered but I've never seen another man like you. Your hair! It's like your head and shoulders are both on fire, even in the moonlight. I take it this is not a common trait in Athens."

"I was the only one, not only in Athens, but in all of the peninsulas. I've heard people far to the north sometimes have golden hair, but they are pale and I am not. Are there any Minoans with golden hair like me?" I winced at the mention of my family name, but

86

I then shook my head in response to his question. After a moment of silence, I continued.

"That must have gotten you a lot of attention."

"I suspect you had it worse." Thesius frowned, deeply, and added, "No, I'm certain of it. What was that, back there?"

"The Labyrinth?" He nodded. "Power. Greed. Madness. Darkness. All of it."

"And you've been living there? For how long now?" He was so curious.

"18 years." Had it been so long? Saying it aloud... I'd spent the life of a young adult, living in that pit.

"So as long as I have been alive? Trapped in a murder cave? Putting on a show for your dad?" He shook his head, as if to shake out some moths, "It's not right."

"Many things are not right around here."

"Except for you. You seem like the only good Minoan I have met so far, except perhaps Ariadne." I winced again, and did my best to keep a straight face.

"My sister. You know, she almost got you killed." Thesius considered this for a moment.

"So, the sound of the lyre I heard, that was not your harp... You have had some communication with the palace above?" This man was very smart. I was impressed.

"Yes, I had a secret channel with my mother, all those years. A hole in the wall. Ariadne's face told my mother something was awry, and Elaía pried everything out of her. Warned me that the final Athenian was armed, and was there to kill me. I was not told you would bear such wonders, though." I smiled, and he smiled back. Fascinating.

"Athena herself gave them to me." He seemed troubled by the thought of his goddess, "Somehow got them to your sister, who hid them in the Labyrinth, in the first room."

"In the hole on the right side of the dias? That's a great hiding spot. I've used that one before."

"Well, if you had found them first I don't think that plan could have gone any more sideways." Thesius stifled another laugh, "I'm glad, though. Athena had no idea what was going on here." He stopped in his tracks, in a slice of pale blue light, and gazed up at the moon. "If I'd killed you… " His locks shimmered, as he shook his head. He seemed to be on the verge of tears again.

"Then I could hardly have blamed you. I'd almost welcome it." I was also choking up. Our emotions were feeding off of each other; I looked away.

"I had been trained to come here and be a hero. Die for Athens. It was all stupid." I felt his hand on my shoulder. "You're the hero. You were the hero before I was born… I could have killed you."

"What heroics have I engaged in?" I scoffed, and pulled away. "I'm an actor on a bloody stage. I play a monster for the sport of a madman. I lead youths around in the dark with words and promises. What is that?"

"You saved all of those lives."

"Not all of them." It hurt so much to think of it. I leaned against a tree for support, and crossed my arms. Thesius considered my words, before he spoke again.

"How many people did that chasm swallow up?"

"From Athens, three. Two from the first group, one from the third. They ran off, into the black. With so many coming in at once… I can't be everywhere. There is always so much fear and chaos, in those first moments in the dark. Before that… the entire crew that built my home. Including my dear friend and teacher. He was the master mason. Ma'aht." It felt so strange to say his name here, in the moonlight, rather than in his presence. "I lost two others. The ones who failed the test. Father had them butchered… for me." I had to sit down. Thinking about all of this hurt so much.

Before I could even catch my breath, Thesius had taken a seat before me. He was so quiet, on those bare feet. Nothing was said for a long time, while the insects continued to sing their song of love, oblivious to the drama taking place below. It was so peaceful, and in that moment I wanted to believe that it was all a bad dream, and I had always been sitting here in the moonlight, feeling at peace with this strange golden man.

"Is Ma'aht... is he the one who taught you how to be so unlike your father? It seems like most everyone is cursed to take after their parents, in one way or another."

"Yes." I inhaled, and tried to gather together all of the things he had taught me, as we wandered those twisting passages. I simply spoke from my heart. "It was he who taught me to consider the perspective of others. It was he who taught me to consider love before fear. It was he who taught me to consider the consequences of greed. I owe him everything." Thesius considered this, for a long moment.

"Perhaps Ma'aht is the real hero, then. Gods bless him." He gracefully rose to his feet with startling, practiced speed. It was like a magic trick, as if he had become weightless. He extended his hand to help me up, and I took it. I nearly pulled him back off his feet, too; I'm not sure he anticipated my mass. We both had a little chuckle, as we steadied each other.

"You have yet to see his real masterwork. I think you can hear the falls now, if your ears are as sharp as I think they are."

The roar of a waterfall does strange things to your hearing. If you don't pay it mind, you might not hear it at all, even as you come right upon it. Even a great and powerful thing, one that can carve the landscape up simply by standing in place, can sneak up on you if it does so steadily. But it can do other things. That dull roar dulls all sounds, and if it is in a basin, such as the one we were approaching, the effect is to cut off the inside from the outside. I knew all of this, and it was my custom to relate it about this point, as I gave the young Athenians their tour. I figured I had given Thesius enough of a hint, so I held my tongue.

We entered the clearing before the final barrier. I paused for a breather, and found a good tree to lean on. "Well, you've been reading us like a scroll so far, what do you make of this?"

He took a look around before speaking. Such a rare quality in men, to think before you speak. Somewhat less rare in women... still pretty rare. I had noticed by now it even tripped him up sometimes, as he thought twice about something even as he spoke. He faced me, and grinned under his fluffy beard.

"First off, disguising the path as deer trails, just brilliant. If I didn't know what I was looking for, or the direction I needed to go, it wouldn't have meant anything to me."

"I have to give credit for that to the centaurs. Well, and your fellows, they work at night to maintain things. I'm afraid to say, I seem to have turned everyone into a night person. Our little production needs to have all the set pieces in place by daylight, yes?"

"And what of the extraction? That must happen in the evening, usually."

"As is convenient, since most people take their time to get their night sight, unlike you. Think of our path, and where the evening shadows would lie."

"I can see it. Brilliant is actually the top superlative I know and I'm right out of them now." He followed this up with a laugh, unrestrained. I smiled at him, and he smiled back again. It was so nice to be unafraid to do that.

"And here, what about this puzzle."

"Oh, this." Thesius confidently strode over to the door, a delicate framework of nasty thorns and vines that was disguising, protective and repellant, and swung it aside with ease. This was great fun. "Chiron would use these things to hide his forest caches. That's my teacher. A centaur. Less tragic than your teacher, I guess. He yet lives."

"Ah, but that is their tragedy, is it not?" We shared a knowing look.

Our trip down to the camp took hardly any time. Most of our journey was behind us. Even as we approached, it was barely visible. High above, the stream met its broken path, and fell into the pool below. That water was life, for all of these people. There, against the cliffside, was the village, made with the leftovers from the construction of the Labyrinth, under a cloak of midnight and bonds of secrecy. It hugged the wall, protected from all angles and every prying eye; a single long building, shaded from most weather by the cliffside, with outside doors on two levels. Most of the birds probably didn't know it was here.

It was a cruel irony that my father's choice to murder the workers at the conclusion of the construction made maintaining this secret much easier. Too many people probably knew of this place, but then it was only the centaurs and I who needed to maintain the secret. That and the growing crowd of Athenians who were compelled to silence by their situation. That crowd was coming out to meet us now.

I could see a moment's hesitation in him, as he saw their local dress, but then he broke into a run. Their faces must have told the story. Tears and hugs were shared all around. I wanted to give them their moment, and slip away, but there was one more task to take care of. A young woman, from the new group, beat me to the punch.

"Ok beautiful, you're probably real sick of hearing this by now, but you need to undress." Everyone laughed. There was no need to maintain quiet here. "You can go find a private place if you like, we're not a bunch of assholes."

"Is that my skirt and belt? Give it here, I can't wait to get out of this creepy thing." I had to agree with that, at some point the entire front of his outfit had been dusted with dried blood flakes. It was much more obvious in the firelight. In a swift motion, Thesius tossed off the white tube of linen and pulled on the skirt he had been offered. He must have gotten very used to people appreciating his appearance. Most of the women and about half the men had *such* a look on their faces.

As he fumbled with the belt, and its complicated clasping, Mantes approached with the goat. Procuring food was the biggest task the centaurs had taken unto themselves, but the livestock had a special purpose.

"I'll do it." I always did. A life for a life, it was the only way. I bent down, on one knee, and took the goat's head in my large hands.

Stroked it down the neck, and around the ears. I grabbed it by the skull, and rubbed it gently. "Sorry for this." Then, swiftly twisted it once around, with a loud crack.

"Let us do the butchery. You have enough blood on your hands tonight." Mantes was so kind. They were all so kind.

"Try to do a sloppier job about it." Thesius laughed, now fitted in his belt. No one else got the joke. "Though, I still need to carry it back. My hands will be bloody no matter what." I also needed to tell my mother that I yet lived, though she would have to believe the worst of me for it to be true.

Just one more hike before dawn, and I could draw another act of this sordid play to a close. As I made my way back, I was filled with an unaccustomed joy, and my fast hops had a delightful spring to them. Was it because I had managed to save them all, for the first time? Yes, it must be that. Though my mind did keep returning to his melodious laugh, and his golden fur.

Nine

About half an hour after Asterius left, my torn and bloody outfit in hand, all of the surviving Athenians were gathered in the garden and leisure space on the other side of the waterfall pool, to trade stories and catch up as we awaited the coming of the dawn. My elation at this turn of events may have masked it, but I couldn't deny my own body any more; I felt most unwell. The world spun, and my stomach seemed both painfully empty, and nauseous. Everyone else noticed when I almost fell off the log I was sitting on.

"Thesius, can I assist?" It was the same man who had brought the goat earlier. Manny? There have been so many names so fast. I wish I'd paid more honor to the dead, back in Athens. This thought process did nothing to settle my stomach.

"Yes, if you can." He took a knee before me, and steadied me with a strong arm on my shoulder. His hand moved down to my elbow, where he felt my heart.

"Let me look," He pulled down my eyes and checked my pupils. I bet the centaurs have been teaching him the art of the physician. "What have you eaten in the past three days?"

"I… " Wait… was that all? "Basically nothing? Some bread and fish yesterday, not much. A few carrots today, before I was tossed into the… the murder cave." Everyone laughed at this appellation.

"Hah, right on the target."

"That's what it is. Damn murder cave."

"Ah, we got a new name for it."

"Don't you worry," the physician continued, as everyone else chatted about their new favorite name for their least favorite place, "This is very common. Most everyone loses their appetite when they think death approaches. I'm gonna give you a small bowl of the centaur porridge and send you to bed. You'll be fine soon enough."

This prescription seemed like the worst idea in the world, given the nausea I already felt, but I was shocked to discover that this rendition of the food centaurs were forced to eat, for the sake of their delicate stomachs, was very different. While it shared the basic grains and vegetables that I was used to in Chiron's version, it had spices! And it was salted nicely! And it wasn't mush! Most of the vegetables had even been roasted and placed on top. By the time I had finished the bowl, not only was I not nauseous, I was very ready to sleep. I asked for the second half of my treatment, and Mantes, whose name I had caught as I ate, escorted me to a bed. It was in the second level of the structure everyone seemed to live in, in a room that was clearly occupied.

Mantes explained, "We'll get you a room for yourself, there are actually lots of empty ones, but we are short a few bits of furniture right now." I was delighted to discover the bed was of the Lapith design, and I slept better than I had in weeks.

I awoke to a delicious aroma, as the sun was begging to set. I had desperately needed sleep, but now I was awake, and the meal still wasn't drawing me in, no matter how good it smelled.

Helea and Miletta were in the workshop I had passed on the way to my room, probably for some privacy while everyone else was eating. As I laid in my bed, I could hear every word of their conversation. The waterfall might have made this arrangement, living atop one another, more tolerable for most of the Athenians, but my overly sensitive ears were happy to reveal every detail.

"No, it's just... I feel like every eye is on me. I'm not accustomed to this." I could even hear Helea sigh, and sit down on a wooden chair, as it scooted a bit across the floor.

"I know this is not what we expected, but I mean, look back at them! Athens really did send their best to this place." Miletta seemed happy. I'm not sure I'd ever heard her voice in that state.

"Speak for yourself, I... "

"Oh come on, I didn't mean we're all as beautiful as Thesius, don't be silly. And I mean, look at me, some men favor this," she paused, as she must have been gesturing over her sturdy frame,

94

"Sure, but I look down on most of 'em." Another pause. "We're all young and… Darling, I've been starving for years and this place is a feast. The centaurs even got us silverseed so we can live without worries." Wait, what? Do the centaurs piss out that stuff or something?

"I'm not just big, Miletta."

"Well, I... I mean, it's not that bad I... "

"And I honestly don't want to be bothered." Another long pause.

"The one is more than enough, if you're blessed with twins they can take turns." Miletta seemed to be making light of this, but I wasn't sure that was wise.

"Men aren't looking at them for the utility of it, you're being ridiculous." Helea's voice was raised, and there was a definite edge to it, "And… what of us?" Ah, there it was. There was another long pause. Enough of this, I couldn't bear to eavesdrop any more. I got up, straightened my new skirt and tried to get the belt back around. I gave up after the fourth buckle, you really needed help to get into these things, and walked two doors down. I got a sharp look from both of them.

"You are not a part of this conversation." Helea was sitting in the chair where I had visualized her.

"Yeah, beautiful, I know you're not on the menu."

"Forgive me." I rubbed my eyes; getting up so quickly had left me with a headache. "But I heard every damn word of it. I'm sorry, I can't turn these things off."

Helea cast her hand into the air in frustration, "There's no privacy here."

"Naw hon, I think Thesius is a special case." Miletta must know of all the tricks I used to get up to when I was younger. "Did you see the ovens, they're so clever, the flues go right up into the waterfall and there's no smoke at all."

"That would be a great subject to change to, but like you said, I'm not on the menu." Despite this perfect joke, no one laughed, largely because no one had noticed the perfect joke, not even Thesius. "And I heard everything so... Maybe I'm the only man here who could give an unbiased opinion."

"What is there to talk about?" Helea crossed her arms, and winced for a moment in pain.

"We could talk about that. That old wound. Or we could talk about you two." They both blushed and looked aside. "Look, maybe I'm different enough to see something most men would miss, but..."

Helea stood, a bit of fire in her eyes, but before I could think I had made a terrible mistake, her face softened. "You care, I can see that. I spent years being angry at the injustice of our situation. And now it's all so strange. I still want to be angry and I am constantly checking myself. Moments ago, I almost yelled at the person I care most for, even as she was trying to help me. And then you come, and I almost yell at you." She turned to Miletta, no longer embarrassed to speak before me, "Am I being jealous? We never did share anything physical, besides what I might observe in my amusement. But I love you. I do."

"No, I... I love you too." And they embraced, the one practically towering over the other. They half broke the hug, but were still arm in arm. Miletta continued, "It's not even like sisters, too. I mean, if you'd wanted... The ladies at the temple of brewing weren't shy."

"I'm glad you never pressured me. I'm just... maybe it's the pain, I can't escape it." This was very sweet to see. I had tears in my eyes as well.

"Well, I'm here for you no matter what. If some man insists on being my husband you can tag along as long as you like. So long as he doesn't mind that I prefer talking to you."

"What if he does mind?" I'm not sure I'd ever seen Helea smile before, but she was now.

"He goes in the ditch. If I can't toss him, I'll roll him." We all had a good laugh at the visual, and I took this as an opportunity to wave and go. I'd meddled enough. Besides, I felt my appetite returning.

Down below, I could see everything I could want; tables of food, sparkling waters, a fine little forest and pasture to play in. All ringed by stone in this marvelous little valley. Everybody seemed to be doing their best to enjoy the idyllic scene too, here at the close of the day. Music and laughter called me down, but even this close the effects of the waterfall and the canyon walls dulled their sharpness, as if it was far away. The fields of Elysium I expected to be experiencing by now would only be a slight upgrade.

I went down, and dined. We had adopted the Cretan way of dress, but not so much their diet. I was thankful for this. I loved meat, but besides the lack of fish, this was like a taste of home. As I ate I mingled and talked, and learned a few things. Everyone had concluded that the falls we had the company of continued down into the caves below. I had wondered this myself, as the pond at the base of the falls had no clear drainage. There was even a sink at one end of the pond where you could see a small whirlpool. It didn't seem dangerous, but everyone avoided it when they swam or bathed.

The ovens we had on hand were excellent, and everything that came forth from them seemed ambrosial. Just as Miletta had described, their exhaust was piped up into the falls, where it practically disappeared into the haze of water vapor it threw. The fire was kept in a separate box from the cooking food, and everything they produced was never burnt or smoky, just cooked and good. And when you heated them, the top stone also got burning hot. You could heat or cook more things on that! I resolved to learn more about how they had been constructed, as I bit down on my third flatbread. My appetite was somewhat dampened when I realized I'd have to go to Elysium to ask the designer personally. If he would end up there. His name sounded like it was of the Nile. What happens, when a man dies in a foreign land? Do the gods give him passage, or judge him by the local custom? I hope that either way, the hero who gave us all this would get some reward.

But then, my thoughts moved on to our other hero. The one who yet lived. My heart broke for him, and I felt ashamed that I had once harbored such hatred for someone I knew nothing about. What could be done?

The centaurs were on the edge of the clearing. They never much liked mingling with people, besides their own kind. It was strange to see them so close at all. I felt their eyes upon me, several times, and as the sun set and the people of Athens prepared for their night's work, I walked over to greet them.

"I am Thesius. I was trained at Chiron's school." They exchanged a glance. They knew this name, of course. They were a small community. "My debt to your people can not be understated, and I wanted to thank you. But I also know your people well enough. You may not enjoy my company, if that is so I will take no offense and give you wide berth."

"No, stay. For now." This one had lighter hair than my teacher. His whole form was thinner, as if he were built for speed. "I am Chianten. This is Tileron. He will not speak much."

"I am pleased to meet you both, and honored by your forbearance." I took a seat in the grass, and got comfortable, as they were, "As I understand, you were involved in this plan from the beginning?"

"Not the beginning. Nearly. We caught these men doing work at this sacred place. We were going to kill them for the profanity of it, when a wise man stopped us, and told us it was to save many lives. We listened to him... he was convincing." Tileron watched, silently. He seemed made on the same blueprint as Chiron, big and strong, but with light grey coloring to his fur, beard and hair. His skin was a bit darker too, where it showed. On the horse half, this coloration seemed almost dull, but on the half that was modeled on a man it was extraordinary.

"Was this wise man, Ma'aht?" Tileron, who had shown interest but little comprehension of the conversation thus far, opened his eyes wide and looked to his companion. They exchanged a few words in a completely unfamiliar language. He knew the name.

"Yes, and we are puzzled as to how you know of him."

"Asterius spoke of him. Very highly, as his teacher." The two of them exchanged more words. I still couldn't pick out one I knew.

"Asterius speaks not of his teacher. His death left a wound that has not fully healed. Might I ask the context in which it came up?" I thought about my experience last night, and tried to get my mind around it before I spoke. My audience gave me the time to think, and I appreciated it.

"I figured out he was saving them. I mean, us. Just as we emerged. I mean, I found his room first." I was failing to explain this in any way.

"We thought there might be trouble, but it was clear you had reached an understanding. He did not aid you, in finding his true home?"

"No, I found it. I had the lamp."

"I saw it. Speak not of it, and don't attribute your achievements to a tool. Unless my understanding of the maze is wrong in every way, finding that room is difficult, by design."

"I give Chiron credit for my training. We did spend some time in caves. That was... more useful than I thought it would be." The whole experience was dreadful, really. If I never saw another cave so long as I breathed I would be a happy man.

"Even so, that must have impressed him." Did it? He seemed amused by it. I remembered the incident with the harp, and my cheeks must have gone red. Enough light remained in the day to betray me. "What else happened, there?"

"I... I'm not sure what came over me, but I played his harp. I was confused, nothing added up, nothing was as I expected it to be. He must have been listening to me for a while." Chianten related this story to Tileron in their chirping, bird like language, and spoke back and forth for a minute.

"Forgive us, Tileron has no talent with languages and gave up trying to learn new ones long ago." I waited patiently for them to finish.

"And then, when you spoke, was it speeches, all ready and finely tuned?"

"No… I mean, he is a fine speaker. He seems to command the tongue better than I do. But, there were no speeches. We talked back and forth. He seemed to be testing me a bit, at the end. He is… he seems to be very sad. I mean, I understand."

"I'm not sure that you do, but then again, you have shown remarkable understanding of so many things, so far. There is only so much I can attribute to Chiron." Chianten smiled, and I knew this was a rare blessing. I took the opportunity to ask a question.

"Are you the artist, or is it your companion?"

"Tileron… you might say he was a born artist."

"Made to that purpose?"

"Art and leisure are not a purpose so much as… " and he broke, as he understood the implication of the question. He had to recompose himself. "I am unaccustomed to this level of understanding. How much do you know of us?"

"You're older than everything. Evil men made you for their amusement, and you persist against your own will."

"That… that is not a normal part of Chiron's curriculum, and I should know. I helped him develop it." He stared me down, looked right through me, but I felt no fear. "You are mostly right. Though, we are not older than everything. Your light, I used to hand out those things by the hundreds, at parties. Everything they made lasted longer than it should… I would feel guilty about you having to clean up our messes, if we were not ourselves part of the mess."

"You owe us nothing, less than nothing, and yet you continue to help. As I said, I am grateful." Tileron interrupted. There was something he wanted to communicate to me, and Chianten related it.

"Tileron worries about Asterius. He fears the chasm calls to him. In my years of knowing him, I have exchanged a few dozen sentences with him, and he is always so practiced and controlled. He seemed… different, in your presence. Tileron, he has tried his best to communicate with him, in his way."

"Asterius values his friendship. He said so." Chianten related this, and it elicited another rare smile, this time from his companion.

They spoke more. A plan seemed to be forming, and I waited to be included in on it.

"Well… You play? What is your favorite instrument?"

"I think they call it a baglama around here. Three strings, you can do harmony or percussion on it. You play with your fingertips, not a coin."

"We have one, and I think it will be yours. But that word, it just means musical instrument. Someone might hand you one with the paired strings. Round here, they call the one you want a kopu. Far to the east of here, that word also just means musical instrument… This is why Tileron has given up on languages." We all had a brief chuckle at this, even Tileron, who didn't find his lack of words to be too much of a barrier to communication, even though words themselves almost always are. "There is a glade, where Asterius goes to play his harp and enjoy the moonlight. It is safe, and secluded. Tileron draws with him there, sometimes. Normally we don't let the new ones out for a year or two, until we are sure you can move undetected in the night. Your disguises will only go so far. But you, you should be able to move safely through the forest, trained as you are. We will show you where it is. Perhaps music will bring him some peace."

"He deserves so much more than peace." I felt a fiery anger rising in me. "That chasm might bring him peace. Is there no justice in the land of Minos?"

"Men are bad at justice, you don't have the patience for it. If you find even a moment of joy in your brief lives it is a rare thing, so don't cast away joy for justice… Will you help?"

"Of course."

"It takes a few days for things to calm down after the sacrifice. Make yourself useful, as I'm sure Chiron taught you to. We will get back with you when the time is right."

I bowed low to them, my face to the grass, and left to do just that.

Ten

The days after the sacrifice were the most dreary part of the production. I am forced to sit in the dark, or shuffle about in the distant corridors while the priests conduct their rituals. I have to be present, but not myself, moaning or making some other spooky sound in the background, as a dark chorus to the priest's workings. At least I did not have to harden my heart; I had no fresh tragedies to mourn, this time. I was worried about how I would communicate to my mother, but this was a foolish concern. The priests knew I was there. Mother would just have to assume the worst of me, as always.

Sometimes I would watch in the shadows, more out of boredom than anything else, as the priests conducted their rituals. The Principle, who wore the mitre of the old god of knowledge, did most of the work, chanting and drawing symbols on the dias in the lamplight with fresh blood. It was hard to take him seriously with a fish jumping out of his head.

My own reading of the relevant texts suggested that their old god of knowledge wasn't so much a fish, but a being that resembled the flightless birds that live on the southern half of this sphere. But, things get handed down, and over time a bird that swims in the water becomes a fish. The fact that I knew he was drawing those symbols with a goat's blood, while uttering words he barely understood, gave me no small joy as well. I tried to channel that feeling into some well timed howls and groans. The whole thing was a parody of what might have to be done, if they were to succeed in their fowl rituals. But, who was I to tell a priest what to do? I was merely the 'god' they were trying to raise.

On the fourth day, I rested. I always gave it a full day, to be sure the clerics had cleared out of the Labyrinth. And then on the fifth I had my small purchase of freedom back, and the energy to use it. I showered my stink off in my hidden lavatory, and changed back into finer clothes.

My harp in hand, I hiked down to my hidden glade. Well, it was more of a fast hop. I was thrilled to be free of the Labyrinth. My glade was about halfway to the Athenian camp, and was protected by a small crescent shaped hill. It may have been an amphitheater at some point in the distant past, but now it just served to reflect my music away from the palace. The centaurs had also effectively spread many rumors about these woods, and no one would dare investigate strange music in the night. I was safe here.

As I turned the bend, I relaxed my shoulders, and breathed a sigh of relief. I surveyed my kingdom; moss and grass, a few lovely weathered rocks, and the ancient stands, long since covered in greenery. In the thin sliver of moonlight, I could see my friend Tileron hiding in the shadows at the edge of the clearing. He knew the rhythms of the show well at this point, and I was glad to see him. Moments later, my heart jumped straight into my throat as I saw that Thesius was there with him.

"Greetings!" He had done his neat levitation trick, and was approaching me. He had a kopu with him, and was in his disguise. It looked great on him. Someone else must have adjusted the belt properly. It was wrapped around his hips right, and was trim about his muscular trunk. It dawned on me that he wanted me to say something in response. I'd been standing mute like a fool for who knows how long.

"Uh, Thesius. Yes. I'm surprised."

"If I am intruding, I would take no offense to leave." His baritone voice was so sweet, how could I take offense at it?

"No, don't leave." I felt like I had to make some sort of excuse, "I'm not used to seeing the first years out and about." This was true, but it was almost a lie; none of the Athenians ever came here. I wasn't sure if they knew where it was, or even that it was.

"I get along well with the 'taurs. They knew my old teacher, in their day. So they know I'm not going to make a mess of things. I know my way about the woods, at night." Tileron was watching us both, intently, in his customary silence. I could see that he was at ease;

he must trust him. I couldn't imagine how Thesius had earned that trust, so quickly, given the barrier of language. Chianten must have helped. "I was told this was a good place to come and play. I forced you to watch me perform once, maybe you'd like to see me on my favorite?"

"Yes. I would. That would be wonderful." I was already wavering on my feet, so I took a seat on the incline, and watched. He took his cue, and began playing. It was mostly just a rhythm, but it was a good one, infectious. Before long I was tapping my toes on the ground in sympathy with his vibration. He finished, and shifted his stance, before looking me right in the eyes. I noticed how his eyes sparkled, as they seemed to reflect every bit of light back at me. "I didn't come here just to perform, you know. This thing doesn't really sing unless I have someone to play melody with me." I wondered who would... oh, me. I had a harp. Why was I being so dull?

I changed into a less laid out posture, and balanced my harp on my lap. I placed my hands upon the strings, and for a moment I blanked out completely, as if I had never held the thing. Thankfully, Thesius started back up with his infectious rhythm, and my hands remembered before my mind did.

The first song was over before I knew it. It was complete, yes, but my hands itched. This time, I led, with a simple repeating scale, as people would sometimes play in the background at feasts and functions. When I was young, I lived for those things, which gave me a chance to pretend I was just a normal child, enjoying the same things as everyone else. The performance house had a box, for the royal family, and the evenings of music and theatre were always the highlight of my week. I often dreamt of taking the stage myself. The divine gives you what you ask for in the worst ways, sometimes.

I returned from my reverie to find us playing furiously. Thesius intentionally miss-strummed a foul note, and grinned at me through his fluffy beard.

"We were doing so well there, but then it was like you got mad at the song and tried to chase it down."

"My mind wandered. This... is a joy I am not used to."

"I'm sure the other Athenians would be happy to accompany you, if you ever feel like making music."

"Yes, but, I mean… it's farther. Not convenient." Why was I stretching the truth so much? I didn't do that because I was afraid for them. If I were caught there, the play would be over. The set dressing would fall right on us. I shot a look at Tileron. He seemed to be enjoying the show.

"They care for you, as the centaurs do. You might not be ready to credit yourself for your heroism, but they all do. No one blames you for… for the ones who didn't make it through." A somber moment passed, and he began playing again. This rhythm was slower, more considered. I built off of it a mournful melody. I couldn't help it, they were on my mind. By the end of it we both had tears in our eyes, but they were mixed of joy and sadness. It felt like a funeral, when the worst of the tragedy is over. I struggled to speak. Such a strange affliction for me.

Before I could shrug off this odd feeling and continue playing, Aeolus, or perhaps it was Enlil, interrupted us with a peal of thunder. Or not, it was probably just a storm. Neither of us cared to risk our instruments to a soaking, so we bid a quick farewell and made our way back to our respective homes. My feet were so swift beneath me that I easily beat the rain. The time it took for the storm to finally move in felt like such a waste.

I awoke the next evening, holding my harp in my arms. Such an oversight, that was terrible for it. I checked the tuning, and everything was in order. Lucky. I couldn't remember going to bed, was I that out of sorts? I dressed, and had a small meal of nut cakes and dried goat meat, before resolving to hit that nice patch of summer berries on the way to my glade. The ironic knowledge that I was eating goat before and after the sacrifice ran out put some salt on the jerky, if only in my mind.

This represented the last of the meat they would deliver in the years between sacrifices. They had some hazy concept of my provision, up there. They tried to starve me, in the months before, but they really had no idea how much I truly ate. A lot of the fresh meat would end up in Athenian bellies. More irony for me not to laugh at, in the dark.

As I approached the exit, harp in hand, my prominent nose was telling me I would be disappointed before my ears confirmed it. I went on to the portal to see for myself. The storm raged on.

I returned to my abode, and pulled out a few of my favorite scrolls to read. These were in the looping script from the east, but I had read them so many times there was no effort in translation. They told tales of a long time ago, in places far away, when man flew with strange beings from one sphere to another in fantastic conveyances. Their many wars and treks in the stars were always entertaining to read of, if perhaps somewhat exaggerated. It made me wonder, though. If any of it were true, how far had man fallen? A side glance at my friend's depiction of his old home, hanging on my wall, was enough to confirm that it was quite a way.

As I laid down to rest, after my morning tour of the maze, I failed in my meditations and fell into the dreaming. In the misty realm I found myself on the stage of my childhood, before an adoring audience. They looked up at me with love, not fear. No one was disgusted, no one turned their gaze aside. I took my bow before the next scene. Behind the curtain, I stood astride my stage prop, a shining silver circle with a cutout and a seat. As the fabric parted, the stage hands lifted me into the air on ropes, and I cried out, hands aloft:

"Away, to adventure!" The roof peeled back and the clouds came upon me with thrilling speed. The sky shifted through the violet end of the spectrum, into purest black. I looked back, upon the world below, blue and beautiful and so very alive. I turned myself, and my silver steed, towards the stars, yoke in hand, and let out a cry for freedom as I sped towards them. My joy at exploring strange worlds, seeking out life and civilization, wasn't dampened at all by my certain knowledge that there was nothing new under any sun.

Eleven

It seemed like that storm would never end. I should have been thankful; Ma'aht's masterwork was better protected from the weather than any home I'd ever had. Even the outer walkway, built as it was on the roof of the first level, hardly saw a raindrop in the shade of the cliff. The people of Athens preferred to spend their time playing in the glade or the shade of the trees, but in a storm most everyone would be in or around the kitchen or the workshop, the two largest rooms, as they were now.

The rest of the rooms were a vast crowd of small, identical chambers, each with a curtained door to the outside. To one end on the ground floor was a bathing room, which had similar conveniences to those I had been witness to before. No shower, though. Gaia had provided us with one of those. And unlike the prisoners in the House of Minos, we had to share the three mechanical whirlpools between us. But it was still luxurious. They had enough empty rooms here to host the sacrifice for generations, especially if they doubled up. So far, that had only happened by choice.

The overflow crowd at the workshop was sitting out on that walkway and talking merrily as they worked on crafts. The output of the workshop had increased significantly the past few days, too. I could be thankful for that. Everyone's enthusiasm for their usual favorite activity was dampened by both the clammy humidity and the prospect of dodging lighting bolts for a wash. Not that it was fully dampened; my old friend Estius was absent from sight, as always. I walked down the stone stairs from the second level, my new bench in hand, walked to the end of the row, and entered my new home.

The weather did give me time to set up my living quarters some more. For that I could be thankful. I looked over my space, larger than a prison cell, but only just. To the right were the standard fixtures. A stone bowl was inset in an alcove, with a flagon for water next to it. The bowl itself could be removed and cleaned; there was little sense in cleansing one's face and hands with dirty water in a dirty bowl. A hook protruded from the wall, to hold our disguise, which was very close to a uniform here. The only other feature in the room was a large bed. These rooms were primarily for day sleeping or privacy. I set the bench down next to it. Now, this space would also serve for my contemplation.

That bed was a source of endless comfort to me, and they had it finished within a day of my arrival. It resembled my old cot in construction, but it was huge. My cot could barely hold two very familiar people, but the Athenians had taken the form and stretched it to the size of the sea of woolen cushions so many of them had grown up with. These beds could hold three people. Maybe four. I'm sure, sometimes they did.

The bed might have been some whimsy, but the instruments they were currently at work on were deadly serious. As luck would have it, the first two sacrifices included four people who grew up crafting such things. They had trained everyone else, as there was time, and the facility. In the end, this had aided the camp greatly in its comfort and safety.

They were musical instruments. The centaurs were able to use their trading chain to obscure the source of these beautiful tools of music. Centaurs in the woods with strange wares was a common thing. Most of what we got in return were raw materials, as it was easier to obscure their transport. The leather that was so critical in making those beds was beyond our ability to craft, and came from elsewhere. The House of Minos paid careful mind to the movement of goods in its borders, to keep things like weaponry out of the hands of the rowdy border regions, so we had to take great care in what we traded in.

Some of the things that returned to us, along that chain, almost certainly came from Hellea. The finely decorated bronze flagon on my shelf was not unlike one I had used throughout my childhood in Athens. I sat on my new bench, my now closed curtain blowing a bit in the breeze, and contemplated the thought of the people of Athens playing beautiful music on tools crafted by their dead children. But no matter how much I tried to immerse myself in the joyous irony of that, my mind kept returning to my strange, sad friend. Tileron's worry had become my own. He deserved so much better than his lot in life.

I found myself with tears in my eyes. This was the opposite of my intention. So I just hurled myself into that bed and tried to out sleep the storm.

The grass was still damp, but was quickly drying in the summer heat, as I walked up to the centaurs on the edge of the glade, my knot in hand. I had performed my duties in a hurry, which everyone thought was amusing, as I had to insist upon taking an even measure of them. I was no prince, here. The centaur's heads were ringed in smoke, as was often the case. Tonight it smelled of the scent glands of a badger. I nearly gagged as I approached, but I kept a straight face.

"Greetings, my friends!" The two of them gazed lazily up at me, their eyes bloodshot and sleepy.

"Aren't we eager?" Chianten grinned through his thin straight beard, as if he had heard a funny joke but was too sleepy to laugh. "You know, he comes out on his own schedule." The thought that Asterius might not be there had not crossed my mind, and I must have frowned. "But he does like his freedom. Tileron?" Tileron shook his curly locks and let out a sharp chirp. The head-shake was a universal word, but as usual his utterances were a mystery. Is that what a bird curse sounds like?

"Oh, I supposed we can just let you find your way there, on your own." He said this in my language, but Chianten beaconing towards the gate must have communicated enough to his friend. Tileron arose, sleepily. He trusted me, but not enough to go unescorted, not just yet.

The night had fallen fully by the time we arrived there. The new moon mirrored the waning light I had seen the glade by before. Asterius was already there, seated in the way that seemed most comfortable for him, with his thick tail tucked between his crossed legs. I was relieved that my worries were unfounded. He was tuning his instrument, and playing a few notes. I was quite surprised we hadn't heard a thing until we turned around the hill into a direct line of sight. This spot was well chosen.

"Greetings!" I called out. Asterius looked up, and a broad smile broke across his face. I smiled back, and he laughed.

"No one else smiles back at me. Not when I really smile. Are you just unimpressed by my teeth?" He dropped one hand down to the grass and leaned upon it to look at me without moving from his seat, and smiled again for emphasis. I took a good look at his face. One might mistake Asterius' face for that of a bull, or an ox, with his short curved horns and his snout. It was mostly covered with the same tight coat of dark brown fur as the rest of him, but the hair atop his head and upon his chin was longer. That, and the high dome of his head, gave him the appearance of having a mane, like a bear, or a mountain lion. His ears, never at rest, poked out from below those decorations of curved ivory, in the same fashion as a bull. But his mouth was filled with teeth much more akin to that of a boar, and when he smiled his long crossed incisors were very visible, and very sharp. They didn't stand proud from his face like a boar's teeth though, more neatly laid too. I walked around so he wouldn't have to crane, and took a seat about six feet before him.

"Not unimpressed, but not surprised either."

"Everyone finds everything about me surprising, why is that?"

"Chiron taught me that when you see an unfamiliar creature, you should look to the eyes. If the eyes are on the sides, they are looking out for things that might eat them. If the eyes are on the front, they are looking for things to eat, like you." I used two fingers to point at my own eyes, and then his. "Your eyes are on the front. You are either a predator, or a creature that eats all things. It's good, you would have died here if you couldn't eat meat." Not to mention, his father's plan would have been utterly ridiculous.

"An omnivore." This was an unfamiliar word.

"I take it that is a special word you Cretans have for it?" I was thankful I had not referred to the people here by the newer word for them. He clearly hated to hear his family's name.

"Yeah, we have words for many things. Mostly curses." We both got a good laugh out of that.

"It seems like such a limited case, why bother? Just describe things." I leaned back upon my hands. Crossed legs weren't as comfortable for me as it was for him.

"It takes up a lot of time to do that, especially when you have a lot to describe." He thought about this for a moment. "I've got a good example. Tell me what the color of the sky is. Not now, in the daylight." Is this a trick question?

"It's green, as the sky is green. Or the sea near the shore." I humored him.

"It's blue. Like your eyes." This new word meant nothing to me, but it was the color of the sky? "See how much less time that took? You people from Hellea, you describe everything in relation to red and green. Not only does it waste a lot of time, it's a poor reflection of reality... I mean, it's dark, they could be grey, I guess, but... "

"No, they are... blue." Another smile, "Ok, tell me how your way is better." His face brightened; he had already formulated an answer to this.

"Imagine a rainbow. What do you see?" I was unsurprised, at this point, that his answer took the form of more questions. I wondered, had he learned this method from the centaurs? Or from Ma'aht? I closed my eyes momentarily, and visualized.

"Bands of color, in an arch. The sky is dark with rain."

"Ok, so those colors, they have sharp lines between them, yes?" He was showing me a lot of teeth again.

"Yes. I mean, they waver in the air, but they are distinct." It must have been many years since Asterius had seen a rainbow, but his vision of it was more clear than I. I had not paid so much attention.

"So the natural order is for those colors to stand distinct from one another. We simply named each one. From the top, red, orange, yellow, green, blue, indigo, purple, violet. There are colors above and below the rainbow too, but most people can't see them." I thought back to the first time I saw him, in the light of a more full moon.

"Your eyes would be yellow or orange. It's not so exact." I noticed the hair stand up on his cheeks. I'd seen this before… is that a blush?

"Yes, well, there are more possible colors than there are possible names. I concede that you have to stop somewhere."

I pondered this new concept, "Is that why the women here dress in such extraordinary colors?"

"Maybe? It's easier to ask for something, or desire it, if you have a name for it." He placed his hand upon his chin, somehow both furry and bearded, and thought for a moment before continuing, "But also, dyeing techniques was one of the things we dug up. Trading our fabric to the east made us rich."

"So, how do you know so much about rainbows? You've been stuck in the murder cave for so long…"

"Murder cave? That's the second time you called it that. Is that your name for the Labyrinth?"

"Now it's everyone's name for it. Sorry about that, it's my fault."

"It's a very good name… Rainbows are a favorite subject of mine. I have several scrolls that detail how they work."

"So, you sat in the dark with a lamp and learned how rainbows work, just to pass the time?" I wasn't trying to make fun, but it was a touch funny.

"When you are trapped in an endless darkness, any bit of light is a relief, even if it is merely reading about how it works." Oh no, that wasn't funny. That was terribly tragic. I had no reply to that, besides to stand up and play. I stretched a bit first. Asterius watched intently, and picked up his harp.

I started with the same rhythm he had such ease with the other night, until he didn't. Maybe this time the song wouldn't tear off into the air like a scared bird. His mind was more on the music, and he wove a fine melody around my rhythm. Before long I had enough of a hold on it that I was providing some harmony with my other two strings. We extended the bridge, and kept on playing. Neither of us wanted it to end. But I decided to speed up, to see how he would react. He turned it into a natural, furious ending to the song. It was thrilling. Tileron applauded from the edge of the clearing, and came to join us. He had his board and his parchment in hand.

He turned this towards me, and I saw myself. He had somehow taken his stick of charcoal and frozen me in a moment. There I stood, on one foot, balanced. My wooly face looked almost like a reflection rendered in grey and white. I had to search my mind for the moment he had depicted, before I realized that it was when I was stretching my legs, just a few minutes before. It was astonishing, I couldn't believe he had produced it so quickly. Not only did it have the magical drawing technique where I could look into the page, but I had never seen the portrayal of such a dynamic pose before. I must have had quite a look on my face, enough to make Asterius laugh again.

"Amazing, huh? Tileron has some neat tricks." The centaur had an idea. He waved for Asterius to take a place on the green, near a large weathered stone. Following his silent gestures, Asterius moved into position and placed his left foot on the rock, with the sharp pleats of his skirt hanging off his knee. His enormous body wavered, unbalanced, so I ran up next to him, and he placed his right hand upon my right shoulder for support. He gripped my exposed shoulder with surprising tenderness, and I tingled as my hair all stood on end. I looked up at him, his face a full head above me. I was growing rather fond of that face. Tileron seemed pleased with this arrangement, and had us move just a bit closer together. Then he gestured with his hands about his own countenance.

"He wants us to smile and look at him. And be still, it helps." I did so, confused. Then, the centaur held his head steady with his left hand on his heavily bearded chin, and flicked his right ear with his finger. His eyes flashed, with a strange glow, not unlike what I had seen with Athena's eyes, but brief. "That's all he needs. You want to play some more?" Before I could answer he was already in a seated position, harp in hand. Moving must be much easier for him than standing still. He was exceptionally good at moving.

Our next song was slow, and leisurely. The warm night air was heavy, and we were a bit heated from the last one. Asterius would allow his notes to hang in the air, and I would intersperse them with a slap or a pluck as I saw fit. It was so natural and easy, as if he and I had always been playing this song. He paused, to take a swig from his canteen. He offered me some, and I obliged. I noticed that the moon had moved across the sky by a fair bit as we played. I would need to start carrying a few more things to these meetings, if they should continue to stretch out so blissfully. Tileron approached us once again with his tools, a giant smile on his broad face. He turned the board to show Asterius his work, and I got up to get a view.

"Impressive! You've outdone yourself, old friend!" He had, and I was sure that Asterius' tone conveyed the message well enough without words. The moment had been caught, perfectly. We both beamed out from the parchment, smiling and happy. Every detail of our attire, even the tiny toenails on my bare feet, could be seen. His wonderful feet were captured in full detail. I supposed that was the purpose of the rock. "Tileron has some sort of thing in his head that lets him freeze time, and then see a moment in it. I think he can see things from the past, too."

"Like his old city?" That drawing had been on my mind, that I understood so little of it forced me to think of it. I couldn't imagine drawing something like that from memory.

"Yeah, when he drew that for me, it wasn't like he was remembering it, it was like he was looking at it."

"He even got your wonderful feet!" I pointed out his foot, splayed across the rock with each toe finding its own purchase.

"You mean my ugly feet." I gave him a side eye.

"I've seen you run. When you left here the other night the wind couldn't have caught you. And you are very big."

"Yeah, I noticed."

"Seriously, Asterius, anything that is so functional is not ugly. It can't be."

"Still, they aren't beautiful, like your... like normal man feet."

"Oh come on Asterius, our feet are just slabs of skin and muscle. They function really well if you don't coddle them, but you are just accustomed to them. Here, let me see." I dropped down before him, closer this time. He had a blank look for a moment, but then he shifted his position and extended a leg to me, so I could take one of his feet into my lap.

He had three 'toes' to the front, each nearly the size of my own foot and capped with a thick nail. The oval pads of each toe were rough, and callused; I ran my fingers over them and his ears twitched. I didn't want to tickle, so I turned my attention to his... ankle? The positioning of the fourth and fifth digits just below it suggested an ankle more than a foot, but it also seemed to do the work of a second knee. The 'heel' certainly never touched the ground; instead he balanced on those three front toes.

Above this ankle, his calf was dwarfed by his foot. It was more or less the size of my calf, and I had a lot less to support with mine. It was tight and firm, though. There was a spot here, just an area of darker fur. Does he have many spots? No more I could see.

Rather than go where I was uninvited, I retreated back from his skirt and down his leg, once again. One of the two smaller toes towards the back of the foot was topped by a cruel claw, in the shape of a sharpened crescent pointing towards the ground. I had hardly noticed it before, but it was a potent weapon. As I ran my hand across it, I wondered: if men were born so well armed, would any of us be alive? I doubted it.

I thought back to the remarkable experience of seeing him run, and tried to see how it all worked together. Judging by the way it swung back and forth while he was standing, his thick tail probably helped him balance. The strong muscles on the tops of his toes probably had a lot to do with it too. They were as hard as stone. Everything about this confirmed my suspicions. This was a masterwork, the sort of thing that only Gaia could make by her endless labors. Asterius had not been manufactured, like the centaurs, whose form compromised their function in countless ways. This comforted me, somehow.

I found a soft spot between the pads, and gently pressed. Asterius lost his balance, and fell back onto the hill. I continued, and he let out a loud groan. I couldn't tell if it was agony or ecstasy.

"Should I stop, does that hurt?"

"No… Gods, no. Don't stop." He never called out for the gods! It was so odd that it had been noticeable. So, I didn't, even as he began writhing and moaning. Having such a huge person twisting at the ends of my fingers was amusing. I accidentally glanced up his skirt, and was also pleased to see that his feet were the strangest part of him. "No, stop, I can't take it." I did, and he sat back up, breathing heavily. I glanced about to see how Tileron was reacting to this, but he had left. Chiron was not the only one who had eons to practice walking silently. "That's enough… Phew!"

"Have you not had anyone rub your feet?"

"No, that was a fresh experience." I did my best to not show how sad this made me, on my face. "Thank you."

"Well, we're not done, you've got another foot and it's bad to work just one. You need them both."

As we left to beat the dawn, I was pleased at the toothsome smile Asterius couldn't get off his face. He had pranced about the glade for a good time in appreciation of how nice his feet felt, before the color of the sky warned us that our time was through. I couldn't wait to tell the centaurs that it was working, that he seemed happier than I'd ever seen him. Though I didn't know whether he was the happier one, or I.

Twelve

My day was restless. When I had returned home from my latest trip to my glade, I crawled into bed, and found myself floating, freed from aches and pains that had become such a part of me that I had forgotten I was even in pain. I immediately fell to sleep. I awoke, earlier than usual, and I was still in bliss. My feet, which Thesius seemed to admire, must require this sort of maintenance.

Was it the same for his feet? Was that why he tried to mask his concern over my ignorance of these rituals? I'd missed so much, so many fundamental things. The more I thought of it, the more I understood that the garden walls I had enjoyed when I was a child were just as much the prison as this place, and the cold respectful distance with which most people regarded me then, in that warm light, was almost as much an abuse as this monstrosity. This murder cave. I risked a quiet laugh in my true home. That was such a perfect name for it.

I had known the Athenians held me in high regard. Well, Thesius had been careful to remind me a few times of late. These reminders always felt unnecessary, but also felt good. It was true, on the rare occasions I did visit, they were kind to me in every way.

I realized, in horror, that I had probably come to reflect some of the coldness I had been shown as a child. Had I missed their signals, or rebuffed them? Part of me desperately wanted to play music in a great lively band with them, as Thesius said I could, but... Thesius.

I had lost grip of my mind for a moment, staring off into space, just thinking about the sound of his voice. And then, I saw him, so beautiful I could hardly look, or look away. I couldn't deny the effect he had upon me, not now. I cast off my skirt, lest it rub me uncomfortably in my current state, and left for the bathing room to relieve myself.

That night, even though my trip to the glade passed by in an eye blink, Thesius somehow beat me. I found him lying on his back, eyes closed, inclined on that kind hill. I felt so out of place. What was I even doing, coming here and playing with him? This could only end in torturing myself further. I had nearly decided to leave when he opened his eyes and spoke.

"Oh, I thought you were a deer. It was an odd pattern, though." He sat up. I noticed his kopu about four feet away, and the moonlight glinting off his shoulders. I looked away. "Is something on your mind, Asterius?"

"No." I lied. I took a seat, and tuned my instrument. A minute passed, and I could not even look upon him.

"But, you have so few words... I pray I was not too forward with you last time."

"No... my feet." I stretched my toes out a bit, and they sang forth their appreciation. "They feel great. I don't want to ask too much of you."

"Too much?" He laughed, but there was concern in his sweet voice, "That was nothing. I'd do that any time you like." My heart leapt, at the thought of that. It seemed too fine a thing to be real. He had his hand on my foot, but I pulled it away, and then I doubted myself. "Everyone's feet hurt... People have been so unkind to you."

"I never asked the Athenians. I'm sure they would have, had I known. I didn't know to ask."

"Yeah, that. I can imagine being unkind one day, but the sort of consistent abuse that leaves you..." He was struggling for words, and there was anger below his concern, "You saw so little kindness you don't even know how to ask for it." Did he know me so well he could mirror my concerns? Or was it so obvious?

"Perhaps not even accept it... "

"Yes, the other Athenians have wondered why you are so distant." I was mortified. It was true, I had missed things! "But they think you were trying to protect us. I think so too." This was also true.

"I will do better to accept kindness." Thesius smiled, and I felt blessed. I blinked, and he was on his feet, with his instrument.

"Shall we play?"

I rested my harp against my left shoulder, and answered with my left hand, a four note arpeggio that had been on my mind. I followed this with a slower rhythm with my right, on the lower register of the instrument, at half the speed. I played for a minute before I realized I had no accompaniment.

"Sorry, I was going to jump in, but that was too lovely and I ended up as an audience. Try again?" His smile was brighter than the moon. Why did I keep looking? We tried again, and our notes were reaching up towards each other when he stopped and I felt his hand on my shoulder.

"Someone is coming." I heard them, just then, myself. Thesius was peeking over the hill behind me, and I turned over on my stomach, and crawled up to the top to look. With as much grace and practice as he could rise to his feet, he threw himself down by my side, and pointed to the trail head at the edge of the clearing.

"I see them. Two men." I was keeping my voice as low as possible, but I knew I was loud. It is why I spoke so rarely in the maze when it was not necessary.

"One of them has a shield on his shoulder."

"Can you see his hat?" My voice cracked, straining to be quiet and form words.

"No tassel." This was good news, this was not a search. A pair seeking their fortune in these rarely hunted woods?

There was a familiar noise, beyond the fields and the trailhead, but close. It was horrible, bloodcurdling, neither human nor animal, but I found it comforting. Thesius did not find the noise comforting, and he pressed himself against me. Neither did the poachers, who turned tail and ran.

"What horrible thing…"

"We will have to thank Tileron for that, later." I didn't bother to keep my voice down, they were gone. I turned on my side and somehow my arms were wrapped around him, and he was pressed against me. He was laughing, gently, against my chest.

"That was way scarier than those men. They wouldn't have stood a chance against us."

"I'm glad we were able to spare them." How was I even talking, with my heart in my mouth? The words did not seem to be my own.

"Me too." He pressed his head into my neck, and, gingerly, I squeezed him. He sighed, joyfully. Then, he looked up, and kissed me. It was over so fast, and yet I was stunned.

"Will you… accept this kindness?" Thesius' face was so filled with concern and care, and his voice was no less sweet at a whisper. I answered with my own kiss, our beards touching, and mingling, our lips brushing. We breathed for a moment, looking at each other, and tried again, and again. I gripped him, tightly.

"Ow, ow ow!" I released him instantly, shocked. He rolled over, and pulled at his belt. It had been poorly latched, and was pinching him. I helped him up.

"Someone else needs to help, Thesius, you can't do this yourself without practice." I started adjusting the buckles, but he pushed my hand away.

"I know how to get it off, at least." He unbuckled it and tossed it away, in one swift motion. It fell to the ground with a clank that would have caused us endless trouble minutes earlier, along with the rest of his skirt. He was glorious, I couldn't look away. He smiled upon me.

"I'm glad that revealing my deficiencies hasn't dampened your enthusiasm." My skirt was doing very little to conceal my enthusiasm at this point.

"What, is there a flaw? Am I blind?"

"Well there's that rude thing. I have to wear my wrap low to keep my shame concealed." He couldn't possibly be talking about that.

"I…. uh."

"But that's a shame we share it seems. I don't mind it. Some people turn aside though." Oh, he was talking about that. What madness is this?

"Because it's…"

"So prominent. It's an absurdity. Everyone wants them small and manageable." It was that? I don't think this is madness, so it must be fashion.

"The scrolls I've read say it's better that people seek compatibility in size." It's amazing I remembered that when I was mostly looking at the illustrations when I used to reference that scroll.

"You've got scrolls and texts, but your clothes are still on." He smiled. "You've taught me so much, Asterius, but I think I've got the experience here. I'd be flattered to have you as a student." His hands were working down my side, unbuckling my belt one buckle at a time. My heart was beating so fast.

"I will learn." These words were not my own, but came from some higher place. "I want to learn… Just, be patient with me?"

"Oh, Asterius, we have so many hours until dawn."

That night I learned more than I could even imagine about what I had been missing, while I sat in the dark. Dawn found me broken by joy, as I wept in his arms, at what I had experienced, and at having to let go. We parted, and came back together, night after night. Our songs grew shorter, and our dances grew longer. He'd whisper such sweet things to me, as we held each other. I'd never known such bliss. But in the cave after each night, it grew harder and harder to accept. How could I be so blessed? The darkness that pressed in upon me made it so hard to believe in my joy, or that such a shining, glorious man could be real.

Thirteen

The trip back was usually so uneventful, but tonight was a little different. A quick rain shower found me under a tree, for the sake of my knot, but it did little to save me from a soaking, and the cold I was enduring stood in such sharp contrast to the pleasure and warmth I had left. It was not the first time I had wished I could somehow stay in that glade, and continue my studies with Asterius, until our strength gave out and we fell into a blissful sleep together. With all the joys I had shown him over the past few weeks, the simple joy of sleeping together had escaped us.

When I returned, most of the camp was already preparing for bed. Miletta was with a small crowd, contesting with a bow in the early dawn light. The bow was the one weapon we had access to, as it was used to hunt game as well as man. That, and the materials used to produce one were too common to control, unless you were to set the whole island of Crete alight!

I considered joining the contest, but I knew that Miletta would defeat me. I was no poor shot, but she was… better. I could hardly think of a time she missed, except in jest. This was a hobby she had taken up at the Temple of Brewing, but a hobby done with such skill feels more like a vocation, or a calling.

I gave a friendly wave and smile to the group, and went to the shade at the edge of the clearing. The centaurs were there, wreathed in their foul smoke. When I greeted them, they seemed to be in a particularly good mood, so I hazarded a question.

"You know, the centaurs take incense and smoke it right in their faces, and I always thought it was a harsh ritual to perform. Is that something you are just more hardy for?"

"No, child, that is merely knowledge. There are two leaves in this world that produce incense you can smoke directly into your temple. One quells fear, and is good for battles and negotiations, but it can enslave you and kill you. The other is more kind. It relieves your pains and aids in your meditations, but releases its hold if you walk away from it."

"So, you just know what plants to use? You make it sound like it works on man too." Tileron passed me his pipe, but Chianten smacked his hand away. They exchanged a few words. He must have understood some of that.

"Tileron is far too fond of relaxation, and I don't want to start something around here. As it is you take to your leisures, you Athenians, though I am pleased to see so many of your favorites are so... athletic. That may be our fault, with our generosity."

I wasn't sure he had read this crowd right, in that regard. They were very experienced at not violating that one rule, and without the centaur's generous gift of silverseed they would have found a way to enjoy themselves. I felt like I was less welcome in light of this, though; their smoke was not the only foul thing in the air, and the companion centaurs were frowning at one another. So I thanked them again, bid them a farewell, bowed, and left.

I was headed for bed when Miletta waved me down. She led me upstairs into the workshop. Was this just the place to be conspiratorial around here?

"Hey beautiful, how you feeling?" I appreciated the concern, but I didn't understand it. I didn't think I was showing any weakness. Was it because I came in soaking wet?

"Oh, I'm good. Great, actually."

"Great, great... so I'm just gonna skip beating the bush and kill this bird. When I said you were off the menu, I thought that was for, you know, me. And the other girls. Not, you know... Everyone." Had I been so absent? "Not only that, you're just absent most of the time. I know you're good in the woods, but we're starting to think you've got a pack of satyrs you're running with or something. We ask the centaurs and they just smile at us. You know, 'cause it's not you talking to them." Suddenly, I saw my activities of the past several weeks from their perspective. I'd been far too secretive, even to my true friends like Miletta. I was ashamed, but I also didn't know where to begin.

"I have been busy in the woods… "

"Yes, we covered that. Poor Theo is walking around down there like a sick puppy all sad about you, it's killing me." Oh gods, Theo! I'd forgotten about that. And that was a lot of fun. She hit her main point again. "Are you going to run off with a bunch of satyr?" She seemed genuinely concerned for me. Not that I had seen any satyr to run off with. With all the time I had spent in the woods at night of late, I realized how odd that was, and I wanted to contemplate why that might be, but Miletta waved her hands in the air. She wanted an answer.

"No, it is Asterius."

"Is there something wrong with him?!" She was much less relaxed all of the sudden.

"No! I'm… I'm having sex with him." She laughed, then saw my face. I wasn't joking. She took the wooden chair, then looked up at me with a crooked smile.

"You know, back when you told me you met Athena I knew it was true, but I couldn't believe you. Now, you went and topped that. What in Hades, Thesius, did you plan on not telling anyone?"

"I didn't plan. There is no plan."

"So, it's love?"

"I…" Oh gods, it was. "Yes, it is."

"Great, now I want to tell everyone but I can't, because it's not just hot gossip, it's his heart. Everyone here would kill me if I broke his heart somehow." I then realized this was true of me as well. I felt a bead of sweat breaking on my brow.

"How… you're my most trusted friend here. Estius, I can't even get in a side word with him."

"Yeah! Hah, that's been funny." Estius had fallen hard for a woman from the first sacrifice, Egeria. I would say he had been practically on top of her since we arrived if it weren't so literally true.

"Well, how should I deal with this?"

"How serious is it?"

"I'm fairly sure he hasn't been with anyone else."

"Do I look like a baby? Of course. Is there passion?" My heart skipped.

"More than I can fathom. Being with him is like… it's as if that waterfall cared enough to touch you gently. As if the ocean could hold you in it's warm strong embrace."

"So, it's spouting poetry serious?" She leapt to her feet and wrapped me in her arms. "Oh Thesius, that's so immensely romantic. I'm so happy to be your friend but this is gonna burn me up."

"Because... you're not gonna tell everyone?"

"You're just gonna have to kiss him in front of the camp, or something. This is not up to me." She put her hands up in the air to show how much she was letting go of it, even as she let go of me. I was sad, it would be easier if she would run out and scream it into the sky. Her chosen scenario did not seem likely.

"So, that might take a while, what should I say until then?"

"We all see you leave with the knot. They made that here, you know, right in this room. Though the blanket and the oils we noted make more sense now." Have they all been spying on me? I wanted to be offended, but being outside these canyon walls was a risk. I understood. "Just say you're playing music with him and Tileron, and keeping watch on Minos. It's believable, you often leave with the centaur."

"It's true, that's what we do. Well, what we start doing." It began with music and always ended in dance.

"Ok, I think I deserve one prying question for my silence here."

"One? One more? Hit me."

"Does it work… You know, like a man?" I'd expected something more like this earlier on.

"He seems mostly the same. No less capable, certainly. And," I was smiling broadly now, "a very quick student. I've learned a lot from him too, but not in that field. He has so many interesting things to say, so much wisdom and knowledge."

"You're telling me you learned nothing laying in that field?" This was a good joke, she had me. "It's just, the same, with some fur and weird feet?"

"No, there are a few minor differences. Nothing that gets in the way. A few fun things."

"I'm going to press on and ask for an example of something fun." Was she trying to embarrass me, or was she that interested? I wondered how many other people here might have taken the opportunity I was given, if it were offered to them.

"The tail. It's thick and well rooted. Lots of leverage there, lots to hold on to."

"He's so big! Are the biggest men always like that? You'd know."

"No, I mean. Yes. Um… "

"So you're fighting over position?"

"It's never a fight." I sighed wistfully. Oh gods, it was love.

"And that is how you turn one probing question into four." She started heading for the door. "Love you, Thesius. Have fun, and tell the others the outline of what's going on? So they don't worry? You can leave out the whole reason you're depriving us of your affections."

"I'm just so delightfully exhausted." She stopped in the doorway, and pointed at me.

"He clearly needs this, so don't mess it up. It's love, you're good at that, everyone always loves you. Just… don't." She shook her finger in emphasis, and left.

"Love you too!" I called out, knowing full well that would start a rumor. Serves her right for being so good at asking questions.

I left, and practically sprinted down the stairs to my room, before some other clever wordsmith could find me and pin me down. Or worse, Theo, so I could break his heart some more. I already had too much to think about. I peeled off my wet wool skirt, hung it up on the hook, and took to my bed, and the soothing arms of Hypnos, which would have to do in Asterius' absence.

The rain came down, unrelentingly, for two days. With it came my customary fall sniffle, and I had to borrow a small pile of rags to contain it. It was nothing, it would pass in a few days. What was worse was staring out into the sky, and hoping for it to open.

Over our evening breakfast I told everyone the truth. Most of it. Theo was so relieved; he was sure I would disappear into the woods and never come back. That night, as the rain fell, we shared a few affections in his room, and I made sure he knew I wasn't mad at him. Theo always did enjoy my foot rubs.

When the sky broke the following day I was elated. I had my things all bundled and ready to go hours ahead of time. It was foolish, I could have been sleeping, but I couldn't quiet my mind or my heart. As I walked out of my room, I almost ran directly into him.

"Manny?"

"Mantes." I never did that! If I'd been lashed it would hurt less than my own judgement in that moment. "Are you feeling well?"

"I... uh." I really didn't want to have that same conversation with him. I sniffled in a bit of my fall affliction.

"You come home wet, and now you have the sniffles and you can't even remember my name." I noticed that Chianten was standing in the grass behind him, a bemused look on his face.

"Mantes, look I'm sorry about the name. The sniffles, it…"

"Chianten thinks you have some affliction related to the trees, and you are fine, but I think you should rest today. There is no sense in taking a risk."

"But hold on... Chianten!" I looked over Manny… I mean Mantes shoulder for some help.

"It seems to me that the physician is usually in charge around here, and you decided that you weren't going to be a prince any more, so I guess you will rest and have some porridge. I could go get some now?" This was not the way I liked to be blessed with a centaur's smile. That being said, their version was so good that it didn't sound bad. But it was not nearly as good as the feast I was missing out on. I decided to sulk in my room instead, and catch up on some of that sleep I was so fond of when I was not around him, or anticipating him. It felt nice to sleep at night, for once.

I felt a presence, and I awoke. I looked out the curtain, and saw the night was full and dark. But then I heard breathing.

"Hello?"

"I'm sorry… Chianten told me you weren't well, and… I should go." Everything about that was wrong except for the smooth rumble of his voice. I leapt to my feet and pressed him back down onto the bench, which he had somehow come to a rest upon without waking me. I lifted his chin and kissed him. This was familiar, and he pressed back against me, but I felt tears on his cheeks.

"Why do you weep, Asterius?"

"The rain and the darkness… It ended, and I got there, and you weren't… " He was crying, sobbing. I held his head to my chest, and stroked his ears, "Some madness came over me, and I convinced myself you weren't real. That everything that had happened… all those magical nights… even that first night with my harp, and your light… after I thought I lost you in the pit… I imagined all that… " Now there were no words, only tears. I held him, and wept myself. My heart wanted to curse the heavens, that such a shining star could be so terribly hurt, and then cast into a pit, not even to die, but to cease to shine at all. But I knew the fault was not in the heavens, but in that palace up on the ridge. I broke my hold, found a rag, and blew. I found a fresher one, and offered it to Asterius, but he wasn't done crying, so I grabbed a cushion off the bed, put it on the ground at his feet, and took a seat there. The bench was sturdy, but it wasn't worth risking it. I took his foot into my lap and started to work, but he pulled away.

"Why do you give to me? How do I deserve you? What could I possibly offer to you?"

"You saved my life, Asterius."

"So this is a reward, a payment?"

"No, Asterius... I love you." It was true, and it hung in the air. I clutched his leg, and pressed my face against his thigh. How could any of us have deserved *you*? He put his hand on my head, and rubbed it gently. I relaxed into him, and wept some more.

"I've loved you since the first moment I saw you, in that cold blue light." He was so calm now, and his peace flowed through me. "I didn't even know, not until you tied me up with your song and forced me to understand. Everything was telling me, but I was so used to everything being the same that I couldn't hear it. Even as the earth moved beneath me, I thought I was just a bit off balance..... But then, I found your shoulder." His large but soft hand moved there, and caressed me tenderly.

"Things sneak up on you sometimes... Like that waterfall, you sometimes don't hear it until you're right up on it." He laughed, and it rang off the walls, almost uncomfortably.

"Did someone tell you that line?"

"No?" I was genuinely confused.

"It's part of the speech I tell as I walk up to this place. To the Athenians. The ones who aren't as clever as you." The room was dark, but I knew he was smiling. I could hear it in his voice. "We are of one mind, so much. I love you too." I arose, and kissed him again. I wanted nothing more than to be of one body with him, as well. My kiss must have told, as he had me fully in his embrace moments later. We fell into the bed, and made our best time against the dawn.

The dawn nearly caught us. After I helped him don his belt, Asterius bounced off so fast I convinced myself that no one could possibly have seen him leave. After I managed to, sort of, buckle my belt, I walked out of my curtain to see... the entire camp having a snack on my step. I had been wondering why the kitchen sounds were so close. Miletta was there, of course she was, everyone was, and she looked like she was a cat who was having a noisy bird for breakfast.

"Good morning? Or is it good night here?" No one answered me, except with the corners of their mouths.

"So, I must apologize, I think it is clear you are in perfect health." This was the best joke I had ever heard Mantes say, and everyone else clearly agreed. Even the centaurs, who were lounging with us and out of their usual shadows, laughed. I laughed with them. It was obvious that Asterius and I had not been as discreet as we had thought. And here I had thought a mere kiss before the camp was unlikely.

"No one likes the cabin on the end 'cause you hear everything." Theo seemed to be very entertained, "When you went and chose it, and then took your contemplation bench in there, some of us started joking that you wanted to be back at the temple like Helea," Miletta and Helea both shot a look at him at this point that would have killed him, if it were an arrow. Especially from Miletta. "But I knew better. Now we all do." Apparently, everyone was very entertained. At this point my mirth at my little social mis-step had transformed into intense mortification at what had occurred. How much had they heard?

"Now, I want everyone to be honest with me, I know you humans have a problem with that sometimes, but did anyone tell him that line, about the waterfall?" Everyone simultaneously shook their heads. "Just brilliant, Thesius. You almost got my rope to go up, and I don't even have one." Oh gods, even the centaurs heard everything! Every single word!

If I wasn't the most social person in Athens when I was a child, and everyone didn't seem so happy for Asterius and I both, I might have just drilled down to the River Styx right then. As it was it took a full hour for my shade to return to my normal red from the... purple hue it had taken. Mantes actually seemed a bit concerned about it, but he could hardly contradict himself now. Could I turn from red to purple and back? Those weren't next to each other. Or did that only matter for raindrops in the air?

"I almost feel the need to beg forgiveness." Chianten had snuck up and surprised me, which was unsurprising. I had my bench in hand and was hard at work, so I set it down and took a seat. I was tired.

"I'm racking my brain, but you've done nothing wrong, so I'm almost confused?"

"You don't know everything. Neither do I, but I know that I do not." He took a seat on the grass. The centaurs around here seemed to be much more fond of sitting than Chiron was.

"You can demure and give me some wisdom. Or you can tell me what there is to be forgiven. Then I'll do it. No one deserves forgiveness more than you."

"You're wrong, I've done some things in my time. Some horrible things, sometimes even voluntarily. But you should know by now how much we love to speak of ourselves... I did not know Asterius was in such a bad place." I slammed my hand down on the bench. My mind had turned, and I felt like there was much to be forgiven.

"He isn't in a bad place, he's in the worst place. A nice little bedroom just off the worst place, right now. Are we going to leave him there?"

"No, that is not even what I meant I... " What I had said must have just washed over him, because he stopped for several seconds and a look of appalling pain passed over his face. "Oh never mind." He got up and left. So did I.

I fell wearily back to bed, a full hour after everyone else, the sun nearly full in its heat. I had moved my collection of things from the end room to a much better place on the second level that, I was told, would spare the camp the details of our most intimate whisperings, should Asterius feel lonely again. Though I was sleepy, I laid for a while in contemplation of what had happened today. Knowing how united everyone was here, and how much they loved the two of us, planted a seed in my mind, that would take weeks yet to sprout.

Fourteen

He loves me.

"He loves me." I said it to the darkness, and it whimpered. I could swear I heard it.

"He loves me, no matter how I look, or stand or run. His song calls to me, and mine to him." Was that a cry of suffering, or a whistle of air through the caves beyond? "You won't tell me he won't come back, or he never was. And if you do, I won't believe you." This was unfair, but it deserved it. "You can press in on me but you won't ever crush me. For now, begone!" I struck the flint, and lit my lamp. The flame shone, though not as bright as he did, and the shadows did flee my true home. I turned, and had the fright of my life.

He was standing right there, tears in his eyes.

"How?!"

"I did not intend this to be such an intrusion, I just… "

"It's daytime!"

"Chiron taught me to move in the day, as well." He had left his belt behind, and tied the skirt in the way that the threshers in the fields do. I saw that he had a length of fabric with him, colored roughly as mud, or rotting leaves. It was an unattractive color, but I instantly understood. Clever.

"But, you!" I realized the tone of my voice, and lowered myself to a harsh whisper, with difficulty. "If they catch you here."

"If they catch *you* here! Everything in this room is a forbidden joy. I've just come here to join them." He sat down on my bed. "Aren't I pretty here?"

"The tiny fire does nothing for you, next to the light of the moon."

"It doesn't do very much for you, either." I wasn't sure what he meant.

"It does its job, I can see around and I can read."

"No, Asterius." He flopped down backwards on my pile of furs. He looked so enticing there. I could, so easily… ah, but that would certainly be heard if some hapless cleric was throwing meat through the door or something. Instead, I dragged my stool over, next to him.

"There are so many things we might be tempted to do, that would call out our doom if we indulged. This is not wise." I was trying to be peaceful, but beside me Thesius was a ball of energy. At least he was, in my mind's eye. A ball of energy, reaching out to me with a thousand strands of light. That was very odd.

"Yeah, I know. Do you think I intend to stay here?" There was an edge to his voice.

"What? No... I…"

"Do you intend to stay here?" He was looking me straight in the eyes, now. I had lied, that candle was sufficient. But the question begged for an answer. I had none.

Thesius threw himself to his feet from the foot of the slab, halfway to the wall, and silently spun on his heel back towards me. And, he thought *I* moved well. He shot me a look that was… it was love, but it was hard where I was expecting softness. He then took three quick strides over and blew out my lamp. The room plunged into perfect darkness.

"Thesius?" He didn't answer for a long time. On his bare feet, I could barely hear him. I just stayed on my stool.

"How do you know I'm even here, Asterius?" That hurt. It felt unfair. After a long time, he continued. "How do you know you are even here?"

"I think. As long as I think, I am."

"That's profound, and I love how you think. But, what if this place stops that? What if you just stop thinking, and stare into the darkness?" There were so many times I had almost done just that. I felt the tears before I realized I was crying. "It would be natural. It's what this thing was supposed to do to you."

I felt his hands on my face. They brushed along my muzzle, unafraid of my teeth. He stroked the base of my ears, on both sides, and wrapped his hands around my horns. It was so warm. He tilted my head up by this leverage to kiss me, savagely, and pushed me back so hard by my shoulders I fell onto my slab, and my furs. The stool tipped over, and rolled away. I heard it move, but not him.

"How many times am I supposed to send you back here? To your Labyrinth. This horrible pit?"

"The murder cave?"

"Don't you jest… "

"It's your joke." He laughed, quietly. I got up, and walked over to my little alcove to relight my lamp. It was gone! "This joke is not funny. Light it, or your eternal flame."

"I have neither. I must have dropped them down a hole or something."

"Why are you doing this?!"

"Because I love you. I love you so much that I can't stop thinking about you, and the idea of you stopping thinking, and staring into the darkness here forever is too much for me to bear. So you are going to tell me you want to get out of here, or we can sit here together, and face the darkness."

"Of course I want to get out of here, but how? It's impossible."

"As I see it, you have 50 people, including me, who would fight to get you out of this hole." Did he mean the Athenians? Was my math wrong?

"52?"

"Aeraeta died years ago, I'm told. In her sleep. And Telys is not doing well, he's not up for a fight. You keep a good track of the people you fail to save, my love, but what about the ones that just run out of time?"

"I'm doing all of this to save you, and them. To keep you all alive. If anything goes wrong… "

"And something will. Something always does. You know that." I thought back, to the lone cleric who had found me in my secret home, and how he came to rest next to my old teacher. "But is just living, enough? Sure, back there in the valley, the new meat loves the stew, but the older pieces in the bowl are looking a bit weary by now. The days stretch on, and there is no goal, no real achievement. Your father built a Tartarus for you, and Ma'aht, bless his shade, built an Elysium for us. But both of these places are prisons." There was a long pause, and the darkness closed in on us both.

Had he ever existed?

Had I?

His voice pierced the darkness, "I want to break free!"

"... I also want this." A tiny cry of joy came forth from my Thesius. "But, we have no arms."

"Bows. And we have a backdoor."

"It only opens sometimes."

"And, unless things have changed much from when I was there, you can walk forward from that backdoor about two hundred paces into a beautiful room, with a nice black and white floor, that has enough axes hanging up on the walls to arm more than half of us." Oh wait, that might work! Oh no, it wouldn't.

"Axes aren't enough."

"The burning light can't be that good at close range, we just need to..."

"No, you don't understand, Thesius. I will fight, but you have to know what we would be up against. Please, turn on the light." There were a few moments of silence, and a sharp blue line of light broke through the gloom, before spreading all around the lower half of the room with a series of clicks. He was sitting under my desk, against the pile of scrolls. He carefully slid out my oil lamp, that precious thing, stood up and placed it back on it's shelf. As he was standing next to me now, it was natural to embrace, and so we did.

"You have got to be kidding me." Thesius was picking at a nut cake at the table, with his lamp by his side. With that thing here, it seemed silly to light my own lamp, but I missed the flicker of the flame, and its yellow-orange color. This light was efficient, but harsh.

"We jest all the time, but I don't care to lie." I leaned back against the wall, my legs crossed on my bed.

"Please don't think ill of me, it's just Chianten told me... if I wanted to convince you of what had to be done I would have to lie to you so hard that I was telling the truth, and I didn't know what he meant. But then I got here, and I did." I wanted to go over there and stroke his hair, but it was best if we stayed on opposite sides of the room, after what we almost did over by the alcove.

"Are you avoiding the subject?"

"The subject of something even worse than the burning light? Yes. I would prefer to eat this mummified nut cake."

"Better than a lot of what I get to eat." He was drawing me into banter, and I wanted to stay on topic.

"You seemed pretty eager to eat something rather precious to me a moment ago."

"I don't bite. You know that." Oh, we were bantering. "No, stop it. It's a warrior that can jump over the castle wall and make a bow, or a sword, or whatever just right out of his hand and kill you. And it can see in the dark, and hear your heartbeat, and run forever faster than a horse, and..."

"Minos has a warrior that can do that?! Why in Athena's name would they need you?!" His voice kept creeping up to volumes I was uncomfortable with.

"It's not a warrior, really, I mean it's attached to a warrior, so…"

"Are we going to define words for a while now while I consider this invincible warrior that might pop over the camp wall at any time?"

"They would have to know of it, first… It's more like armor. I think the people of the Heaven's Gate got it in trade for something. Probably a lot of people. I never saw any texts directly related to the armor, but that would be the usual form of one of their sales. They definitely did not make it, that thing is beyond them. But it attaches to a warrior for life and as long as he lives we can't fight them. I've thought this through a lot."

"So, we have to outlive this man, and then we get the news fast enough, and then the new invincible warrior trips on his new sandals or something?"

"If it happens around the Solstice it would be even better. Most of the guard goes home to see their families then."

"Oh, wonderful, do you happen to know the name of the god of long chances, because I think we need to start praying." He was smiling, but the edges of his eyes weren't. I didn't want to crush his Hope, even though I know he'd be better off without it lying to him. He continued to think aloud, "We have to figure out a way to change the game without having any beans on the board… I have to ask, when you were challenging the darkness earlier, did you hear it reply too?"

"I thought I had imagined that." How many other things, through the years, had I not imagined? Suddenly, I saw this place a lot more like Thesius did. "I think the moon beckons, unless my timing is off."

"Oh, blood and darkness, let's get out of this murder cave!"

Fifteen

Asterius was clearly pleased to see I had my kopu hidden around the bend from his cell, but made sport of it. He had one instrument in each hand as he hopped ahead of me to the secret glenn, taking single strides that I had to multiply by twenty, or thirty. I was fast, but I knew I couldn't catch him. I wanted to have my strength with me; it would make the night more amusing. So I paced myself and kept to the shadows. I was almost there when I met him coming back my way.

"I thought you were running." He rubbed his head sheepishly, "Thought something had happened?"

"Your ears are as good as mine, or almost. I'd call out for you." I kissed him on the cheek. Snout? Whatever.

A few minutes later we were settling into our familiar positions. We checked our tune, and began. I was standing, as I preferred, and Asterius cradled his harp. But perhaps I had been too effective in my arguments, as music was not on his mind. When he put his fingers to the strings, I could tell it immediately, and I just stopped my rhythm.

"Try again?" Asterius pitched his head to the side in emphasis. It was so like what the Centaurs would do, and yet the dog-like expression looked more like a man on him, despite his face.

"You are thinking. Do it out loud so I can hear."

"There are a lot of nearly identical words you don't know in there." This was adorable, but he was dodging my question. I just gazed upon him, and loved him. After a long moment, he spoke again, flustered, "Now I'm not thinking at all, thanks!"

"I'll beat the darkness one way or the other." We laughed. It felt so good to laugh at the darkness, out here in the pale blue moonlight. He got to the point.

"I keep thinking about your god of long chances. You were joking, but... is that a bad idea? Could we pray our way out of this?"

"The gods aren't welcome here. Athena told me so." It had to be true. Athena was clearly capable of not knowing, but not of lying. But it played to Asterius like an out of tune string. He looked skeptical. We were done with songs for the day.

"I don't see how all the texts I've read could be wrong. The witness of so many people. They go where they want! The only thing that seems to stop them are other gods. Barely that." He was letting his hands talk, as he would often do when he was going to play the teacher. I turned it around on him.

"Have you ever seen a god around here?" I set my knot aside and stretched out, enjoying the late summer breeze. In the heat, my disguise was down to a skirt. They actually had little ties on the inside, and I had been relieved to find that they didn't live in those restrictive belts at all times. Between that, my bare feet and the length of ugly fabric, I was cool, clothed and invisible.

"Maybe once? When I was young. He was a very unusual man, at least." He put his harp aside and laid back, his vast chest contributing greatly to the pleasant curves of the hill he was on.

"You could tell me?" I continued stretching, working out my shoulders, and then my calves. I took my time, and gave him time to gather his thoughts. When I straightened up I noticed that Asterius had sat back up and crossed his legs to get a better view. "Or you could just watch."

"Yes. I mean… I will just tell the story. I was out playing by the back pond, in the garden. You haven't seen it, it's behind all the parts of the palace the public might see… Or prisoners. You weren't really…" I gave him a kind look, and he caught his breath before continuing. "You distract me so easily. He was a tall thin man. Looked like he was from the peninsulas, small nose, olive skin. Middle aged, with a bit of grey all over. He also looked poorly kept. Thin. He was wearing rags. All of that was not the sort of thing I would usually see in our walled garden."

"You went to talk to him." Of course he did.

"Yes. I was chatty, and I didn't have much company. He was a new face, and I know I've never seen him since. Honestly, thinking about him now he reminds me a lot of my teacher, but he was definitely not the same person. Much taller... I don't remember everything he said. Kind things I wasn't used to, mostly. He... said he would be at home here, more than any other place."

"Would be?" Odd word choice, even for a god.

"Yes, it sticks in my mind. I didn't know what he meant, so I asked him where his home was, and he laughed. Part of me wants to think he was some sort of hermit or madman who somehow sneaked in there, but I don't see how."

"Yeah, the palace is not the sort of place you would sneak into. More like the sort of place you run from." He shrugged, it was true. I knew it wasn't his fault.

"Here is the rubbing point. The thing that bothers me. There were other people in that garden, but no one else saw him. I remember I told grandpa. He seemed interested." Lightning struck me, and it all came together.

"Have you seen any nymphs around here? Satyrs dancing about in the forests of the night, anything?"

"A few times when I was very young. Not since."

"Not since you told your grandfather about the visitor in the garden?" His jaw dropped, and he stared off into space. I continued.

"Athena told me about this thing, a machine. Some sort of sphere in a tower." I held my hands out in an approximation of her demonstration, "Athena said it stopped her, well all the gods, from even seeing what was going on here... But the centaurs seem to have no problems."

"The centaurs are physical beings. Gods, satyrs and nymphs are the physical manifestations of spiritual beings. Well, in the case of nymphs they are the physical manifestations of the spiritual being that is embodied physically as a... "

"Whoa, that's a lot of priest talk. You're gonna have to write down all of these alternate words you people in Crete have. It's bewildering."

"Oh yes, I'll get on writing a giant list of nearly identical words for you. I'll call it a Thesaurus, in your honor." He was smiling broadly. Gods I love him.

"You're right. That sounds boring and useless." I joined him at rest, leaned back against the hill, and threw my foot across his exposed foot. As if in return, he rubbed my ankle and calf appreciatively with his large soft hand. Or was I resting on his leg? It was hard to tell where the one stopped and the other began. Whatever.

"Maybe not useless. Definitely boring." Asterius didn't seem at all bored.

"Tossing aside the priest talk, if they don't need flesh to act and exist… Maybe they can't be here? Could some sort of machine do that?" Now that I said it out loud, it sounded like an impossible lie.

"Machines only seem to be limited by the understanding of their creators. And the more I think about it, I can see how this could be something grandpa somehow did. He didn't show me everything. Any wonder he brought before me was brought down out of the tower. The shorter one. I never got to see the tower myself. All his best men worked there, and they did have a lot to work on… " Something was bothering him. My hand was on his knee, when did that happen? "There is a hole in my knowledge."

"You look like you have several holes in your head. I may have no idea what you mean." He tossed his head back and let go. I was glad that one hit the mark.

"No, when I am thinking about this god problem I can see a hole where there should be knowledge, but there isn't. Everything I read when I was younger was selected by grandpa, and mom grabbed whatever scroll she could get. I'm starting to think I didn't get everything. There must be another library, in the tower. One I never really got to read from." Something was bothering me about this theory, too.

"Satyrs can bleed. They have flesh. As far as I know, they can't just up and vanish. Why aren't they here? I mean, I know they aren't exactly like the centaurs. New satyrs pop up all the time, usually with familiar faces. That's nothing like the centaurs. Not at all."

"Yeah, they're dead." Asterius delivered this apparent contradiction flatly, as if it were obvious. But then it dawned on me: of course! It made perfect sense.

"It's an afterlife?"

"It's an afterlife. They are spirits made flesh, but they are still spirits. They die in the woods, the god of the woods likes them, they are reborn." I had indeed figured it out, and I prayed we would never run out of puzzles to solve together. "Only men for some reason. It seems to happen everywhere, too. Up north, they turn into plant men." Asterius held his hands about his face, as if to imitate leaves.

"That sounds like less fun." It really did.

"I'm sure that plants have some kind of fun."

"Not like the satyrs do, or the nymphs might let them win the race every once in a while."

"I don't want to be shocking, or terribly provocative, but you know, a lot of plants do it," he raised his fuzzy eyebrow, "With themselves!" And he blessed me with another big toothy grin.

"You did it with yourself until you were 33!" Now my whole leg was over his, with no ambiguity in the words.

"Yeah, but I never had any offspring from it." His arm was around my shoulder, as thick as a coiled net, so hard, and soft, and warm...

"You and I aren't gonna be having any kids either, unless you're hiding more under that tail than I thought!" This brought us fully to an uproar of laughter, and I ended up in both of his arms. Moments later, we were making another futile attempt.

142

Sixteen

After our confrontation with it, I felt much less at ease with the darkness. The eternal flame, a second hand gift, was always alight, even when I slumbered. Even then I felt it, gazing at me from the corridor beyond. My mind was at war with it now, as I now knew there was a war that had to be fought, but I was suffering for it. This was its home, uncontested, and I had lost an advantage against it I never knew I had. My new home was in his arms, and I was far away from home.

Thesius' knot, his word, but I loved it, was living here now, alongside my harp. He said they needed to keep each other company after our last encounter, and he had instruments at the camp. They were cuddled up beside my bed, and I was jealous of a pile of wood and dried intestines. It was ridiculous, I knew it was, but I was still jealous...

I could smell, even here, the rain. I was so tired of rain, even after a single day it was enough. I went out to gaze at it. It took me but moments to make my decision. The rain might fall, but I couldn't stay trapped here for another day! It had only been one, but it felt like a lifetime. The harp and the knot will just have to fend off the darkness alone.

I knew the path to the camp, so well, but nothing looked the same under the storm. It was if the darkness had reached out of my former home and tried to follow me to the Athenians. I increased my speed, as if to outrun it, but then I missed a landing, and slid on some leaves. I tumbled, and smashed into a tree. Some bird left, cursing at me for waking it from its rest. Tileron might be able to tell me what it said.

I seemed to be unharmed, until I put some weight on my left foot. It was pretty sore, but I could walk on it. Not hop, or run. I walked to the camp, through the storm.

As I entered the Athenian camp, every inch of me soaked, battered or smeared, I thought about Thesius' soup bowl, and how the broth was slowly turning rancid. Looking up at the canyon walls, I could see it. But then, as I stood at the far end of the pond and watched the water draining into the chasm below, the whole of this place seemed more akin to the hammered piece of bronze I had been shitting in for 18 years. I heard muted signs of life, and I sat down and cried. These people didn't deserve this. What was I doing, how could I have ever thought that keeping them here was some kind of solution?

I don't know who saw me first, but Ada and Nysa, from the second sacrifice, joined me first. They were like sisters, well, more than that, and they did everything together. I think it gave them courage. I must have been a scary sight, in the dark under the storm, looming.

"Asterius!"

"You look dreadful, big guy. Were you attacked?" Nysa placed her one hand on my shoulder. She came without the other, but did better inlay work with one than anyone else here with two.

"No, I just tripped."

"And fell into a bog?" Ada was skeptical. I had picked up a good part of the forest floor.

"I think I'll be fine after a rest."

"And do you intend upon resting out here in the cold autumn rain?" It was Mantes, who was approaching with a small crowd of others.

The workshop was a cozy place with almost everyone packed into it. All the lamps were lit in the alcoves, and people were seated everywhere they could be, including out on the walkway.

I was still a bit wet, and wrapped in a pile of blankets. Mantes had insisted I disrobe and take a dip before I entered the building. There was no lightning to make that risky, though I was dismayed at the crowd that formed to watch me, as I used the waterfall as all of them did. I suppose I must inspire curiosity more than disgust, here. I

144

could only pray I had no wet fur smell, as my nose was always strangely blind to it.

Thesius was there, but after greeting me he had melted into the shadows. It was probably easier to just step back and let everyone else work around me.

I was embarrassed by their care. It wasn't bad! I healed fast! But they had bandaged the cut on my foot, and placed it on a large warm stone. It was almost as pleasant to my aching paw as Thesius' hands were. The crowd didn't thin until everyone got a chance to greet me, and say goodbye before departing to their work. I had been such a stranger. I had not spoken to many of the Athenians in years. Nysa's rendition of this unusual greeting/farewell stung me, but it also stuck in my mind.

"You see this?" She was pointing at something that wasn't there, so I didn't know how to answer. It was rhetorical. "I was 16, riding on my horse out behind the temple of brewing. Went off track, for fun. Got tossed onto a tiny stick. No bigger than any of my fingers. I didn't even think I was in trouble when I pulled it out... They had to cut off the arm three days later. Used the stuff they make there, to keep the rot from taking the rest of me. I survived, to be sacrificed. That was more fun than I expected, thanks to you, but if you are careless, who knows." I realized she was meeting my eyes, as so few people could, "Many people love you, Asterius. You should act like it."

Once things cooled down, Thesius emerged from his shadow and came to me, wearing his brilliant smile on his perfect face.

"I told you they hold you in high regard." People sat about, mostly playing the Nine Beans and trying to not look like they were listening in on the two of us. "Are you cozy?"

"Do I smell bad? My big nose can smell everything but myself, and I..."

"No one cares. Also, no. You're fine." He sat next to me on the long bench, and laid his head on my shoulder. It complained with a creak, but held. Two of the first years, young women, moved their board a bit closer. They didn't seem to care if they were being obvious. I really needed to get about learning all of their names.

"I couldn't take the darkness…" Not for another moment. I didn't bother to try and whisper, or to hold back my tears.

"I know." He took my hand in his, as much as he could, and squeezed. I took my other hand and wrapped it around them both, and held his hand with both of mine for a while. "Every moment I have to leave you in that place wounds me. I've come to hate the rain… I used to love it."

One pair of players either grew tired of the certainty of their game, or were embarrassed to be listening to our pining for each other, and left their board behind them. The next people would clean it up when they started their own game. The young women remained. I replied.

"I no longer doubt you, my love. Not even for a moment. But the darkness seems to be at war with me. As if it knows I will never be an ally, now. It's wearing me down." He let go of my hands, and his warm lean changed into a side hug. My arms were tangled in blankets so there was little I could do to return the affection.

"I almost gave into that grasping darkness once." Can the light give in to the darkness? Or are we only a light in each other's eyes? "I can see now that it's always been my enemy, just as you have always been my friend. I just had to get to know you both to see."

"When?"

"Back in Thessaly, at the school. I had someone dear to me, there. He betrayed me, by trying to save me. Brought a girl from the other camp, after I met with Athena and knew I had little chance of survival. Chiron kept the girls away from me, you see." I snickered at the futility of this. I knew by now that Thesius had a clear preference. "I think my dad intended Chiron to abandon his women, and their studies, but they were most of the school! He wouldn't do that. He kept them aside. Or us aside?"

"Your friend. He intended that you would violate the rule and escape?"

146

"Yeah. He said I didn't have to like it, I just had to do it, and we could run off together. He said we might join a band of satyr in the wood. I didn't know how mad that was, then. But I wanted to. I didn't want to die. And he didn't want to lose me."

"Why didn't you? Your father may have even found a substitute?" Thesius gripped me tightly, and spoke very quietly. I envied him, this ability. "Speak not of that. My friend was not the only one who grasped, but Athens' honor…"

"It seems… such a minor darkness. This little grasping. Didn't he do it out of love?" I left it ambiguous as who I was speaking of. It hardly mattered.

"No. He did it because he feared losing me. Like I would have done it, for fear of losing my life. And yes, it was a minor darkness, because we were grasping at minor things, just ones with terrible consequences."

"You never know the magnitude of your actions, when you make them." I thought about all of the decisions that had led me here, into this room full of light and love. These people could even turn my mistake into a joy.

"Well, saying no was the best decision I ever made. I would have abandoned the best person I've ever known without ever having known him. I can't imagine anything more tragic."

"Then what of my darkness, why does it have such power? Yours, it just swayed a few men to do selfish things."

"My men failed when they grasped at little things. Your men failed when they grasped at everything… Your father and grandfather both. They were such good friends with that grasping darkness that they ended up building a perfect home for it. And they trapped you there." He choked up, and buried his head in my shoulder while I replied. It was true. Grandfather put me in a cage, as well.

"I denied it. I had a light in the darkness."

"You coexisted with it. Did you truly deny it? When you used to walk those halls, did you listen to it whispering?" So many times. Too many times. "Did you carry your light?" No, never, for fear… of losing the Athenians. It had taken a grasp on me. Of course it had. I didn't need to answer, he could read my face so well.

"I almost did give in. I had weeks to contemplate the offer. But I'd had a visitor, the year before. My mother came up, on a cart, from Athens. She seemed so fit, but she died that fall. Somehow, she knew this was her last chance, that she wouldn't be well enough to travel soon. I wasn't tempted then, but she knew I would be, somehow. After she died... I had to honor my love for her. She would have wanted me to stand proud, and do what is right. So I did. I'm so glad I did. You never get anything good by grasping at it, and the very best things... I don't think you even know what they are until you have them."

"You're my very best thing. And you walked into my room."

"After you sacrificed everything again and again for people you could easily have taken as enemies. People who didn't know you well enough to not... hate you."

"You never hated me, you hated an idea of me my father made up. I hate that thing too."

"No, I hated you..." I didn't know what to think of this, "The two things, the idea and the... person, were the same until I had the courage to pick apart the difference. If I had listened to the darkness, I might have cut you down. That night, in the moonlight, the horror of that possibility almost broke me."

"I felt your pain, back there." I had. His face was the most tragic and beautiful thing at the same time. Now, I knew he was thinking of me.

"As I felt your pain, back in the murder cave. When I trapped us in the darkness." The two young ladies were not even attempting to play by the rules now, and were just moving the pieces around the board in a circle. "There was a moment when I saw you. Sitting there, on your stool, like an image of light. I could feel your fear, but then, your love, and I saw you stretching forward and backward, forever and ever. I felt like nothing could ever pull us apart as long as we remain ourselves."

"I too, saw you, like a ball of energy connected to everything. Connected to my own heart, in a thousand places." Had we bared our shades to each other? Could even that eternal light stand against the darkness? A part of me knew that I had risked everything to stay. But, as I looked into his eyes, I knew that we had already won. "Worry not, my love. The worst thing they could do to me now is kill me, not destroy me utterly. Your light saved me."

"Oh, I can't bear it." One of the two young ladies jumped up, a large woman who matched Thesius in height, and almost in his shoulders. "You two need to stop being so terribly romantic in here. We've been playing the same move for 20 turns because neither one of us can think of anything but you two. And I wanted to listen but now it's annoying, I'm tired of leaving my pieces on the board. Go to your room."

We did. The bed bowed under my mass, but that just made Thesius press up against my side harder. It felt so strange to sleep at night, but I knew I would be awakened in time to get back to the cave, and so I felt myself drifting off. He was already breathing peacefully beside me. My mind kept returning to random things. The beans I kicked off the vacant board as we ran off to hold each other in privacy. The night flames on the balcony, which reflected their light up onto the wall behind us, under our closed curtain. Thesius, and his sweetness, and his mother's good advice. A loud sound of passion interrupted my thoughts, and brought me back to a fully awakened state.

"Oh... yeah. This cell... I get to hear everyone now. I don't think it's so bad for anyone else who has stayed here. I'm sure you heard that."

"It made me a touch jealous, but the rare joy of sleeping with you sounded nicer."

"Yeah." He snuggled under my arm, and the blanket, and I squeezed him against me tighter. But there was still something... The beans on the board... The love of his mother. I sat bolt upright in bed, almost throwing Thesius out of it.

"Wha?"

"Elaía!"

It took him a few confused moments, as he woke up, to reply. "Is that... your mother's name? I think you mentioned it once." A second later, I saw all of the color drain out of his face. He had figured it out, and I was ashamed.

"Have you... talked to her?" His voice was low, as if to conceal my shame.

"No! Thesius..." Mine was panicked, there was no concealing what I felt.

"Since when?" He must have read my face, "Since that night, when I heard her playing in the maze?"

"She told me you were there, down the hole, and the... the priests were there after the sacrifice, and I knew they would tell her I yet lived..." What must she think of me, of what I had done?

"How often would you talk to her?"

"Every few days. She knew so little. I let her think the worst of me, to protect her."

"It's been months, Asterius!"

"I know! You... your love was so bright it blotted everything else out. And I stopped walking the maze... I've been a terrible fool."

"She won't think the worst of you, she'll think worse than that! That the thing in the cave has finally eaten you! That you have no more words to give!" He was already on his feet. "She's your mother, you said she loves you."

"She does, I never doubted it..." Now he was pulling on his disguise.

"Morning comes. It is overcast, and we should be able to move without being detected. Can you walk?"

"I'm fine. I might need a rub, but later."

"She has waited long enough."

Seventeen

He ran up to the marvelous lamp on his table, and cupped his hand over it, as if to conceal it, as if I had not seen that it had been left on in his absence. "What is the point of that, my love? Will your hand pull back the light that thing released?" He realized how silly he was being, and we both hazarded a low chuckle.

"Is it love that has made me such a fool, Thesius? I would never have been so careless before." His bashful look, with his hand on the side of his face, made me feel a bit a fool myself, but I spoke wise.

"It was fear that made you careful before. You just need to find a new justification to take care." The truth of that stung him. I remembered he had gotten a similar lecture earlier... Was I overdoing it? "When does the royal house rise? I assume she won't be in her chambers all day?"

"We beat the dawn, so we have an hour or more yet. They tend to be late sleepers. I should check the maze, make sure I have taken care of any offerings." Did I hear him right? Did he hear himself?

"We should check the maze. Together. I won't send you into the dark alone, never again. That's how much of a fool love has made of me. I'm going back in there. I choose to."

We made it one room into the murder cave before we turned back.

"We'll have to turn off the lights, there are no lights in the Labyrinth." I complied, and the darkness pressed in. But then, I did not move when he tried to walk away, his hand in mine.

"Why?"

"They might smell the lamp oil, and then all would be lost." He winced in pain as I turned the light all the way up. It was way too bright now, but I didn't care.

"This thing burns without oil or flame. For thousands of years. You smell that, the nothing it is giving off? You know all of this, Asterius. You might be the smartest person I've ever met."

"You've never met yourself, Thesius." He was silent for a long time. "Why? Why did I think that?"

"You're still obeying the rules this place imposed on you." I could see the tremendous pain on his face, as he realized he was. "No, we need more than a light. This place scares me. We are going back to your room."

We had no holy symbols, no gods to watch us, no priests to cast out the demons that hid in the shadows. But we did have our harp, and our knot. Our love, and the love of the Athenians, was there. It would have to be enough. We re-entered the maze, armed with our flame, our love, and that knife I always had with me. It didn't feel like much.

We made a line for the big central chamber, hoping that our haste would help us to escape the dark influence. It did seem easier, knot in hand, like I was heading to my hidden glade of joys rather than this pit of misery. I thought I heard something, like a nightmare from my childhood, but it faded. Before I could think too much of it, we saw something at the end of the chamber.

Laid before us, just on the other side of the rolling stone door, was a tremendous feast. Fruit, bread, cakes, and meats. As much as I had seen up in the court, on the day of my sacrifice. I looked at Asterius for some sort of explanation for this, but I could see by the look on his face that this was something new.

"Didn't they feed you meat? Just meat?"

"Mostly goat."

"So?" He had such a strange look. It was like he was trying to unthink something. I picked up a piece of bread, and tried a bite. It was far too sweet, but it was fresh. I spat it out. "All the bread here is so sweet. Why is that?"

"They put honey in it."

"Yeah, but why?"

"You expect it if you are used to it." I looked about this forest of blood, as countless empty eye sockets stared down at us from their screaming bony faces. Once, my darling Asterius expected to wake up to this.

"I think it is probably better to avoid something bad, than to accept it so long that you expect it. I also know that you have figured this out, but it is disturbing you. Out with it."

"The god. The one they thought I was. There was a harvest festival in the fall."

"They never celebrated it with you before."

"Yeah, because I was Asterius, before." The look on his face was unreadable. I was disappointed, but perhaps it was just too many emotions. "Oh, Thesius, what have I done?"

"I don't know what you did, because this is beyond me."

"I always was in mourning. Every time this happened before, I hid in the far chambers of the maze and bemoaned my failure, and cried. This time... I was happy. About you. About the fact that I saved everyone, for once. I think... I may have been excessively theatrical." It took me a moment to figure out what he meant by this.

"They think they have won... "

"I have achieved apotheosis." I had heard that word before. I remembered the conversation on the ship, as we approached our fate.

"Or, the opposite of that."

"Yeah." This word came out like a choke. Again, I heard a repeating chord.

"Do you hear that?"

"Yes, lost songs from my childhood, twisted and mad, carried on in the darkness."

"Is that one way it spoke to you?" He nodded, "Did it ever speak to others?" His eyes got wide.

It was coming out of the hole, near the bathing room. A twisted melody. Not even a song, more like ten of them, torn asunder and thrown in a pile.

"She should not be up yet." His voice cracked, but I couldn't tell if he was going to cry, or if he was struggling to maintain a whisper.

"Did she often play things that make you want to die? Or go deaf?" It wasn't a pan, it was factual. Listening to this semblance of a song was painful.

"No, never." He rapped on the wall of the hole, with the golden ring on his finger. The music ceased, for a moment, before resuming with an accompaniment of loud sobbing. Asterius pressed himself against the wall, clutching his harp, and sank down to the floor. Now two people were sobbing.

"Try talking to her."

"She can't hear if she doesn't come up." He spoke between his tears, "She doesn't want to hear what I have become." He put his head between his hands. I didn't know what to do, so I took a seat beside him, setting my lamp on the floor, and threw my arm over his broad shoulders. I listened to this chorus of sadness, and thought; this is comedy. Everything went right to get to this point. But even with everything going right, this place could only make tears. Imagine, if it had gone wrong? The wrath that would have broken free from here. The horror. The tragedy.

I knew what to do. I began playing a simple rhythm. It was awkward sitting, so I stood.

"What are you doing? What if they hear?" I stopped, but only for a moment.

"It seems like there is a lot of music being played up above. A few stray notes, would that attract as much attention as yelling? Especially since you're so fond of your stage that everyone knows what it sounds like when you bellow?" I knew what it sounded like, but only from ecstasy. "And tell me, love, you are talented, but have you ever been able to play both rhythm and melody?" His face shifted, to his beautiful toothy smile. He understood. It was mad, but it might work.

"Oh, my shining golden bear!" I'd never heard such a thing. I felt such joy, like he had given me my new name. "Yes, let us play."

As usual, I took the rhythm. Nothing somber for this place, I played out my joy at every moment since I had been by his side. I started with my slaps and harmony, as Asterius was already weaving

154

a furious melody, both of his hands moving as fast as they could, plucking out one chord after another. It was not a long song, it didn't need to be. It just had to be more than any one person could conceivably play, and we played more than two should have been able. I collapsed into his arms, laughing, at the end, forgetting our place, and this place, as I sat on his lap and nuzzled into his firm soft chest. The darkness had left the Labyrinth, if only for a moment.

"Asterius?" We were tangled together, and it took several seconds to rise to our feet. Asterius pressed himself against the portal.

"Mother, I am here." He struggled to contain his volume. Then, she was weeping again. But these tears were different.

"Oh my sweet child, my gift, can it be true? Or have I gone mad?"

"I yet live."

"Not you. How many?" I realized what she meant, in context. She was smart, like her son.

"51. Most of them." I never thought that a choke could be joyful. But, if that choke is holding back a scream of joy? More tears, and then a response.

"I always knew you were poorly suited for what they had planned for you. I should have done more to stop them... Return on the Solstice. Be ready. The door will be open. I will do my best to make it easier." The two of them, had they discussed this plan before? No, they had just come up with the same plan. Or something very close.

"I love you."

"My darling son... I thought you had left me. Take care. Both of you." And she closed her curtain.

Asterius insisted that we collect some of the food before we leave. Making haste, we stuffed it into a spare skirt he had in his bedroom, with the ends tied off. The too-sweet bread was left behind; no one would have liked it, not even Asterius, after what I had said.

We took the path through his false room, and we briefly set aside our burdens so Asterius and I could kick his pile of treasures over with glee. The pile crashed down, bounced and flowed across the floor, like it was trying to run away from us. We had chosen not to respect the treasures of this murder cave, as it would want us to. Truly, no one could hear, and even if they could, would they come see?

The Labyrinth seemed so drab as we left it. The shadows were flat and dead, and lacked their usual threat, like they were tired. We had won, for today. We had found a spare bean on the board that no one was using. And she was a queen.[4]

---

4 Chess hadn't been invented yet. This is set in the 9th century BC, by the extremely arbitrary method we use to mark the passage of time. This is only a joke for you, and I. Though, it is true, our two heroes had much to laugh about at the berry patch on the way back to the camp.

Eighteen

The entire character of my life changed that day. No longer was I fighting for purchase, holding onto reflected bits of light in my cave. Now I was running for the exit. I could see the light before me, even if it were only the light that greets you upon your death.

I was ready. Everyone was, disturbingly so. When Thesius explained what had occurred, to the crowd of Athenians assembled in the idyllic green, I swear I saw bows in hands before he finished, even though so many of them had been awakened from their slumbers, as it was mid-day. I hadn't even realized we were walking together in the light until we had almost reached the berry patch. It was easy to miss, with my real light ahead of me.

Even when I explained the problem of the powerful armor, and the cruel man it wore, and how we might have to face him if my mother failed, no one wavered. Even the new sacrifices, who were still having a lot of fun, had no hesitation to leave when they saw how much Thesius admired me, and cared for me. They had all grown up with him. How could they not love him?

There was one person here I was apprehensive to face. Thesius had some brilliant idea he was working on in the shop, so I walked down to the edge of the green, to the shadows there where the centaurs always lounged.

"Chianten."

"Asterius." We sat in silence for a good while. "So, still lacking in words? I heard you speak to the Athenians, earlier. You could be a general, or a lecturer in a great hall that probably doesn't even exist on this sphere any more."

"You were always telling me what I could be. It was hard to imagine being anything other than what I was." I smiled at him, he feared not my incisors.

"I fear I was too interrogative with you. You didn't need someone to show you wisdom. You sought that out, of your own accord. Deep wisdom, in that sort of behavior. The sort that springs from the shade, not the mind. But I told you all these things you could be. And then we were silent, for so many years."

"I couldn't face what you were saying."

"I was pointing to a door that was fully closed. It was foolish. Someone needed to kick it open, first." He smiled, a rare gift, but then he frowned, "Please forgive me."

"For what?"

"For not doing this sooner." And he pulled me into a warm embrace. I leaned on his shoulder, and spoke to his ear.

"You never ceased to be my friend."

"I was a poor friend. But thank you." And we broke. I stretched my arms, as Thesius had taught me, and bounced around a bit on my feet. "You certainly have a spring in your step."

"Thesius gives the best foot rubs!" And there he was, now! He was running up with what looked like the back of a kopu, but it was carved a bit different. He was swinging it around like mad, and laughing.

"I think this is close, but I've never held one. You have, right? Try it." And he handed me an odd piece of wood. It was heavier than the back of a kopu, and had some extra wood attached to the wide part. The narrow part had been modified into a grip. I had no idea what it was for.

"What is this?"

"Oh, I get to explain something to you, a delight!"

"It's not that rare."

"It is while our clothes are on." He smiled. I wanted the clothes to be off, so desperately, in that moment. "It's a training tool. Chiron didn't give us real blades for the first few years. Just carefully carved sticks. I thought he didn't trust us, or he was being cheap, but it worked great. They were balanced the same and we focussed on form rather than chopping at stuff like mad children." I understood completely by now, but he continued. His voice was a delight. "Well, none of these people have held one of those double axes you have. We can train them, so they'll be ready. I think we can make 20 of these by tomorrow."

And so, we did. His first attempt was pretty close, a bit too heavy, and the weight popped right off the end after a bit. One of the more experienced crafters built the second attempt, and it would have served well as an improvised club on its own. Everyone was swinging one around soon. Although, there were some momentary missteps.

"I will take a bow." Miletta was adamant, and it wasn't an argument to me. I knew her name now, I was compelled to learn it after the previous night, and I had learned a lot about her. She was the best archer amongst them. "I'm good with it. I know it won't be much use in the tight spaces, but that's a big palace. I know the three of us, together, can shower the upper level with arrows. That would give us a better chance." Oh, she had some other choices for the bow? It's true, we needed archers to counter their archers.

"We're not taking the women, right?" This was one of the first years, he was a stranger to me. But, this was a question? My years with the centaurs had taught me that their subtle training made great athletes of everyone. It only seemed like a game. This was certainly true of Thesius, though his teacher worked his mind as well. Almost everyone here that wasn't ill was in fantastic shape. Peak athletic form. "I won't risk my love to this!" Egeria stepped forth, one of my favorites from the first sacrifice. She was such a gentle soul, that group was almost children, and the centaurs and I had to raise them a bit. I was shocked when she slapped him hard across the face with a resounding crack. Everyone gasped.

"Oh gods, why did they curse you with a perfect rope and a fool for a mind? What are you protecting me from, Estius?" She flipped her hands in the air in outrage. Estius was holding his face, and my own cheek felt warm in sympathy. "We are all dead here, and if we should ever leave this place it will only be by a stroke of luck and the skill of everyone. Everyone here! Or do you think we are so great a force that we can tie half our hands to protect your feelings?" There was no further discussion of it. She was right.

When we were not training and otherwise preparing for the raid with the Athenians, Thesius and I were in the field. Not always at our secret glade, though often. There were a lot of things to put in position, and many positions to try and take, before the winter solstice. Maintaining surprise meant we had to reinforce the deer trails for use by many people who were not as fleet of foot, or as subtle, as my golden bear. And we had to do it without raising suspicion, as some of those woods were still hunted, despite Tileron's best efforts. It would have been hard work, but it was an exaltation, to do it in such company. It also gave me the opportunity to share one of my favorite scrolls with Thesius, under the light of the full moon. Well, it was a favorite when I was getting big and growing my beard.

"I like the art that comes from your hand better." He was turning the scroll this way and that, as he examined the illustrations. "These are so flat. You've got that 'looking in' trick down."

"Yes, well. You were wondering how I was being so innovative. I remembered that thing and dug it up." He leaned in closer to the scroll to examine an illustration, and then recoiled. Some of those people were very flexible.

"These are all men and women. I think… I think they are. Some of them look very odd." It wasn't hard to get the general idea, though. A face provides little difficulty, if you can look upon it with love. Thesius and I had been so blissfully overjoyed to discover that.

"In a lot of the oldest scrolls people had weird teeth and noses. Sometimes hands and feet, not as often. Don't know what to make of it, it's not like now." Except for me, of course. I would be extreme even by that standard, though.

It always puzzled me. Even the centaurs have a human face. Why should I look like a beast? Why should some of the people on these scrolls? A fox ran by. The creatures hardly paid notice to us now. Our faces had some similarities, I thought. Is it the human face, flat like the image of the moon as it passes through the air around this sphere, which is an aberration[5]? I gazed upon his face, amused as it was, and it was hard to find it out of place.

"Well, I suppose things work the same with us. I mean, positions."

"Only roughly." It was true! There was a difference of at least 33 to 42 degrees in the angle of attack, depending on how he should hold his torso.

"Gently works too." He was not at all paying attention to the scroll now. It was a silly thing, barely worth keeping. We had no trouble innovating previously, it was just a more patient process.

"Or, we could try both, by turns?" This was an invitation, and Thesius had no intention of saying no.

I even had a few opportunities to play music with all of the Athenians. As the air first started feeling crisp, and we had only a few more weeks to go, we had a little concert in honor of their goddess. I am not a person of faith, but joining together with them in that joyous music might have made me one, if I didn't know so well what the gods were. We then had a funeral for ourselves. This was more cheery than I expected, apparently they dance a lot at funerals on the peninsulas.

Even so, I felt the restriction of life in this bowl, in their music. Their orchestra had no horns, no large drums. We had to maintain a certain level of propriety. Our chance was so close, it would be such a shame to ruin it all now.

If anyone had seen us, I wonder what they would have thought. I'm pretty sure no one did, the other Athenians had learned how to

---

5 Asterius would absolutely use this joke, if he spoke English at the time, or if he were writing this now, and he wouldn't care that literally no one got it. But then, he would be delighted that Thesius did get it.

Also, it is worth noting that the animal that passed our heroes by was actually a rather plump marten. It turns out, when man find themselves on an isle without the fox, they just name some random animal a fox rather than live without them.

traverse the forest better than I had given them credit for. But the group of us, 50 strong, would have probably turned aside any curious eye in dread. Uriel, who had drawn the black straw to stay behind and care for those too sick to fight, wept bitterly for us as we left. They were such true tears, and it is always nice to have a mourner at your funeral.

They were dressed almost as if we were going to harvest, in the chill night air. My communications with my mother had been very brief, but she had selected a time, after the start of the great feast of the Solstice, for us to enter. That it was at night was to the liking of most everyone, at this point. The light of mid-day seemed harsh to all of them now, not just I.

The band of Athenians were without belts, their skirts tied in place with cords, and we were all wrapped about with a length of rotten leaf colored fabric, just to be sure. The only one to wear a belt was I, as it comforted me somehow, but I was the strangest sight of all. Surely this was a procession of spirits, especially on the Solstice. Best to leave them alone, right?

My golden bear's shining shoulders were disappointingly covered in the moonlight under that fabric, but several people pointed out how much his gift stood out, and that it needed to be masked. There were so many other ways I could tell him from the crowd, but also distinguishing him was his fine leather harness, made by some godly smith in some place far away from here. I wondered about that, as gods had a greater tendency to take things than to make them. He did not have his blade, the chasm did, but the harness had a hook for an axe now, and a good place for his knife thanks to my sister. He also had his lamp, hanging from his harness in a leather harness of its own, that one of the Athenians had made. It was loose enough he could still operate it without worrying about dropping it.

We assembled at the mouth, in the woven path. Most of these people had only seen this place once. Hopefully, the door would be open, and it would be a quick passage.

162

Thesius took the lead, with his poorly named eternal flame, which was both breakable and had no flames at all involved in its operation. It was best for morale. I knew the maze, and so I took the rear, with my little dented oil lamp in hand. I could keep the line together that way too. I would not lose anyone else in this place. Not on my life.

There were noises in the dark. There always were. I once preferred to believe I had been imagining them, but I had not been. The Athenians were warned, they even knew the path up and into the castle, we had run it out on the field again and again. But it was unsettling. The darkness was defending the palace above, as best it could. But the band made it through with our love in our hearts, and our lights in our hands. We were in the main room before I knew it. Thesius turned the beam of his lamp sideways in the colonnade, where we assembled, to spare the crowd the sight of our audience above. Or perhaps that was the angle it was meant to be used at, it was hard to know. Everyone was a bit scared now, as we assembled, not of the murder cave, but of what was ahead of us. We could see the door was open.

We lined up, with Thesius and I taking the front, and three in each line behind. We had trained to press against the walls if anyone started to fall, to prevent our doom from being a comedic one, but we had to reach the walls, so we had to rely upon each other. It was decided I would lead the way, by a vote, which seemed to be the way everything was decided amongst them if there wasn't immediate unanimity, which was often. If there was resistance at the top of the stairs I could play it off as a procession of the new god. That would probably give us a bit of time, critical time, if they had any faith in me. That Thesius would stand by my side was no question, then. None of the band could imagine it any other way.

Nineteen

The first thing we saw, at the top of the stairs, was Ariadne. She was in some new elaborate dress I didn't have time to look at, and she was as white as an undyed cloth. She stood there, looking at Asterius and I, her hands held rigid to the sides. I looked to Asterius, but he was confused, not concerned. Of course, how could he know her face? She was just another well dressed girl in the audience, from his perspective. Before I could speak and make things better, Ariadne beat me.

"Father was right! You've returned as the god of death and harvest! Remade the sacrifice as your retinue!" And she thought of this, and what that meant. I could see it on her face. I thought she might throw herself to the ground, and grovel in worship. Instead, she just looked at me, in my strange rotten leaf shroud, and screamed, before running away as fast as her feet could take her.

"What madness is… I guess we're going to get that a lot."

"Asterius, that was your sister, your mom must have sent her to open the door." It probably would have been better to not share this information, and I knew that as soon as I saw his face collapse into shock and grief. Thankfully, he didn't go running after her. There was no guard in the… Asterius had a word for an open field in walls. The ward. This whole space was full of people, screaming at me, the last time I saw it. I liked it better like this, empty and in the moonlight. When I looked back to him, Asterius seemed concerned rather than sad. More than I would expect.

"Where is everyone?" He wasn't bothering to keep his voice down.

"It's late?"

"It's the solstice festival. Late is the idea. It's the whole purpose of it. Stay up late and defy the night. I knew there would be people, I just figured there would be fewer guards."

"Where would the most people be?" I thought this was a good place to start if we wanted to solve a mystery.

"The grand court? That's where they serve the food." Asterius would know. I would too, for that matter. I could almost taste the honey and carrots.

The rest of the Athenians had filed in behind us now, and we made our coordinated run for the front hall. Before long, we had a band of heavily armed warriors, just as planned. Most of them had not seen the grandeur of the palace, and were gawking about. Mantes and Helea were doing their best to refocus them while we planned the next move.

"I say we go for the court." I'm biased towards mysteries.

"The place with the most people seems like the worst choice. I say we go for the armory. We might do a lot better than axes with what they have there." This was Mantes.

"The most people of what? This place is giving me the creeps." Miletta was not keeping her voice down either, and she was very loud. It rang off the stonework a bit.

"Nothing about this is right, there should be people everywhere. We discussed this." We had, our planning was as meticulous as it could be with Asterius' 18 year old information and everyone else's continuous input and votes. So many votes. "This is not how the festival goes. I know, I was kept at the periphery of it, but I know it wasn't silent like a tomb. The court is defensible if the warrior is here, and it might tell us something. I'm with Thesius but that's dumb so I'm not voting."

"That's not how voting works." Anyone could have said this.

"I am clearly biased, he could say we should march right into Hades and I would walk right by him." Asterius is adopting our curses, now? Given how fond the Cretans are of curses, that was a deep compliment, to all of us.

"People vote through their bias all the time. We just hope that all together it balances out." Only Mantes could have said this. It was perfect. Asterius took his vote.

Either many of the band were emotionally biased towards me, or it was actually a good idea, but either way we headed towards the court after the roll was taken. Not so much a roll as an instant win of the ayes, actually. Both Asterius and I had axes now. Most of us did, except for seven archers, led by Miletta.

Asterius felt somewhat uncomfortable with the thing, not because he wasn't trained, but because it was the symbol of Minos. I couldn't think of a better thing to use, myself, but I understood. But he held it like it was a hot turnip.

"Grip it tight, love." I didn't want him to fumble his weapon for symbolic reasons.

"I would grip you more tightly. I hate this thing." It was clear.

"Just use it for a bit, to throw it away. For good."

We turned the corner to the grand hall before the king's court, and we saw the first revilers. They were elaborately dressed with a pattern of white and black squares all across their skirt, and silvery renditions of the ubiquitous belt with a bundle of wheat, and the bull head on it. This bull looked... angrier than the one I had seen before. Now that I saw the detail, I realized that a few of the heads downstairs had been changed out to this design as well. Besides the position of the chest and how it was thrust to the sky with little concern for the comfort of the women, the style was uniform. Under it the skin of the legs was the shade... purple. Was it some tight cloth? They were all wearing white leather masks above the nose, which made the fact that they were very dead and lifeless considerably less disturbing than it would have been otherwise. It felt like a favor.

"Someone has done all the work for us?" Mantes was pleased, this was good for our strategy. Most of the Athenians were horrified. I couldn't read Asterius' face, which meant he was feeling everything.

"We should take the court." I said, as I pushed aside a corpse with my bare foot. It was wrapped around the door and keeping that half of it from swinging open. When it did, crashing into the wall with a clap that made everyone wince, we rushed in and saw the grandest party that any of us had ever been witness to. Actually, I first checked the huge bulls on the wall, but they were the same. I realized I was being a fool; changing them would have taken a very long time, and would be very expensive. They would have to take up a collection or something. Then, I focussed on the party everyone else was staring at.

Food was everywhere, lines and lines of plates and cups. It was a crowd in the hundreds, every single bit of space in the court was taken up. Any one of the participants had more jewelry on than everyone in Athens owned, except perhaps hidden in a pot in a field somewhere. Also, everyone was dead. Their faces were twisted, their mouths were foaming, their hands clawed at their own throats. Extremely dead. Many of them did not have masks on. It felt like a punishment.

But then, applause! Even one pair of moving hands is stirring, if the space is right. "My congratulations on the performance." A grand older woman, dressed in a torn purple dress, was standing at the head of the room at the largest table. I quickly judged she was in the queen's position[6]. Elaía. She must have been another face in the crowd at my party.

"Look at all of these people you had convinced, Asterius. You could take a bow, if you like... You had me convinced for a while too." The expression on his toothsome face was not hard for me to read, though I had seen it so rarely. Shame.

"You can't blame me for this." I still had no idea what this was. A number of the Athenians were crying, openly. I noticed a large pile of jewels over by a big punch bowl with a scale model of an angry bull head, on a plaque. Aha, there's the collection!

"Oh, I know who is to blame. Such a shame he only had a few crumbs of your ceremonial cake. And even less of the god's sacred

---

6 This is ~900 BC, so this is not a chess reference. This is not 1250 BC either. A few storytellers make a crossover issue where all the heroes can have an adventure together, and people a few thousand years later find that fan fiction and try to put that on a timeline, without trying to make it make sense. Our ancestors weren't all liars, that's an impossible lie, but a lot of them enjoyed a bit of fan fiction every now and then, just as we do.

drink, I'm not sure he had any." Note to self, do not try the punch. Though, I may never want to eat or drink again.

When I was done making jokes with myself to retain my sanity in the face of the most mad thing I had ever seen, by far, I decided it would be better to look at my light rather than hide in my cave and tell jokes to my own shadow. I was dismayed. He gazed about, madly, at all of the bloated faces. He was in so much pain. "Everyone else was too afraid to offend you, Asterius, or is it Bael? But Arbias isn't really a man of faith. He doesn't believe in gods, he just makes them... Or failed to!" And then she laughed, wild and mad, almost a scream.

"Stop it!" They were my words, but they came out without a choice. I heard them, and then I realized it was the perfect thing to say. "You're his mother, can't you read his face? You're tearing him apart!" Her face blanked; she had realized what she was doing. She sat down, and she poured herself a drink. He was upon her in a flash, and he flipped the cup away.

"It's wine, Asterius, the poison is over there in the corner." I was right! "Look for the pile of jewels, given in offering." Also right. "Those are yours, I guess. Mind the bloody skirted gentlemen all around the table," Wait, what? "They couldn't get enough of your drink."

"Mother, I thought... " Stop thinking, Asterius. This is a battle. I looked around and most of my band wasn't even thinking, they were crying.

"I should have lived better by you, my son, but I'm not going to die for you today. I might die another day." Something about this statement made me intrigued, happy and infuriated at the same time and that just made me confused. My light's face was shaded with grief.

At this moment, Ismene, who came in the second sacrifice, let forth a bloodcurdling scream. She had flipped one of the men around the food table over with her foot. He was one of a large crowd there, all face down. The whole front of his skirt was red with fairly fresh blood.

168

"What happened?" Mantes was holding his face. The physician in him was cringing. The warrior in me was bewildered.

"Oh, when I told them that the glorious return of Bael was nigh, and you were going to walk up those stairs tonight, a lot of them got some very curious ideas about what would be the best way to show their devotion. That group sought to impress you by cutting their roosters right off. I think it made the poison work on them faster, but they may have just been too enthusiastic with the drink." Several people vomited. Asterius just barely kept his lunch, and I was considering. I decided to focus upon strategic matters. Something she had said was bothering me. More than all the things she had said that were disturbing me.

"Might?" I had to interject, again, addressing Elaía, "I don't think any of these people are going to kill you. Is the great warrior alive?"

"You mean Grildon? Oh, here he is." She tipped over the man at the seat next to her, who flopped to the floor. He seemed to be a short bloated middle aged man, but it might have been the poison that was bloating him up. "Not too impressive without his shell. I've seen that man kill so many people. For sport, they would do it out back, rebels and such. I really did enjoy watching him die. He had enough that it just seemed like he fell asleep, though. I wish he had suffered more. Did you see, one of them tore my dress, thrashing about!"

"Is that it?" Asterius was pointing at a curious object on the table.

"Yeah, it crawled away from him and sat itself in the middle there. Poor thing must be afraid of heights and ledges." It was a twisted, mad smile she was wearing. I couldn't imagine what living here was like. I was just worried for her mind, after our performance in the darkness, but she seemed to be more sane than most of these people were.

"Well then!" I cried it out, to cheer the crowd. This news had made all of us happy, though most of us were still shocked and nauseated. "I think we can stay abreast of the burning light. We can do this!" Everyone cheered, but quietly. This was still a battlefield, even though it looked like a mortuary temple.

"Oh, Thesius, such spirit. But before you run off thinking my husband is just one man, and die before him as so many others have done, you have to know what you would be up against." Gods I hated that phrase. "But before we talk about how we are going to die... Asterius, please introduce me! To the one you played with. Surely you love them."

Asterius responded by throwing his arm over my shoulder, and pulling me close. I had been moving to his side this whole time, as a plant moves towards the light. I couldn't help but lean my head on his firm, soft chest.

"Him?! I mean, we all loved him, with his maddening songs and his locks. Your father wanted to keep him, but he decided that... sacrificing him would be more fun." She sighed, and turned away. Had I disappointed her? "It's the golden crabs."

"But, those things are useless in a fight. I mean, that's what they were made for, but... they don't have the expendables." Asterius knew what we were talking about, which was good, because I thought this was a recipe or something for a moment.

"Yes, but your lovely father decided to give them knives, and what do you know? They rather took to them. Really, they seemed delighted to finally have a way to spill blood again." And she laughed again, that mad laugh.

"I never did find them amusing. They were so... aggressive." His ears were pulled close to his head. Those things, whatever they were, must have left him with some hard memories.

"Asterius, I am having quite a hard time following this, and so I'm sure all the other Athenians are too. Could you make it more simple?" His arm was still over my shoulder, so I wrapped my arm around his back from the rear. He needed a hug.

"These things, they are inside..." Asterius lowered his tone, as he had noticed everyone was already pretty close, "... inside two metal bowls, and they have legs sticking out in between. They stand about knee height on most of you. The whole thing looks kind of like a beetle, or a crab. They were killing machines, they shot little arrows

170

out and killed... people I suppose, it's not for hunting. The arrows had their own little bit of fire in them, and the fire let them fly very quickly. They also had run out long ago and no one could make new ones. Grandfather spent so much energy trying to do so and he only managed to blow up the workshop twice."

"But now, they have knives!" Estius was thrilled, or at least that's what the tone in his voice said. I'm sure that tone was a liar.

"Yes, and they can run very fast. Up and down walls, too." This sounded appalling, like a nightmare. I must have looked crestfallen, and I saw this spread through Asterius' gaze to his face.

"It's just one thing after another." Asterius released me and collapsed into one of the bronze chairs, which was so sturdy it didn't say a thing in response. "I'm so sorry I drug you into this."

"Asterius, stop it." It was bad enough that his mom was tearing him apart earlier. He didn't need to have a try at it.

"I've done everything to keep you alive and now..." I grabbed him by the horns and turned his gaze to mine. "Uh, ouch?" I released him; that was too rough.

"Sorry..." I made sure he was fine, rubbed his neck, and continued. "You didn't drag any of us into this, you didn't even drag you into this. The man who did is upstairs, and we're going to go get him. I don't care if I have to be stabbed by a murderous version of one of your shitting bowls to do it." The band cheered. This was a feeling we all had in common.

"They move so fast, and nothing we have could penetrate their armor. We can't just do this on your high emotions, Thesius." He had a good point.

"What about... that thing?" I pointed to the forbidden jar, sitting on the table. It was such a strangely beautiful thing. It seemed so simple, just two thick golden loops, surrounded by and somehow melding into an oval of inky blackness.

"Pretty, isn't it. I've never seen it off the neck of the bearer. It's also bad. We can't use that."

"Actually, under the circumstances, a warrior that could jump over the wall and…" Anyone could have said it. The warrior had been the talk of the camp.

"No, bad as in… it's a terrible temptation, Thesius." Actually, I was the one who said it. The warrior seemed like a good idea. "Everyone I knew who had it was a killer, and they were worse after than before." Only Asterius could have said this. It was perfect. Also, wrong strategically.

"So, do we wait until your father figures out how to martial his mechanical guardians to come down and kill us here? You know he's working on that right now, he loves killing so much." Elaía laughed out loud at this.

"You saw him for, what, a few minutes, and you know him that well?" I was happy that I was impressing her. She seemed put off by Asterius and I, at first.

"I also saw his creation downstairs. Several times." My hand was on his shoulder, as he sat, and we supported one another. "That was all I needed to know about him. He delighted in the suffering he was inflicting, on the people who he threw in that murder cave…" I was interrupted by a loud peel of laughter from the queen.

"Murder cave!" She tossed aside the dead hand of a former general, and grabbed the flagon he was grasping for. She poured herself a drink. Asterius let her have it. "You Athenians have such a way with words, despite the fact you have so few of them."

"I can see the virtue of both ways of speaking, to be frank. Thanks to your son. He has taught me a lot." So very much.

"I bet." She had such a look on her face. Was it good wine? No, it was us. She was happy about us. Asterius noticed. He crossed his chest with his arm, and held my hand in his, on his shoulder. There was a moment of peace, in the midst of battle. "I am impressed with you, my son. To have taken the hand of such an impressive person. The Athenians are blessed to have one such as you, Thesius."

"Actually, if you don't mind me interrupting, Queen of Minos," Asterius winced at that word, though it was both accurate and in the mouth of his friend, Mantes. "We all thought that we were blessed to have your son, Asterius. Without him, all of us would have surely perished. He sacrificed everything, except for us." But now, the look on my lover's face made my heart sing. The queen laughed, but then she looked ashamed.

"You Athenians, and your words... " She took another drink, "I thought you were too good to be remade into… that, but I had no idea how good you really were, my son. Given the apotheosis thing, I half wondered if you hadn't regurgitated them and put them back together again. I'm happy to see that isn't true... That isn't true, right?"

"Oh, that's appalling! No, of course not." The curl in his lip at the thought of eating and vomiting us all showed every one of his fangs. A few of the Athenians recoiled, but most didn't. His mother didn't either. "Ma'aht built them a hidden place, not far from here."

"Ah yes, him. Lovely man. When Arbias had him tossed in that pit I wished I could have thrown him in after. Oh yes, the regurgitating thing." It was such a specific word, related to birds, that Chiron had taught me she was using here, and while it was marvelous to hear it in usage, the image it produced almost made me do the same, but without a hungry brood of chicks to appreciate it. My stomach held firm. "He'll probably scream something about that to you. He's fully convinced you are Bael. You have his faith, you know? I mean, now. I think that nibble might have put him in an odd state of mind." She took another drink. I was a bit worried for *her* state of mind, at this point. I did not feel like drinking, in this charnel house of death. I'd never seen so many corpses in my life, let alone in one place.

"So, who takes the armor? Should we draw a lot? Or take a vote." Estius was eager to get to this point, it seems.

"Asterius, I remember you saying it could make a bow and arrow, out of the air?" I had a preference already.

"Indeed. It can fire a good number of arrows before it needs to eat, too. I'm fairly sure it would work against the golden crabs, the arrows are very fast and… destructive." Asterius had apparently been witness to this. How often did they kill people for sport, here in this rotten country? But most everyone had a more pressing question.

"The armor eats?!" Several people said this simultaneously. I might have said it, in my mind.

"Yeah, the thing loves bread. Nothing but bread." This was one of the many things Elaía found hilarious at the moment. I wondered if it expected too much honey, but I held my tongue.

"Then my vote is Miletta." I looked at her face as I said this. She looked shocked; this was clearly not her preference. "She is the best shot among us, and if it can jump over the castle wall it can jump up onto the walls too. She would have the best view and purchase. And it's armor, it might protect her in the exposed position."

There were a few people who wanted to draw a lot, but that was most likely because they were hoping to get the armor themselves. It was disappointing. Most everyone else saw the logic of my choice, however. She was the best shot, there was no doubt of it. She didn't like it. But still, she reached for the thing, nervously.

"Wait, wait! I saw this the last time." It was Elaía, "The first one failed. He was wearing clothes and it really didn't like that. Tore him apart. My father didn't manage to tell anyone about that little condition, before he died." This was another horrible thing that was only funny to her. It seemed as if she could write a whole book of humor that was only funny if you were mad, and call it her Elaíarus. Also, I was jesting with myself again and I needed to focus, before she stopped laughing at least. She composed herself, and continued. "That fool was the second choice, after we roused some old cleric out of his bed to explain what had happened."

"Oh you've got to be kidding me, I have to strip for you Minoan sons of bitches again? Gods damn you and your…" She squeezed her mouth, her eyes and her fists shut, and continued. "Fine."

"We'll turn around…" Anyone could have said this.

"Why? You've all seen me naked countless times." Miletta was right, except for the queen, and maybe Asterius.

174

"Because we want to give you the dignity these sons of bitches denied us the last time." This was Helea. Only she could have said this. It was perfect.

"What will happen?" Miletta was addressing Elaía directly.

"Grip it and put one thumb in each of those golden holes. It will flow over you. You'll scream. And then it will say a bunch of nonsense words to you while you recover. It was fascinating, really."

"Does it hurt?" Miletta didn't care, she just wanted to know.

"I don't think so, it's just terrifying." Mercifully, she didn't laugh.

We all turned our backs, even Elaía, and the first thing we knew of her donning the armor was a scream. I'd never heard her scream before, and there was an odd gurgle to it. We all whipped around to see this horrid black ink, spreading all over her from her hands. She fell to the floor and writhed as it covered every inch of her.

"Don't touch her! It has defenses." This was Asterius, and it was a good warning, several people were going to help. Now she was a black form, more an outline than the shape of a man. It reminded me of the difference between Asterius' drawings and all the ones I had grown up with. The black form rose to its feet.

"I can hear lots of talking. Like a grocery list, or a shipping manifest. Really fast. Not a word of it…. Yeah, just a word now and then. Not much." She was keeping herself calm, this was a good idea.

"Keep talking." I encouraged it.

"So, that was weirdly loud… Um, now I can't hear anything." Miletta tapped the sides of her head. I noticed that she had cruel claws on the ends of her fingers once she moved them around enough that I could see the outline right.

"Poor Grildon was nearly deaf without it." She clearly had no sympathy for him, her tone said more than her words, "Walked around with it clinging to his ear the past few years, like a black stain on his head. Give it a minute, darling, it will adjust. I'm happy to see that it accepts women, I was hoping that wouldn't be like it's dislike of fashion. That was such a mess. Got all over my shoes!"

"I heard that. Messy shoes?"

"There, it adjusted, didn't take long." Elaía took another drink.

"Everything looks odd. Like it has a color over it?"

"You should try moving around a little, but slowly." There was a great deal of concern in Asterius' voice. She took a few steps, and then was sliding into the wall in the blink of an eye. It was so fast I could hardly track her. Precious gems rained down off of the decoration, and a cloud of ochre powder was tossed into the air. She got up, apparently unharmed. Even as the ochre fell down about her it seemed to repel it, and she was still just a black outline.

"I started walking, and then I thought about how I wanted to walk to the wall over there, and then I was there and I couldn't stop." Miletta was continuing to talk through this.

"Yes, it can move very quickly over long distances. If you don't want to suddenly be somewhere, don't think about being there." Asterius said this as if it was the easiest thing to do, when it seemed like a steep hill to climb. But then again, that fool over there managed it.

Miletta surprised us all by taking the opposite of his advice, brilliantly. She walked calmly into the center of the room, and then she was standing on one of the huge bull heads on the wall, in a streak. She waved, and then she was on the other. Then, back by our side. The second bull decoration came crashing to the floor, only harming a pile of corpses. It must have been poorly attached. Well, they got the collection for that. I was pleased; this final time I could see the jump, because I was ready for it, but only barely.

"That was easy once I understood it. It even makes sure your feet are in the right place to land! Everything seems to slow down, it's amazing. What else can it do?"

Before Asterius could answer, Arbias did with a monstrous, shrieking howl.

Twenty

It was the Sun Eye. Arbias must have reached it! But, instead of the wooden roof collapsing upon us in a great gout of fire... nothing.

"Mother, you poisoned him here, he knows we might be here?"

"Yes, I'm puzzled why I'm not dead, but also pleased." She took another drink. I knocked the cup out of her hands.

"Go get some water, I've seen people drink so much wine that it's as good as that poison over there."

"I drink wine every day Asterius, you haven't been here..."

"In 18 years!" I was screaming. I didn't care. "18 years in the murder cave trying to do anything but what it wanted me to do. What he wanted me to do!" She was very frightened. I was close, and I was larger than she had ever seen me, up close, by far. I expected Thesius to pull me away, but I looked to his shining fuzzy countenance and he was standing there, arms crossed. He opened his mouth, then thought better of it. Then he decided he didn't care either and opened it up again.

"My mother gave me up to come to this murderous show, and die. She never knew anything about the gods, or the tools they would give me. But she did good by me. I did what was right." He pinned her with his glorious blue eyes. He didn't care if she were a queen. The Sun Eye fired again, but he did not flinch. He was a prince. "Your son had to have a parent dropped upon him by some miracle that I cannot even ascribe to the gods, because you've figured out some way to keep them away from here... Or, someone did, once, and you stole it. That parent was so good to Asterius that he undid all of your abuse and gave him a backdoor, a home, and a way to save us. And you... Your husband had him thrown in a pit where he died." Thesius was yelling, tears in his eyes. I'd never heard him so angry. It was frightening. I knew my mother well enough to know that this wasn't pleasing her, but I didn't look at her. I looked at him. He was my light.

"I gave him a light."

"The Athenians would have found him ten if you hadn't given him the one. We had them all over camp." Mantes had her pinned too, I could tell by the angle. I still didn't look.

"Scrolls, and cakes!"

"I liked the scrolls." I had to tell the truth. I still didn't have to look at her.

"We would have made him better cakes, and bread. Anything he wanted. He always refused them. But he gave us *his* food." This was Eridice. She so rarely spoke, I hardly knew her voice, but somehow I knew it was her. I also knew who she was staring at, but there were too many tears in my eyes to see.

"Asterius deserved so much better than anything Minos gave him. Anything you gave him. You should be ashamed of yourself, you torn old hag, you don't deserve to kiss his feet." It was Miletta, and I was thankful. But then there was a hiss in the crowd. I looked up, through my tears. Miletta was the outline of a ball of knives, like the sea urchins we would crack open sometimes and eat. It roiled about her. I knew I had to compose myself, and speak.

"Miletta, it gets very, very stabby when you hate someone, and while I don't like my mother right now I would prefer her to not dissolve into a pile of meat." I swear I could see her blink in shock through the featureless void she had become. She turned away from the queen, and the surface of her armor calmed down. "That's right, much better."

I felt hands clutching at my toes. I looked down, and my mother was there, at my feet, sobbing. I was torn. I wanted to help her up, hug her, tell her everything would be all right. But when had she done that? When she did, when had it ever been true? I walked over to my shining golden bear, and took his hand in mine. Arbias contributed to the conversation another horrific release of energy. Everyone flinched, but Thesius and I. I had fired the eye many times. Thesius was just amazing.

"Now mother, if you want to do one useful thing in my entire damn life could you explain to me why we aren't dead now?" There

178

was a higher priority. I turned to the shocked Athenians. "Also, clear the court, this is a terrible place to be, be in the halls! Take to the stone ceilings! Go!" I was screaming to them, in panic, but not in fear. I had allowed my emotions to get the better of me. But not now. They started leaving the court. Before my mother could answer my question, my father did.

"BE JOYOUS, PEOPLE OF MINOS, THE DAY IS ARRIVED! THE GOD OF DEATH AND HARVEST HAS ARISEN! BAEL! BAEL! DEATH, AND HARVEST!"

Thesius was clutching against me. So was Mantes, and Eunice. I was glad that Miletta wasn't, but her noise suppression system probably took care of that.

"What was that?" Mantes was wild in his eyes.

"It's a loudspeaker we dug up, it…. It's loud. It makes the speaker loud." I was just thinking out loud.

"I figured that out from context, my love." Thesius was no longer clutching at me. When Mantes and Eunice saw this, they sheepishly released me. "What did he mean?" And then it dawned on me. Another discharge, and almost everyone flinched. This time, in the distance, I could hear something like a crack of thunder, or a crash. I thought about the view from the high tower, not towards the ridge where I shot grass targets all those years ago, but towards the city, below. I knew. I wanted to cry out, and bellow, as I once did in my bloody costume, but that would be too appropriate. Instead, I yelled.

"We discuss this in the hall!"

All of us did fit, barely. Mother was going to crawl around on the floor but one of the Athenians helped her up and pushed her ahead of him. I was glad I didn't have to touch her.

"My father… King Arbias thinks that I am the god Bael, arisen." I almost choked on my words, but Thesius gripped my hand, and I continued, "The god was one of death, and harvest. The ancients revered it because it made them better killers, by its influence. To kill another is to make the harvest... of their life. They killed so many in its worship."

"Poetic. Dark though." Mantes had his hands on his hips, his axe pinched to his side by his hand, "I might have liked it when I was 14 and kind of moody at the temple. But what does that have to do with anything, Asterius?"

"Father thinks I'm more than some little spirit that can do a few tricks, but something more like whatever oddity your gods are. Something with real power. So he needs an appropriate sacrifice. I think... he may believe my mother began the work with her little surprise attack..." I paused, I could hear it charging. Thesius squeezed my hand, he could hear it too. Another horrid shriek, and I continued. "So now he is sacrificing the city. The whole city of Minos and everyone in it, with burning fire from the heavens." Another shriek of horror, but this time from someone in the crowd. Almost everyone was very displeased by this idea.

"We won't let him do that." Thesius was adamant.

"And why not?!" I think everyone was surprised to hear me say that, after what I had just said, and what Thesius had just said. "I'm not a god. I don't want to suck up their suffering and be sated by it. I could have done that with you all." I gazed around the band. I loved so many people here. Almost everyone in this room. "But think about what they did to you. Your town. Not Arbias, the people of Minos. They cheered on every murder. I'd say letting them burn would be ironic, and you Athenians love irony."

"Asterius, look at me." And I did. How could I have ever looked away? "We can't undo the past by making a mocking repeat of it. Sure, that would be hilarious, and thousands of people would die." He looked away from me, "A lot of those adults down there deserve it, but..." Helea took my other hand. This was a rare privilege.

"Asterius. I could barely walk when Minos attacked." Her voice was very low, but she knew that I could hear her.

"And that is horrible!" Everybody could hear that.

"Yes, but think, there is some child down there under that light. Right now. Just like me. Probably many more children." I turned away from her gaze, but she continued talking. "I will live with pain

180

for the rest of my life. Not like you do, Asterius, I couldn't bear that. But… There are many things I miss in a haze of pain. I wouldn't wish that on my worst enemy, let alone a child who had the misfortune of being born to them." This was also about me. I wanted them to burn. But then, am I better than Bael, with that dark desire? They suffered under Minos too.

"Fine. We should probably stop that." Helea kissed my snout, on the side. I think she must have had to jump.

"Thank you." She already had her axe back in her hand.

"So, Asterius, why is he not in a bigger hurry to burn down the city? It's been a few minutes since the last shot?" Thesius had a good question, as always.

"That's just the charging cycle." Wait… I'm such a fool. "The charging cycle, I should have mentioned that! Every sixish shots it needs to recharge for… a long time. Uh, ten minutes or so? It's not always consistent, it's very old."

"I was really hoping you would say that every six shots it would kill the one who is using it, but that would be lucky." How can he jest? I can play straight.

"I think I've fired that thing a few hundred times." Never at a person.

"Oh, never mind that then." Given his light tone, I'm sure he knew that. Several people in the hall laughed, despite themselves, and then didn't quite know why.

"So, maybe attack now?" Mantes was on point. "Unless we are giving up on the whole 'We won't let him do that' thing." He was talking with his hands, with a touch of mockery, "I, for one, do not want to have to walk through that town to find a ship, not while it stands, but I see where the room is and I will walk by your side."

"I want to go after that loudspeaker thing." Miletta's voice was strange, distant. "That put everyone on the floor but you and I."

"I can fold my ears down… It might be a hard target. It's… well, they are pretty small, about the size of a dinner plate. Dull grey color, hangs off a hook with some cabling… vines hanging off of it. They are hard to see, but they are hanging on the side of the lower tower. They are almost the same color. There are four of them, one on each side. Grandpa found a bunch more but…" I could see by the look on everyone's faces this was not the right time.

"I might be able to hit that, if I could see it, even with a not-magic bow."

"Oh yeah, the way that works…" A crescent of black shifted out of her hand, and the string extended from each end and met in the middle. It then retracted, and she put her hands on her hips. "Alright, you know. Just think about the arrow when you want it. Uh… oh, the targeting system. I wonder if that could find them, the owner before that one was kinda chatty with me sometimes…he said it could paint anything, not just an enemy… target." Thesius squeezed my hand to remind me he was still holding it, and spoke.

"I would bet if you just think about the thing he just described and what it does…" Thesius was so smart. I loved him so.

"Oh, wow, that's odd." Miletta was bobbing back and forth at her hips, looking at a corner of the room. Or at least I think that's what she was doing, it actually looked quite disturbing. "It's like it forced me to look over here and there are… fires that look like the letter Chi… but they are somehow on the other side of that wall. It's uncanny. I move, and it's like I am looking at something far away."

"Talking through is great, Miletta, but I think you should use that informatio…" Thesius was interrupted. I placed my hands over his tender perfect ears, and held him to my chest, as my father presented us with another cheery message.

"BE JOYOUS, PEOPLE OF MINOS, AND DIE! THE GOD OF DEATH AND HARVEST HAS ARISEN! BAEL! BAEL! DEATH, AND HARVEST! HE COMES WITH POISON AND FIRE AND KNIVES!"

Oh, no! Knives! I waited for everyone to recover before I gave them the good for us, bad for them news. I was sure Thesius had already figured it out, pressed tight against my chest. Miletta was already gone, that thing is so bloody fast, I didn't even see her leave.

Thesius also beat me to the punch, as he was on his feet and facing the band.

"There are almost certainly people who are both loyal and unpoisoned. We will probably see fewer of the nightmare toilet things but I think we should be on guard against th…" Before he could finish, he was on the ground clutching his head and I was trying to shield him with my hands again.

"GRILDON, I THOUGHT YOU WERE DEAD, MY GLORIOUS SON HAS BROUGHT YOU BACK! AS HE BROUGHT BACK THE SACRIFICE! COME UP TO THE TOWER SO WE CAN CELEBRATE!" He could just turn down the modulation and… also he could try being slightly less mad.

"How does he know we are back. I mean, here?" Estius had a good question, for once. I looked up in the corners. Was there one here? Yes! "Look, there. That little red light." I was sure he knew what the color red was, "It's like an eye that lets you see far away. He can see us. Not hear us. Just see us." Grandpa never did get the audio transmission down right. Or projection, for that matter. There was a loud crack, and a rumble. It was… near? Oh, the tower. Oh… she doesn't know that she can change how fast the arrows go. Oh… Oh no!

"Was that Miletta?!" This time Thesius was just clutching his own chest, axe in hand. I gripped my own axe. All of this cuddling while armed was difficult, but Thesius was making good use of that hook on his harness to free up his hands… I am just thinking about his chest. I really need to stop looking at his fuzzy chest in that amazing stupid thing they put together to sneak in here….I need to say something.

"Well you can take the head off a blade of grass with the thing but…"

"That was not a blade of grass falling to the ground, darling."

"But she doesn't know that and it can take the top off a tower too?"

"Well at least that horrid speaker that makes you loud is…"

"WHAT ARE YOU DOING, GRILDON! ALL THE GOOD SHIT IS IN THERE, YOU PUS MARKED PILE OF CAMEL EXCREMENT! WAS YOUR MOTHER BORN OUT OF THE VULVA OF A BABOON YOU..." Another crash, this one somewhat less energetic. She is a quick student. The system crackled, and there was feedback.

This was actually worse than listening to my father talk. I was holding my hands over my ears, even with them down. Thesius, everyone, was on the floor, clutching their heads. Then, another crack I felt more than I heard. The noise lessened, but it was still excruciating. Then, one more, and finally there was only buzzing in my ears. Probably everyone's ears.

"Gods, gods!" It could be anyone. Actually, it was everyone, but Thesius and I. Even my mom was calling out to the gods. But they weren't here. I let them cry out. I wanted to cry out, too.

"Thesius!" I ran to him, but one step, and I held him.

"What... What was that... Asterius, it was far worse than the talking, all I can hear is bees and everyone far away."

"That might get better." I hoped it would, or I would curse myself for my lack of diligence. "It was just... failing, breaking down. I think Miletta got it."

"Obviously." He leaned back into my arms away from me, in the large space I could make if I linked them together with my hands. He was shaking his head, and it sparkled. A lot of people seemed to be worse off. A few of them were talking to each other at very high volumes, confused. "Zzzz is gone." Already? I should be more worried about myself. And them.

"Not for me, yet. We should try to focus half as well as Miletta is." At that moment, we heard the eye power up, he and I both. Our hearing must be fine, and if we are fine, they are probably fine. Why am I worrying about deafness when I could be incinerated at any moment? He knows exactly where I am standing. Another discharge. That shot went into the city. So nice that he hasn't given up on my sacrifice, sweet even, it's the closest facsimile of a present I have ever received from him. Except that bloody murder cave.

"We really should move on the tower. The one Miletta didn't mangle." Thesius had a point.

"She should just shoot it." Estius did not have a point. It was a very tall tower.

"Yeah, and bring the tower down on us, thank you Miletta for not doing that!" Mantes called it out, as you would call out to a god. It was not inappropriate, her audio enhancement system might pick it up. Mantes probably doesn't know that.

"Do you know where to go, Asterius?" His golden face, sparkling in the lamplight, focused me upon my task. I could hardly bear it, but...

"... I confess I've been dawdling. But yes, let's go see my paradise. The one I lived in as a child. It's the only way there."

Twenty One

The past twenty minutes, ever since we entered that accursed court, have been a series of horrific and confusing things, but we can get through this together. I kept repeating that to myself as horrific and confusing things continued to accumulate around me.

Oh, I was keeping track, in my mind, of each horrific occurrence, any one of which could snuff out the lives of everyone I love the most. I needed to understand the lay of the battlefield, even as it continued to be horrific and confusing in every way. But this chaos was putting my whole band into a state of confusion such that we had hardly moved fifty feet in ten minutes, while we prattled on. We needed direction, and Mantes gave it to us.

"All right then you bunch of deck scrubbers, let's go through gods damned paradise and kill the King of Minos!" Mantes was done with talking. He had his axe in the air, and he was right. Another horrible sound came from the tower, and I could see in my mind countless people burning alive in the town below. And being stabbed by mechanical crabs. I then tried to reverse visualize that last thing, but it was difficult.

Asterius was in the lead, and he was moving quick. We all tried to keep up. Out and around, down the stairs, out the side door, through a long corridor with open places, like many oculi, up above. Everywhere there were lit lamps, and nowhere were there people. This place is almost as much a maze above as below, I was thinking, as we turned the corner into paradise.

The gate was open. I could see a space as wide as the bowl Ma'aht had built for us, between us and the base of the tower. It bothered me how exposed it was. Then I was amazed. There was... so much. Trees, fountains, statues, little places to sit here and there. There were flowers everywhere, but it was the middle of winter! Lamps were placed all over, on posts made of metal. They seemed to be made at one with them, and there was a fire inside that was very bright. You

186

could not look at them. It was not like my cold flame, it was red...
more orange, really.

Paths went all over, and rather than be satisfied with a glenn or a green for this paradise, they made all sorts of little hills all over, and ran the paths over them like their masons had all the time in the world to cut blocks into stupid patterns. It seemed like they were trying to make as many curves as possible. It was maddening to look at. I then realized that this paradise also had paths for water that traveled between each fountain. Their own private river system, to float about on and enjoy. I looked to the face of my companion for the first time in a minute and saw that he was crushed. I took his hand, as we hid in the shadows near the gate.

"I spent all my time here, on the other side of this gate in paradise, until they took me to my new home."

"Don't call it that." It wounded me.

"Yes... this place was pleasant, in a physical way. I never lacked for anything, except the love I really wanted."

"That sounds like a poor substitute for paradise."

"It sure was. It was a trap." I could see the walls, higher than elsewhere, and the way they tilted inward. I thought about how well Asterius could jump... "Just another cage. A nicer one, but I don't think it made me any better than the other place did. If I had stayed here I might just be firing that light. Maybe having fun doing it."

"Don't insult yourself, Asterius." He had a terrible habit of doing so, "You would have broken free. Probably without my help." He knew it was true.

"I would have come and found you."

"Somehow, I know that is true." I had to say it aloud, so he would know. But he probably did, even without me saying. "But what now? That open space will kill us."

"I have an idea. A terrible idea which I hate. But it will probably work."

"I'm open for ideas, we'll vote real quick if there are doubts." Mantes said this, then arranged it quickly.

It was a very good idea, in my opinion, and I voted for it without any bias towards my love. If Estius had suggested it, I would have voted for it too. The tools we needed were at hand. Right around the corner and down the hall was an amazing treasury of musical instruments. My own knot, the one made in Thessaly, was there. I grabbed it, though I preferred the kopu made by the band. It had so many happy memories associated with it now.

We arranged our modified disguises in a more funerary form. Less about concealment, more about spookiness. And we formed a new line, but this time it was four wide all the way, with only one person at the lead. I looked along the corridor, at my band, and felt such love. I wished Miletta could hold up the rear for us, and then she was there, right beside me.

"Hi, uh..." She seemed at a loss for words. So was I, staring into that perfect blackness.

"Miletta!" It was Asterius. He was very concerned, and ran from his position at the front to talk to her. "Are you ok?"

"Oh, great, I've been bouncing around. I used to be envious of you, Asterius, how fast you are, but I think you've judged yourself based on this thing. It's so fantastic, I feel so good, and... "

"Miletta, look at me. I can't tell if you are looking at me." Her head suddenly appeared, almost as if it was floating in midair. That did solve the problem. "That thing can make you feel things. It makes you feel good when you achieve certain... goals. This battle has probably been achieving some goals for you."

"So... it's like drugs? You stuffed me in armor that puts me in front of a thurible, or gives me a cup of wine? That's mad!" She thought about this for a moment, as she considered everyone's shocked reaction to this very true observation, when she corrected a detail, "No, putting me in it made sense, making it is mad. Whoever made this is madder than that guy up there."

I looked to my love, and he had tears in his eyes, but they were tears of appreciation. "Miletta, I am astonished you got a grip on that so fast. Yes, it is terrible."

"You might have filled me in on that before I ran off... ok[7], I grant, it was a battle. I need to take this off, it's creepy. Can we kill that guy?" Miletta was looking at me, and she must have seen the shocked look on my face. She took a step back, instinctually.

"How did you miss that back at camp?" Helea had been listening. "You can't take it off, it stays on the bearer for life." Now Miletta had the shocked look. She sat down.

"I suspect your appreciation for the madness of whoever created that thing has increased significantly, Miletta." Asterius was trying to be comforting, but he was being teachery. It was love, but it was wrong. "I told everyone it was bad. I can't believe it didn't all make it to you. The camp thought that awful thing was a delight and couldn't stop talking about it."

"Be silent, Asterius, look at her face. You asked for her face." I hated to be so harsh with him. He was silent for a moment, while contemplating whether hugging a bundle of knives and death was worth it under the circumstances. He used words.

"Oh Miletta I'm so terribly sorry. I wish... I wish I could tear that thing off of you." Asterius seemed crushed, and here we were, holding hands again.

"No... no. I mean, it's creepy, but it's great? There are worse burdens. I'll try to not breathe too deeply on this thing's smoke pit. Is there any way to tell?"

"It's all in some indecipherable language. I mean, it didn't help that it kept ending up on men who couldn't even read one language." Listening to this, I realized I might have put it on. I know at least two. I stuffed away this thought, and ran right away from it, but then bumped into the thought of Asterius wearing it. Oh gods. Then I thought of the consequences of that. Either he finds apotheosis by

7 You don't get it yet.

other means, or I become something to rival the gods back home, if not stand by them. I think it ended up in the right place. She doesn't want it, and that is… good.

"Thesius!" It was my beloved, and he was rushed, but there was such love in his gorgeous blazing eyes. "You've been lost in thought. Unusually so. Share that one with me later, if we yet live, ok[8]? It took you a while. Miletta is gone. She said goodbye, even. It seemed important, so… " He was of one mind with me, even when I was momentarily out of it.

"Oh, nothing, you know, this and that, where we put the costumes and the set pieces for the show. It would be best to be meticulous." I lied in such a florid way that he knew it, and he raised a fuzzy eyebrow at me. I meant that he would know. I wanted to talk later, if we yet lived.

I again wished Miletta could hold up the rear, but that would be bad for the show. While I was elsewhere she had confessed to taking a few shots at the other tower, much to Estius' delight, but they all seemed to miss. Even so, it was much better that she took a high perch and continued to give us some gods out of that machine she is wearing, to make up for the ones who can't step foot here.

I also wished that I could hold his hand through this, but it was foolish. An actor on the stage has no time to hold hands off script, and we were the backup band so I had better keep my hands busy. All was arranged, and so we began playing the most impressively dull funeral music. Apparently around here they preferred not to dance at funerals, which is a shame, but when in Minos. We proceeded into the yard. I half expected us to erupt into flames and die, but… nothing. We walked right across. There were a few hills, and the twisting paths made it impossible to maintain a properly respectful line, but we did

---

8 A joke in time is only funny at the right time.

our best. I had to resist the temptation to go sliding down a steep part of the stone lined river they had here, it looked delightful.

I couldn't look at him, as he did this. I tried not to hear his words. He could be so impressively loud. He rarely was, intentionally. I could make him. But right now he was belting it out. Everybody could hear it in the back, even over the band. Best to focus on the performance. But how could I?

"Worship me, the great Bael!" That line killed me inside, I hope it landed. "I have come from the perfect darkness, to bring power unto this world!" Give the audience what they want. "Gaze onto my retinue, my damned servants, who I lived and dined upon!" So disgusting, this plan this man made. The place he built for it. "They now will live and die with me, forever!" If he had chosen, it would have been. Maybe not the un-eating someone part that seems terribly unlikely even for our gods back home, where did they get that? I am making jokes with myself while my lover calls out a lie, even as I play the song for my own funeral. Is this what madness is like? But no, something gave me the answer, in that moment. What madness is like. I couldn't give credit to the gods, though perhaps there is some force that is higher than them that can pull aside the curtains at the right time.

Halfway up the tower was an unusually large portal, though as I got closer I could see that there was a balcony there. On that balcony, coming out to greet us, were two monstrosities. They hung just over the side, looking down, and I might not have seen them at all if the front of the train had not ended up on quite a high hill by this point.

My thought of how they might look was accurate in some ways. The body of the thing had two shitting bowls facing each other, with some machine on top that I'm sure would have shot flaming arrows at me at some point, many thousands of years ago. Between them was a darkness, or a cavity, and it brought to mind a clam. Like a clam, it seemed to have a number of eyes peeking out of this cavity, looking in all directions. Unlike a clam, it had nightmarish legs as well. I tried to count them, and then stopped. More than a crab, or a spider. Like a crab or a spider, they were segmented, but unlike a crab or a spider, they were made of an odd orange metal, as was all of it. The horrible things seemed to be heavily ornamented, carved in relief all over both sides and the legs. Except for the ends of the legs. Those were recent additions, I'm sure. Walking out between them was another vision of madness. I'm sure he's the one who tied those knives to their legs.

"Glorious Bael! Glorious Bael!" Arbias cried out. Truly, a performance for the ages. His own father had forgotten his name. I wanted to applaud for Asterius, but that wouldn't be sufficiently funereal. "How can you bless me, Bael!"

"Gaze upon the axe!" Asterius held aloft the symbol of his family, the double bladed axe. It was everywhere, here. Tied behind all of our backs in the folds of our costumes, for instance.

"Yes! Bael!"

"Are you ready for your blessing?" I saw the rise[9]. But, how could he? It was so far above us?

"Yes!" Arbias screamed. Asterius tipped his massive frame back, and with a bounce, hurled the axe all the way up into the balcony. It struck his father on the right side, near the shoulder and he howled in pain, falling back into the darkness. It was a good hit, but it wasn't fatal. I could tell. But still, a hit. Asterius continued to amaze me. Oh, but the encore really bowled me down.

Two things happened at the same time. I could hear a whistle. I'm not sure anyone else but he and I might have. The horrible things started moving down the face of the tower, clacking on their knives. Then a man, a loyalist in a mask and party dress, popped out of a door to the right of Asterius, on the side of the hill we were on. He was atop it, and beside him, in a moment. He had an axe, and had a thought to kill a god. Or perhaps, he didn't find our performance to be as impactful as it was upon the intended audience. All of our axes were tied behind our backs.

---

9 Freytag's pyramid. Thesius knows nothing of this, of course, he is just judging how high the balcony is. It's a stupid joke, lighten up.

As he raised the axe, I saw his life, and mine, and the way we might carry forth, if Asterius would yet live. It all flashed before me in a moment of endless tragedy. I almost missed Asterius grabbing his raised hand and, with a smooth kicking motion, opening up the front of him, like he was a piece of rotted fruit. He fell to the ground, and he died. He didn't scream, or beg, or shit himself. He didn't call for his mother, or his gods. He just... died. It was unlike every scenario Chiron had prepared me for. People don't just die. I knew, in that moment, that if we were born as well armed as Asterius, but with the hearts of man? All of us would be dead. I had no doubt of it.

The other thing that happened in that moment was one of those crab things evaporated with a thunderous noise. Then the other took a fine hit, and flew off the tower to our right. I could see blood as it hurled through the air to the ground. Why was there blood? I put that away in the large basket of horrible things I would have to contemplate later. We might run out of benches, if we survived today.

"Looks like I can hit things on the tower, just not the tower." It was Miletta. She seemed unnaturally loud, even for her, but not harsh like the speaker that is loud. I was glad she had tried. I was also glad Asterius was alive, but looking at his face I wasn't sure he was.

"I didn't... I didn't mean to... " He had that look on his face again. Shame.

"That was two fine hits, better than the best warrior could hope for, Asterius." It was an excellent point. Phyron spoke almost as often as Eridice. I think they both prefer poetry to speech. But in this case, I could see that words were not enough. I grabbed him from behind, not a position we often took in public, and wrapped my arms around his soft belly. It was soft, even through that belt.

"He was going to kill you, my love. Don't hate that part of you that kept you safe and by my side."

"It just happened, I..."

"You have instincts. And I'm glad." I knew he was weeping, even without seeing his face. It was an inappropriate moment for this intimacy, however, and Miletta punctuated this point by causing the front door to the tower to evaporate in another thunderous clap, throwing dust into the air and all over the place.

"Looks like I can hit the door, too!" We all heard her, but the truth was before us. It was time to kill the King of Minos.

Twenty Two

I had seen the tower a few times. I toured there, but I never lived there. So, I wasn't surprised by the grandeur, but everyone else was.

"It has a fire pit. We are at the base of the tower?" Mantes was with us, and confused. Most of the band had moved to other parts of the palace, to fully secure the place and make sure no more party goers were going to pop out with axes at the worst time. I knew there were no guarantees.

"Look above, to the bowl. It collects the gasses... smoke, and takes it out." I was tired, but I was never tired of soothing people's confusion. I looked around at the faces of the people I loved, in the light of the gas fire in the center of the room. Mantes, Ackterios, Helea, Theo, Nysa, and Thesius. He was puzzling at the gas controls on the wall. Thesius turned one of the valves, and the fire winked out. It was considerably darker, and in that moment I felt a sting upon my shoulder. I looked up to see what bee was assaulting me, and briefly saw a loyalist up a level, peeking down the spiral stair that was embedded in the wall. It went all the way to the top of the tower. I was thinking about the railing that should be there, when the loyalist screamed, tumbled through the space it would be placed at, and fell to the ground. He crumpled on the stones, and choked and gurgled. Ackterios ran up and kicked him, as he had a bow, not an axe, to wield, and he had a lot of battle spirit in the moment. But he had already done the job. It just took a while. He gurgled and spat. I smelled something terrible. Finally, he shuddered and died. It was horrible, but somehow it was right, unlike the effect of my perfect sickles of death that I brought down on that man earlier. I could see on their faces, in the dim light, concern, but I could also see that they thought this was right. This was how men die.

I could not see my light, because he was already by my side. I could tell that he felt guilt at succumbing to his curiosity, and I countered. "You might have been shot if you were standing there.

195

Your curiosity has kept us all alive thus far... " In so many ways. "Don't hate the part of you that has kept you by my side." I threw his words back at him, but not in malice. It was his curiosity that had brought him to my side.

"Don't make light of this, Asterius, that arrowhead was as long as my hand and I've seen men die of less." Just now Thesius saw a man die from a single stone arrowhead, so this was true. Or, was it that fall, that was nasty? I always thought there should be a railing there.

"You know me, my love, but you don't know everything of me." It was true. There was too much to tell, and my mouth was often busy with other things. I stood from the seat on a bench I had naturally taken after being shot, and stretched my shoulders. I looked down at the arrow, like a knife on a stick, glistening in the dim lamp light. I had pulled it out, instantly, without even a thought. It hurt a bit, but not bad. I looked down to see the tears. He had taken my place on the bench.

"It's not bad, I tell you."

"You lie to yourself about how bad things are. You did it for years." It was true. Not this time. I placed my foot, the one I injured that rainy night, on the bench next to him. It seemed a flirtatious stance, with my skirt in his face, but he was in no mood for intimacy. "Look at my foot."

"Your shoulder..."

"The foot." He looked, and I could see his face change.

"That was open a few weeks back. I was worried you might lose your foot... I can't even see it now. How did I not notice that?"

"Even big obvious things are easy to miss sometimes." I smiled upon him, and that was big and obvious enough. He leapt to his feet and felt about my shoulder wound. It was a bit tender, but I let him.

"It's closed. It's already closed." Then, shock. I felt a bit of shame, I wish I could give a share of my constitution to each of my band, but sometimes gifts get collected in one place, just by virtue of how long they have been accumulating there. The gifts of my body were not something I could give away, except perhaps to Thesius, in our best moments together.

Thankfully, this moment was well covered. Another loyalist popped out of a side door, and Helea slayed him instantly. Well, not instantly, but she spared him and us the drama with a few extra hits. The last one left the axe embedded in his skull, and she was struggling to remove it.

"Leave it, Helea. There are so many on the walls, just grab another." Mantes was right. There were so many, in fact, that she chose to not grab one, and took a large serving tray as a shield instead.

"There may be more archers. I will cover Nysa, the rest of us can take the rear." There was no need to vote on this formation, it was obvious as soon as Helea said it. "Are you sure you are all right, Asterius? That was a hit."

"I am almost recovered, already." I was honest. This was a battle, there was no sense in keeping my light under a bowl out of my shame for it.

Nysa had a remarkable ability of her own, though perhaps it might seem like a disadvantage. When I had described the towers back in camp, she had pointed it out. It was why she was at the lead. Her missing arm was on the wall side, and her working arm worked very well. The stair made her disability into a strategic advantage. I voted that she should be on the team, back there in the green. The deep logic of this didn't make it any easier for Ada, who was now with the team guarding the spot where the front door used to be. There was a tearful hug at edge of the small pit Miletta had left, between them, before we entered. In that moment, Helea had just walked in with us. I was glad, now.

We advanced up the stairs, in three groups. It was a climb, the room was three times my height or more. Every room here was at least so tall. It was grand, but a waste of space. Our axe and shield walked up, the shield one stair behind and providing cover. The rest of us walked up a few paces behind. And then, on the floor, our archer. We had pushed some cabinets in front of the basement doors so we wouldn't get any more visitors from below, and we had a determined guard where the door once stood.

The second level was easy. It was a storage place, and the guardian had already been slain. I looked over the many crates, covered in cloth. Some things in here might be of use to us, if I had time to open all the boxes and catalog everything in them, and if the reason the thing was boxed up in the first place wasn't because it kept killing people at random. That was the usual reason some wonder would be boxed rather than used. No, not worth the effort. We advanced, in the same fighting form.

The third level was the armory. The real one. Many strange tools of death hung on the walls. I was very surprised to find it undefended, I had expected a fight here. I had to discourage the Athenians' natural curiosity.

"Many of these things are not like swords or bows, if you play with them they can easily kill the user. Please, don't touch, most of these things don't have the expendables, and the ones that still work mostly just explode." This was not just for the benefit of Thesius. It was easy to be fascinated by tools of death, especially when they are so mysterious and well crafted. We advanced.

Now we were on the balcony level. I loved the view from here, as a child. I would have lived on this balcony, looking down on the little paradise below, if I could have. I saw my father's blood, staining the stones in the steady orange gas light. This room did not have a fireplace in the middle, but many tiny places for fire around the walls. This place was for parties, when my grandfather was alive. Only the most elite of Minos would dance here, and look out upon this majestic view. I preferred the band of fishers that trod these stones now. We were half way up the tower. At this time, I heard the charging sound. Thesius did too.

"Is he attacking us, finally?" Mantes said. I was also shocked at how well our little performance had gone, earlier. Mantes must have good ears as well. The shot was fired, and I waited for the horrible release of energy nearby, the screams out in the yard. But nothing. In the distance, a crack and a bang. Thesius and I both exchanged a look.

"He is determined. I'm not sure I would still have faith if my god came and threw an axe at me." Thesius had the choice of many gods. Father didn't think he had a choice. I was here. He had made me.

I didn't answer. I didn't think about the people down below in the town, that these beautiful people had inspired care for, in me, though they never cared for any of us. Except, I did think of them, and I was lying to myself to keep myself on my feet. But now, I was lost in our next move.

"Remember what I said; the fifth level is the worst. It has the most important things in it. It's most likely to be defended. Be on guard." We assembled our fighting form again, and advanced. But there was no one there.

There had been some changes, since the last time I was here. This room was two and a half times the height of the first room, to make room for the model in the middle. The thing had been found, boxed and ready, as if it were to be moved into a new exhibit space. It was now exhibited here, all resplendent with fine metalwork on the supports, and fine stonework on the spheres themselves. Mounted in the center of the model, hanging down from it in a precarious way, was a strange sphere I wasn't familiar with. I considered the chances that a new sphere had joined our local dance since I last saw this model, but discarded the possibility almost immediately. It was buzzing with energy. I turned aside, there was something more important here.

"I need to get the shield down, that's the reason Miletta can't shoot at this tower or just jump in the windows. I'm not sure that thing would even let her jump into an ionic shielding barrier, it would probably cause damage." Thesius was very confused.

"Usually you have new words I am unfamiliar with, love, but now you give me a familiar word and I have no idea what you mean. I see no shields hanging here, lots of axes. And how could a disk of metal or wood stop that thing Miletta has become?" Helea winced. He should have chosen those words more carefully.

"It's a matter of convenience," I was stabbing at the control panel against the wall. "It does a similar thing, but in a different way. So, you borrow a word." There, that did it! My fur stood up for a moment, as the ionic field shifted, and pulled back into this machine. I turned to the room to see all of them playing with their hair, which was standing on end. It was a delightful sight, unlike the vicious crab thing that was climbing down the wall overhead, on its little knife hands. Before I could cry out, it smashed against the ceiling, violently, and crashed over into the shielding control system. No one was in the vicinity, thankfully, except for myself, and I was good at moving. It also did not explode, thankfully. Miletta was there, of course. I hadn't seen her come in, of course. I hate that thing, but I was so glad she was wearing it right now.

"It was amazing, just a few seconds ago there was, like an orchestra? A big triumphant song, but really short? And then it made me look, it does that it's so weird, at the tower and there were little bursts of color around it? Like a celebration? Also, I wanted to keep an ear on you and somehow I could hear everything that you were saying! I had to know what that shield thing was and so I came up and... "

"Miletta, pull back from your smoking pit a little." This was Helea. She was concerned.

"Back when there were a lot of those things... " the thought of that shocked everyone, but I continued without breaking, "... the shield being taken down was basically the end of the battle. It was celebrating, because we had won."

"We haven't won yet." Thesius was right.

"We have to kill the King of Minos." Mantes was also right. I surveyed the chamber to see if anything was of use, before we moved on. My eyes fell upon the strange addition to our local dance of the spheres. Thesius was curious about it too, which was odd because it was in a room full of things to be curious about. He was holding his

200

hands out, before him, judging its size. He walked forward, as if to grab it, and I understood.

"Don't touch it!"

"It's the god machine. It's another shield. They put it in the same place." He was right, and I could see on the outside of the machine, in raised golden letters, words in a language I understood.

"Yes, but it is dangerous."

"Athena told me to throw it to the ground." He reached for it again, and I took his hand.

"That thing has been running, without end, since I was a child. Imagine what kind of energy would be needed to keep your gods away for all that time." Thesius stepped back from it, though he still held my hand. He was looking around.

"The windows are too high." I knew what he was thinking. Good idea, but we would have to clear the space first. I knew we weren't advancing until he accomplished his mission. Father could wait. "Carry it down and toss it off the balcony?"

Miletta had understood everything. She was truly remarkable. "I will run down and speak loud at the crowd. Get them to clear the garden. Uh, this thing won't go off so big it takes down the whole tower, right?"

"I honestly have no idea," It was true.

"Well, Miletta, if it does then you will live to tell the tale." Thesius thought about patting her shoulder, and extended his hand, but thought better of it. "Do so, this tale deserves to be told."

I carried it down, gingerly. Miletta had done her job, too well, it was so loud our ears rang. Properly modulated, though. Thesius was at my back, to steady me should I lose my balance on the stairs. It was heavy, and it vibrated in my hands. I felt so cold holding it, and I looked at my Thesius and, strangely, I felt nothing. The lack was so distinct that it was notable.

"Is that thing also a drug?" Miletta had also noticed. Or perhaps it was her onboard threat assessment system. No, how would she know what it was telling her? It would take a while for her to understand it without knowing the words.

"I feel awful around it, Asterius, like a part of me is being held away. I would hate it, but I'm not sure I'm capable at the moment." I gazed upon the script.

'For the Removal Of and Protection From Spiritual Influence'

They always were so good at labeling things, at the Heaven's Gate. I walked confidently up to the balcony on the firm stones and tossed it over the edge. Thesius looked over, to watch it sail down into my false paradise, but I pulled him back, into my arms. Moments later, dirt and debris showered us through the balcony portal, and a titanic thunder shook all of Minos. I felt the love I had for him blossom, and somehow grow larger than it had ever been before. Or perhaps, it simply came to be as large as it once was, long ago. It was such an immensity. He had accomplished his mission, and I was so happy for him. He seemed less pleased with himself, as he was lost in thought. My father, upstairs, was even less pleased.

We heard an unearthly howl. It was not unlike Tileron's cry, but this was not an act. It continued, for far longer than a man should have been able at that volume, crackling and sputtering and turning over itself in its own infinite agony. A blessed moment of peace as he breathed in, and then more, gurgling and half swearing a dozen words at once through a veil of spit.

The cry was such that we broke our form and ran upstairs. Miletta was already ahead of us. Of course I hadn't seen her move.

There were no defenses. We had defeated them all, I could see that as I crested the last stair. There were lovely arches at the top level, thin, with a sharp peak at the top that blended into the roof. This room went to the top. There was a large bed and some living things to one side, in the shadow between two arches. That was new, no one used to live here. Was there another bed downstairs? I seemed to recall it, now that I thought of it. There were feathers everywhere, even though birds never would alight on the tower, due to the ionic field generator. And that thing was definitely on... Various models of things that once conveyed people in past ages hung from the ceiling. It was akin to the flock of birds that would never alight here. You could gaze at the stars here, removed from the light below, which blotted them out. I rarely came here when I was young. The Sun Eye was usually brought down to me.

There it was, of course. Someone had mounted it on a cart, so you could move it around from portal to portal easier. They were pretty clever at killing people, here in Minos. Father was at the controls, and he had it pointed at Miletta. I panicked. I considered throwing myself in front of her, but what would that do? Even if I had time, the charging noise was over. A bright flash filled the room, and for a moment I saw a brilliant mirrored sphere, or half of one, in between the two of them, with the open side pointed towards my father. My father screamed, a more conventional scream of pain. Then the Sun Eye sputtered, and gave off its magic smoke. Of course that awful thing had a defense against it, these weapons were everywhere back then. I was such a fool.

"Looks like I have a shield too!" Miletta observed, correctly. "I was hoping so, that's why I didn't flinch." She might actually be as smart as my Thesius! I looked at my father, and I recognized him as well as he knew me.

He was in terrible shape, both physically and mentally. The wound I had given him had crusted a bit, but still flowed with blood. Miletta's fresh hit had put a light burn all across his face and hands, and singed off his beard and hair. The room stunk of burning, and it would take a lot of incense to cover that up. But it was his eyes. Not the whiteness of them, the blindness he had just had thrown back upon him. The madness. They searched the darkness, for some thing that could not be seen. I had spent a lot of time in the darkness, and I knew it was a futile search.

"Arbias." I could not call him father.

"Bael! Why must you make me feel! Must I have everything taken from me before you remake me?" He was crying, and I recognized the look on his face, though I had never seen it there before. Shame.

"So you feel it now, all of the things you've done?" It was Thesius.

"Glorious sacrifice! Golden man!" Arbias knew his voice, "Bael remade, you stand by my so... " Thesius kicked him, viciously, across his face. He tumbled into a ball.

"Don't call him that. You threw him away." Thesius cried out. Arbias just cried. I walked forward, to kill him, but I couldn't. It was so deeply unfair. He was without defenses, in every way.

"Don't kill him yet. Let him feel it, a bit." Mantes suggested mercy in the most unmerciful fashion. But he was right. We could discuss, and then he could die.

"What was that thing, we just destroyed?" Thesius was deeply disturbed. I could see it in his eyes. I took him by the shoulder, to comfort him, and found myself steady upon him.

"The label was, in their script, 'For the Removal Of and Protection From Spiritual Influence'." Everyone in the team heard this, I made sure of it. It was of possible tactical significance. Arbias heard nothing over his babbling and his weeping.

"Is my love for you a mere influence?" This was his concern. He whispered it, to my chest. Our position had shifted, and I hadn't even noticed.

"It held away your gods." As long as he lived. This was between us.

"But, our love!" I saw his love stretch out before me, forever. Wow, that thing must have been making everyone feel a bit down in the dumps! Also I love that word Miletta is so fond of using as an exclamation, I need to start using it myself.

"And it did not hold our love away until we were inches from it. Consider what this means, and speak no more of it." It was good, my advice, and well timed. One would not want to offend the gods.

204

At this moment, my love, still in my arms, began giggling uncontrollably. I thought my hands had touched some tender spot, but he looked at me and I knew I wasn't tickling him.

"I was of a mind to try and recover the assault, when I ran from the room that faces the chasm." I knew where it was. Had I stared out into that space for so many hours? No, I had not imagined it. "With my knife." More giggling, and then, "You might have been inconvenienced for an hour, if I got in even a few good hits before the sickle came down." That phrase was new to me, and I hated it already. Before I could raise my objections to this characterization of my abilities compared to his, there was a god in the room.

Twenty Three

I thought it was Miletta, but instead I was gazing at something beautiful, rather than nothing at all. He appraised me, with his glowing eyes in his perfect[10] face, somehow both that of a man, and yet having the appearance of having never seen a shell. His hair waved in some breeze I was missing, and that hair had failed to choose any of the common colors and was simply moving between them.

I chose to appraise his clothing, as that face was too much, to find very little to appraise. He had on a skirt, held in place by a golden belt of cords. It was enviously short. Had I worn my skirt in this fashion I would be accused of, and in fact be guilty of, indecency. On his feet he wore tight shoes, of the same pure white color as his skirt. They seemed to lack the strapping I was accustomed to, but rather had tiny pin pricks all about in solid pieces of material. The lacing at the top, and the general concept of the sole, were the same. On the side was some fine embroidery of a wing, in a red thread. The shoes were very fetching, but the rest of the outfit was as showy as it was minimal. Or that might have been his body. It might have seen a shell to make it so smooth, but I knew it had never. I would have to rub my skin right off. I'd never seen the curves of any being's muscles with such perfect definition. I looked to his face, to see his eyes on Asterius.

"Cousin of mine, good friend, we go way back, he came here a while back and said you were a decent fellow, when he told me of it." How could he talk so fast? I was often accused of talking too fast and I could barely follow him? A moment later, he was right next to Asterius, and when he flinched, chose instead a position right between us, almost perfectly equidistant. This should have been

---

10 In this case, Thesius means perfect in the modern sense, and the word he was using was perfectly analogous i.e. flawless. Note the divergence of perfect and perfectly. The latter speaks of something different, but it is hiding in another word.

206

uncomfortably intimate, but Asterius had released me from his arms and backed away in alarm at some point. I hadn't even noticed. "So many things to stab me or fire light at me or otherwise make my day more difficult in this room I hardly know where to stand. How are you managing it?" I seemed to have far less choice of position. Miletta might be similar to him in her available moves. The one seemed almost a parody of the other, but it was hard to know which was which. Her presence might be what is making his bean so hard to place on the board.

"The Sun Eye has released its magic smoke, god, so if that makes it easier to stand still, I volunteer this information." Asterius was being diplomatic, though he did look a bit astonished. I was the only one who had witnessed the glory of a god. Well, a god of Hellea, that king over there might be on something else entirely. Suddenly, he was looking in the front of the... Sun Eye? Had he ever called it that before? Regardless, I liked it. So did the god, or at least he liked something, he was delighted.

"See, he was right! That one is a good judge of character. What a terrible, wonderful, fascinating, horrible device." He had turned, and was looking at me, in more or less the same position as before. I hadn't seen him move at all, as if straightening up was too long a journey to take. "Don't you think?" I confess, it was hard to think while I was looking at him. He sensed this. "If I thought I could, either one of you would be very entertaining, but I know better than to pull honey away from a bear." I wasn't sure which one of us he was referring to, in this case. It probably didn't matter.

"Great Hermes, God of Trade, Luck and Music, Keeper of Roads. Greetings, and thank you, for these things have served us well through our trials." Helea could be very poetic when she wanted to. It is a shame the temple lost her, but perhaps she will have the opportunity to return.

"Good thing they served you well cause I sure as Hades didn't." He jests? About that?! "Wow that whole thing dragged me down, even getting near here gave me a headache. I mean, the machine. Also all the murder and violence against travelers and such I really hate that shit. But yeah, that big guy looks nice. Seems nice too. Asterius, right? Oh, and you, pretty man with the unfashionable choices," What did he mean by this? This outfit was one of necessity. "I'm supposed to rescue you, you good? Yeah? It looks kinda like you got this under control so let me go see some stuff." He vanished.

"I wasn't done." Helea had more to say? But, she would have another opportunity. He was back.

"Wow, that was some sight downstairs, I just went to go see that art on the walls in the court, that stuff is great the artists were some of my favorites in centuries, and first I see it's all wrecked up, but then I see the place has been turned into some sort of elaborate mortuary temple! I've never seen so many corpses, let alone in one place!" I was surprised to hear my own thoughts in his voice, but then he corrected, "I mean, I have seen that many bodies, it's just been a while. I mean spread out over time, lots of bodies but not…" Athena ends the conversation whenever she sees fit, but a conversation with Hermes seems to never end, even though he's been here so briefly. It's like talking to a centaur that has found a leaf that makes him talk really fast and with entirely too much confidence. Needless to say, this transcript is truncated. Helea had something to say, and she got to the point.

"Do you gods love irony?" She knew the answer. Hermes swiveled his head towards her, like she was a target and he was compelled by the clothing he wasn't wearing. "Because I have a delicious irony for you. But you will have to heal."

"Requesting a god to heal you is gauche, darling." The way he tilted his hips, and the way he placed his hand upon them, was whatever that word he said was. It must be.

"Not me, him. I have a few words to say to him, and there is some set dressing I think he needs to see before we put an end to this show."

Hermes gazed upon her for but a moment, and then he knew her plan. I didn't, but it was hard not to share in his delight. Is this the

208

curse of perfection? He walked over to Arbias, which shocked me because I had not yet seen him walk, just be there, and spat in his face.

"I can do it with a kiss too, but I didn't want to kiss this horrid thing." Was he talking through it like Miletta, or is he teaching us? When I had the second thought, he winked at me. It was most disturbing. Even more disturbing was the transformation that had washed over Arbias' face the next time I saw him. He was healed, from the neck up. Even his beard and eyebrows were back. And he was looking at us with eyes that worked.

"Bael... Hermes. Are you with the gods even now, my son?" I was too far away to kick him, such a shame, his face looked so much more kickable now. "Have you risen? Shall you take Olympus? Let me suffer forever, my son, I will die and live and die and live and die for you, Bael..." At this moment Hermes grabbed the air, and dragged it downward. The opposite effect of the speaker that is loud seemed to fall upon Arbias, and though he spoke, we could not hear him.

"That guy is insufferable, so this play better have the ending I am waiting for cause this audience wants something, which is what you want, but I am the audience, and you'd better give this audience what it wants, eh?" That took a lot less time to say than you would think. He stood aside, for the show. Helea was not going to disappoint him, she just needed a quick costume change for the final scene.

In one swift motion she pulled her cord, and flung aside her garment. This was not the first time she had to bear her wounds before the people who had given them to her. But this time, she had the dignity of choice. A ribbon of horrible, pale flesh wrapped around her, like a garment of misery. I was behind her, but I could see the path of it, and I knew that half her chest at least was in the same state.

"Look at me, you withered king, you pile of rags and excrement." He did smell pretty bad. "I was a child, testing out my feet on the shore, and you sent men to kill, just for sport. And they did, and I just made it out with my life. My mom lost her vision. My suffering is endless, just like the suffering you inflicted upon your son. Now you are healed, so you can see what you did to me. But that's not the thing

I most want you to see." She turned towards me. Her face, so beautiful with her determination, made up for the horror. She had a request of us. Asterius knew. This was improv, but it felt perfectly scripted. He took my hand in his.

"Look upon me, father." I could see him mouth out a foul god's name, "No, I am Asterius." He turned and kissed me. Our beards brushed against each other, and then our lips. It was odd, to feel such intense passion, in such a foul place, but this was our victory. This was his victory. We kissed, again and again, until there was a shriek. He had realized his mistake, and he was no longer un-speak louder. Hermes has great stage timing.

"How?" It was a word, but barely.

"Ma'aht. He built them a sanctuary. Us a sanctuary. With the spare stones from the construction." Asterius said this, triumphantly, as he should. He had executed the plan better than Ma'aht had made it. There was no exit from Ma'aht's plans, but we had made one. Arbias' eyes searched, before he remembered the name.

"The old mason? I had him tossed in the pit after he lost all those stones, we could have used them. The others, when they wouldn't say who they sold the...." Of course, they had not been sold. So many people died to protect a secret from this man. All at once he felt the weight of this defiance. But it was fine. He had killed them.

Mantes had a line, for this little drama, "Tell me, shit king Minos, that lovely little sphere you kept downstairs. I saw the bed, you've been living with it, so it's precious to you." That was a detail I had missed, it wasn't wonderful enough to draw my attention in that room. "What does the text on the outside of it say?"

The king shuffled against the wall, and realized he could not move. He decided to answer. "Auro knew, what does it matter, I knew what the thing did, how to turn it on and off. Why I would ever want to turn it off..." And then his shame came back for seconds, and he screamed. He had forgotten he had lost that thing's protection.

Asterius knew his line, even though this was improv. He waited for the screaming to stop and some tiny bit of sanity to return to his face, to speak. "The sphere read 'For the Removal Of and Protection From Spiritual Influence'. I read it in mere moments."

Mantes laughed, "You fool, you insufferably poor excuse for a king. You went and put your son in a murder cave, and you should have put him in one of these towers! You could have taken over the world!"

He could kill them, but he couldn't beat them. Us? He couldn't even kill. But himself? His real enemy had always been himself. His eyes swiveled, mad. He choked, and then a dark peace came over him. He was no longer Arbias. As bad as that man was, this was not as good as it sounds.

"Your plans are excellent, my son!" I appreciated this semblance of sanity even less than that wretch calling my dear Asterius that. "Even better than mine! Look at how well this worked out. We should work together. Why, you and I have so much in co…" This was interrupted by a scream, of defiance and justice. Helea fell upon him, with an axe she could have grabbed at any moment because there were so many conveniently at hand.

"Stop," smack, "Calling," crack, "Him" splorch, "Your," wet axe hitting sound that doesn't exist in this language because we don't tend to hit people with axes more than three times, "Son!" She continued to strike him, but she didn't have lyrics for that part of her dance, any more than I have sound effects to apply to it. Then, she began screaming again. Blood showered the room. She was getting too much into her performance. Asterius and I looked at each other in a panic, unsure what to do.

Before we could react, or even speak, Miletta's outline was next to her, and then she too was naked. Or, rather she wore only a single piece of jewelry, on her chest. She grabbed Helea by the shoulders, and stopped her.

"He's dead, honey. Really dead. Don't hurt yourself, he won't be any more dead with more hits." Helea dropped the axe, and they embraced, a bloody, naked apparition of love and pain. The very.

211

manifestation of justice. Only they could have ended his life on such a note. It was perfect[11].

The god clearly agreed. He even waited until they broke their embrace to clap. That must have felt like an eternity to him.

"Even better than expected. I am not disappointed, five stars, or however many is the tip top best at the moment. So, uh, hey... I think I might go now. Oh, you might wanna give some attention to that guy over there, he's so out of it I can't even read his name and I'd give him, oh, ten minutes? Yeah, later." Then he was next to me, far too intimate, right in my ear. His sweet words were brief, "A low skirt and fuzzy shoulders are so unfortunate. But he seems to like it. See you later, cousin." And he was gone. Asterius had fuzzy shoulders too! His fur laid down a bit better, but... I realized something. Was this a show? Not everything we had just done, yes, obviously. Was Hermes putting on a show? For me? I considered his perfection. If I had the choice, would I have made myself more perfect? But, Asterius liked my fuzzy shoulders, and my... low cut skirt. His skirt was low cut as well, and I found joy in it. Would I have made myself less perfect in his eyes? Would Asterius have made himself less perfect in mine?

Then, I considered, he called me cousin. The noise fell away and I disappeared for a long moment. I heard something. Helea was snapping her fingers. She had a dress on, again.

"We've got a problem, Asterius is trying to take care of it but I figured you might want to be present for this." She looked me in the eyes, and there was a touch of madness there, but there was in all of

---

11 I must stress that, except for in respect to the gods, no Athenian would ever use the word perfect, even in their own minds, in the modern sense. Which is to say, to be without flaw. But they use another word very often that feels a lot like perfect, so I am using it as a stand in, as we do in English. But I wish to define this lost word here, and it's various meanings, to clarify. 1. To be fully at ease with the environment and situation. 2. To be true to your/its own purpose. 3. To be at one with the purpose of the universe. Which is to say, this perfect feels similar, but is entirely different. Every time Asterius and Thesius refer to each other, it is in this sense.

our eyes at this point. Under her clothes, her skin was a vivid shade of crimson, wet with fresh blood. I was oddly at ease with that. "I know, we've all had a hard day. It's Theo." At that moment, Asterius came up the stairs at amazing speed with a flutter of white beside him. It took me a moment to see they were linen sheets, and by that time I was halfway to Theo, who was rolled into a ball and sobbing against the wall. I immediately realized what was happening, and ran to his side. I almost beat Asterius.

"This is too much for him, too many things, he's going into shock!" I wasn't aware of the meaning of the last word he used, but I understood it perfectly in context and adopted it immediately.

"I know how to deal with shock…"

"Yes, centaurs, help." He was shivering uncontrollably. I remembered my own experience, having met a god not terribly long ago. The second time was easier. We both embraced him, or laid on top of him would be a better word, as the shaking became worse.

"Not sure this is working." Actually, I was sure it wasn't.

"He was pretty bad when we noticed him." I felt so bad that I was looking at that god rather than my poor Theo, but the irresistibility of his face, let alone all the rest of him, may well have been what did this to him. Theo was always easy to stun with a bit of beauty. Then we received a surprising suggestion from an unexpected source.

"I think I can help." Miletta said, improbably. She was no physician, it was not her interest. "With the armor thing." What was that word she liked? Wow, improbable.

"How?" I couldn't conceive of it.

"Let me talk through this." I noticed that the inky blackness was over her again. I suppose it's better to wear armor on a battlefield but it was… creepy. "When I look at you here I can… kinda see how hot you are? I mean, I think that's what it is. And I see he is less hot."

"This man is dying here please get to the point." Asterius really didn't want to lose Theo. I didn't either.

"Well he has some sort of thing on him. It looks like I could warm him up? I'm just trying to figure it out from context, I can't figure out why it would want to single out someone in shock," Miletta learned fast, too, "for immediate execution, especially since I have you guys painted as allies."

"Wait, what? It can pinpoint allies as well as threats?" Asterius seemed genuinely surprised, and this surprised me. I thought he knew everything about this thing. The fact he didn't frightened me, on Miletta's behalf, but I stuffed it down.

"Seems to be able to. I mean, I asked it to, and it did it." Had no one thought to ask before? Probably.

"This is very off topic Asterius." Theo was shaking even more uncontrollably. I could hear his teeth hitting each other and I hated it.

"It makes sense, do it, let us move away." Asterius was right. He was going to die anyway at this point, might as well make it fast.

Miletta walked up, and in a moment he seemed to be enveloped in the inky blackness. And then it pulled away. Theo laid there, still. We all thought he was dead, until he started snoring loudly. We were all familiar with this sound, especially me, and it was comforting. We left him under the blankets while we considered our next move. Before we could get three words in, there was a god in the room.

"So where d…" Anyone could have said this. It was me.

"Hey, so I realized that was the best show I've seen in… well, centuries, and I kinda wish I coulda seen all of it from what I'm hearing from your band all over the castle but the thing is I think you need some boons of the gods it's more than warranted and here we go." Do I need to say who this was? He moved with impossible speed, all over the room, kissing everyone who wasn't the bloody pile of meat that was the former king of Minos. He kissed Theo, which is tragic, not only because he missed it, but also because it seemed like he didn't need it. He even kissed Asterius, but I think that was for sport, his injury was mostly healed. He was at my ear. "I looked at the chart and it's too close, sorry, you'd have to actually be injured." He said it like it was one word but it was 22, in the original language,

214

which is not English. He was gone, and then I considered what he was emphasizing to me. It felt like an insult to my mother. But, I then realized, she wouldn't have, not ever. She must have been tricked. The god was before me again. He winked. Then he was gone. This told me two disturbing things, in a mere moment. Hermes is a great teacher.

Suddenly, there were screams, of joy, of freedom, of knowing a moment without pain and loss. Helea and Nysa were in a full embrace, with a total of four arms. Everyone else was in tears, except Theo who was in dreams.

Twenty Four

The power of their gods astonished me. The amount of tissue damage and permanent disfigurement that god removed from those two women, in mere seconds, was beyond my understanding. The amount of energy that would be required to just make the material that had been lost in Nysa's arm would have required her to eat a whole pig, or could have leveled this tower, perhaps the whole city, in another form. It's no wonder these things inspired such terror in my father that he thought it necessary to fashion me into one, if he were to take on the whole world.

It actually annoyed me to be so in touch with Arbias' rationale. The words that the perfect darkness had spoken through him, minutes before, still stung me. But still, I understood. These gods were something else entirely. Everyone else seemed much less troubled by this development, except for my golden bear, who had been lost in thought with me since the god had left. He returned from his mind, and came to me to discuss. We did so quietly, not that it was necessary with all of the celebration all around us.

"The gods... They are of the mind, are they not?" This was not what I was thinking, but it was true. Hermes had said several things to him and I couldn't hear them. I wondered, at the time, if he could mute himself the same way he did my father.

"Yes. All of them. Normal gods can't do that, though." Thesius was confused by this.

"Normal gods? Other gods are not the same?"

"No. That was amazing. I could almost have faith."

"But, you saw him!"

"That's not faith, Thesius. We saw him. He was right there. He kissed me and healed me, though I scarcely know why." Thesius pondered the difference, as he leaned back into my hands. We were in each other's arms again, and I hadn't noticed it happen. Again.

"If you didn't have faith, would you expect not to see them?"

216

"Except under extraordinary circumstances. This seems to be a key difference. They are the same, just more. And healing someone without faith… unheard of." My shoulder felt great. An old injury in my thigh also felt great. It must have always been causing me pain, but I forgot it was so.

"I'm glad he did. Seemed to get everyone. I bet we suffered no fatalities, and wounds will not take any from our band. It's a blessing."

"Indeed. A boon. I'm glad he was happy with us, instead of angry." What would that look like?

"He moved just like Miletta." This seemed obvious to me, but it was causing Thesius concern.

"What do you think your priests based him on?" This was not the right thing to say to Thesius if I wanted to talk to him for the next few minutes. He was lost in thought, and I held him. This was our victory, and the band of Athenians were in celebration all around.

We opened our embrace. The day broke, and we looked out over our battlefield, and the ruins of my false paradise. A new cry could be heard. It started on the other side of the palace, so it took a bit to coalesce. It was extraordinary.

"Love, and courage! To the people of Athens!" Again and again.

"Love and courage! To the people of Athens!" The cries rang out.

"Love and courage! To the people of Athens!" Miletta joined it. It was loud, and perfectly focussed, but my ears didn't ring. She was good at this.

"Love and courage! To the people of Athens!" My golden bear was crying it out, as if it wasn't his first time. Perhaps it wasn't.

"Love and courage, to the people of Athens!" And now I was crying it out, as the tears ran down my face. We repeated our victory, again and again, until it was gracefully shortened by unanimous consent.

"Love and courage! Love and courage! Love and courage! Love and courage!" And we carried on till most of us were hoarse, then we all cheered and clapped. It was the most spectacular performance I could have ever experienced, or been a part of. I was so proud of each and every one of them. I held his hand, and we looked out into the new dawn.

The cleanup started immediately, but took weeks. First, Miletta went down into the city and took care of the rest of the golden crabs. There were far more of them than I had been made aware of, and they had engaged in such enthusiastic violence once they had a target to kill. Such horrors I don't care to repeat. No one could stop them, even with the ancient projectile weapons some people had. The burning light left only ashes, like a cauterized wound. It was horrible, but abstract. The crabs had left a lot of meat on the ground. It was so lacking in abstraction that the city smelled more of vomit than burning, by the end of the day.

But they didn't stand a chance against Miletta in that armor. She was exceptionally good at using it. She realized the strategic advantage of mobility and placement that the thing offered perfectly. Well, as perfectly as one might expect, given how alien and odd that thing was. There were a few things I needed from the towers to keep people safe through the process, so I began my work. I was searching for something to aid in cleaning up after those horrors, before Miletta had even finished dispatching them.

"Thesius, please stop looking at it so close."

"If this one is leaking a deadly poison that will cause our bodies to rebel against themselves and grow beyond control before killing us in a grisly way then we are already dead so I might as well satisfy my curiosity." That blasted god was rubbing off on him. I would have put commas in there if it had any.

It was easy to be curious about a lethal instrument of such purpose and design. I was curious myself. But there was one tool I needed before I would dare approach that thing. The wand. I found it in a stupid place.

"Hey, there seems to be some pile of treasures under his piss bed. Did you check here?" Mantes had a good point, as usual. That man never failed to prove himself useful. I admired him. Even when he was so young, in that first sacrifice, he quickly became something like the parent. I see now, I was in no place to give such warmth. And centaurs kind of hate people, or at least their presence, and with good reason. So, Mantes was there for them. I was so glad he was here, too. Especially when I found the wand under his pillow. Blasted fool. Thesius was looking at it curiously even as it entered my hands. He has such good instincts as to what is most interesting.

"That looks like a tool. It has a handle. But it is so plain. What could it do?" Indeed, it was plain. It had a handle, which was partially an embellishment. The original was smooth orange metal, with a nice curve. The leather and wrapping was added later. The length of it was the same metal, in a long cylinder. It tapered slightly, and ended in a rounded point. "You couldn't even stab some meat with it to roast." The thought of someone doing that with such a precious tool must have made me cringe, because he was looking at me, now. "You know what it is. Tell me."

"It's a machine for interfacing with other machines. It can control many things. But it also can convey information about the environment in a lot of useful ways. And it has a few things it can do on its own. It's not just one tool. It's many tools."

"So, this many tool… There were a few new words there, I may be way off… but it controls things remotely?"

"Yeah."

"And it can sense the environment. But why?"

"There are many things unseen, unheard, and unfelt… until it is too late. I am worried about something unseen right now." That blasted killing machine over there ran on a foolish source of energy. I wonder why they didn't just crack the things open like eggs over their enemies, but then I remembered that they would have to clean that up somehow. Hopefully, since they were used in battle, the casing the first team of engineers had managed to open, with great difficulty, will be pretty hard to break. Unlike the Sun Eye, the crabs had access panels. They were clearly designed to be maintained, and required it, a bit. That also allowed them access, of course. That whole area of the palace had to be walled off and the walls coated in bitumen. But we will see... Thesius was snapping his fingers.

"So worried... that you left me? You never do that, that's my thing. What are we up against?" I have come to hate the fact I had to introduce that phrase to him, but it was of strategic necessity. It was also necessary to share the worst with him now.

"This is not just a poison, as you understand it. It can fly through the air from where it lies, as the light flies from the sun. Anyone in sight can be poisoned. It's terrible. We need to make sure it doesn't spread around, if it is loose." I hated the look of terror on his face, but the look of determination that followed filled my heart with joy.

"Well, let's start now. Let's see if we are going to die, love."

Twenty Five

The thing did bleed. I had not imagined it. Inside, was something that looked like it was once a dog. Perhaps a goat. It had no skin, and nothing besides a heart and a head, so it was hard to tell. It seemed to have been floating in some sort of closed pot, buried inside the nightmare. Also, Miletta's arrow had torn it up a bit. I looked at Asterius, and he was clearly relieved. This thing wasn't going to kill us, just sitting there.

"No, it would be beeping and flashing like mad if that thing was giving off particles." This last one was a new word, and I picked it up immediately, but I had to ask.

"If this can throw off particles. Can the sun? I mean, does it?" Asterius gave me a look.

"Do you mean Apollo?" His questions were so infuriatingly good. And, I remembered Chiron. A god cannot precede the thing that it represents.

"No, the thing that preceded him, whatever that is." Asterius pointed to the marvelous thing in the center of the room. I had barely looked at it, as it was obviously a thing of beauty and wonder, and was not going to try and kill me. In the center of the thing was a ball of gold.

"That is the thing which preceded it. Or, at least a representation of it."

"Is it worshiped?" Why not, that's amazing.

"No, it's studied. For understanding. The Sun does not need worship, or desire it." This word had been interchangeable with Apollo in my mind, up to this point, but it was blisteringly obvious that couldn't be true.

"I'm a fool, I should have known. If the light of the Sun was the influence of a god, this whole place would have been plunged into darkness." The look on Asterius' toothsome face led me to believe I had come to the right conclusion by a path he had not expected.

"Yes, well. Where do you think we are."

"Crete?" I was right, but I was wrong.

"No, where is Crete? All the land, all the waters?"

"The... Earth?" This word had been interchangeable with Gaia, and yet how could it be? Asterius pointed his thick hand towards a blue sphere in the model. It had been given extra attention compared to the others. I could see the shape and color of land and water.

"The Earth swings about the sun in a grand dance of the heavens. This dance moves itself, but... "

"In circles?"

"No, but it is hard to model an ellipse so they used mechanisms to ensure the timing stayed right."

"The... timing?" I was trying my best to follow this, but I needed a visual aid. Oh, was I to be surprised. Asterius walked over to another panel of switches and levers I had not been paying attention to before because it wasn't trying to kill me, and the dance began. Or, at least a model of it. I stared at it for so long. It was the most beautiful thing I had ever seen, even the perfect gods could not compare.

"So, each of those spheres is an Earth like ours?"

"No. Most of them are awful. Being there for a moment would be lethal. But our neighbor wasn't bad. And it seemed as if this dance were new, and there were a few more dancing partners at some time in the distant past."

"Wasn't?" I had gotten good at picking out these little hints by now.

"There was a war." I thought about his words.

"Is our neighbor the red light in the sky? The wanderer?" I was thinking out loud.

"How?! How did you know that?" His voice was usually only this unintentionally loud when I had a tight grip on him, but he was across the room.

"If Apollo takes after the sun... a war between the spheres would be pretty inspiring. We call that light Ares." Again, Asterius was stunned that I had come to the right conclusion by a path he had not expected. In a moment, he was not across the room. He moves so bloody fast, I wonder if they based that armor on whatever he is. Thankfully, he fell upon me to kiss me, not to slay me instantly. We carried on, until we heard a cough.

"This was a fascinating lecture and discussion until you two decided to interrupt it with a making out session. Could we get back on topic and talk about this dance, this is amazing." Mantes was right, as always. Asterius broke our embrace, and coughed, a bit embarrassed at his loss of control.

"Well, this would be a good time for questions, if this is a lecture?" Asterius was also right, but it was all questions so far? Oh, he wanted Mantes to ask. I will be silent.

"If Ares is not the red light, but is taking its place... What of the white light we call Aphrodite?" Asterius pointed to a yellow orange sphere, closer to the sun. That must be it.

"Another sphere. Long ago, it was like Earth. But so long ago that it is unfathomable. Now it is horrible." Mantes had his head on his chin, as he would when he was lost in thought. I could ask a question now, I think.

"So... why?" It was a crime to consider the motivations of the gods, but it was impossible not to under the circumstance. But then, I realized my mistake. The priests made the model. I corrected myself before Asterius was done formulating his answer. "Why did the priests design them that way?" This question really impressed him. We almost started kissing again, but he controlled himself.

"They were power stacking. Just take every powerful thing and ascribe it to your god. The spheres, in their dance. The Sun, which gives us life. Fire, Spring, Love, whatever. All powerful things that people hold in high regard. To be frank, I thought that was the trick with your gods. Just lie and say your god does everything, even inconceivable things. However, after seeing that god I am... it's hard to imagine." He almost said something, but caught himself. I realized it would be best to wait until Mantes is not around to probe further into this topic. I looked to Mantes, and I was surprised by how unsurprised Mantes was by all of this. I was astonished.

"That's more or less what I thought of it. We keep adding new things into the gods. Even when I was at the temple, we were. Someone, uh, I think his name was Boots, came up with a new plow head and they said that Demeter did, and its power was hers. It was... weird. Any new thing someone came up with, some god had to own it." This addition by Mantes really impressed Asterius, so he risked adding some more information to the lecture.

"Right, they want the appreciation people have for that plow. It might be a little, but add it up with everything else, and..." Asterius was also surprised by how unsurprised Mantes was, but he was unsure it would be wise to share everything he knew. He shot another nervous glance at me, which Mantes didn't notice because he was too busy continuing Asterius' thought.

"You have riches." Mantes had apparently learned some things in the temple that had not been a part of the excellent education Chiron had given me. Possibly only by observation... Mantes was great at that.

"Or, great power. But..." Was this another thing he didn't care to say around Mantes? The hair on his face was standing up, his shoulders too. We needed an excuse to end this lecture, and I had one at hand.

"So, this is amazing and all but how many of those crab things are there? We need to check them all, right?" Everyone knew this was so, and we left immediately.

Our search revealed only one had failed to contain the poison within it, under assault. It was on the beach, on the other side of the breakwater, high up above the dunes. Everyone was thankful that it wasn't in the center of the city. Knossos might be salvaged yet.

As Asterius and I approached, the tool started making sounds like a bird, but more consistent. As we got closer to it, the bird seemed to get angry. The tip of the tool started flashing in angry colors of red and orange too.

"That's bad?" I knew.

"Very. Directional, though. I think we can make it less dangerous."

So we did. We walked up from the direction without particles, and dumped dirt on it, out of baskets, in a great line. It wasn't just the band, many townsfolk pitched in. The immensity of their shame at their behavior was only increased by the continuous help the band from Athens had provided, and eventually we were just working together for everyone's good. It was easy just to see them as people, now, even though every one of them, not long ago, had screamed in my face and wished for me to die in the worst way imaginable, to achieve an unfathomable end.

The line was to reduce everyone's exposure to the particles to a minimum. It was Asterius' idea, and we didn't even bother voting on it. As soon as he explained it, it was obvious. Pretty soon we had a nice burial mound over it. That should keep it pretty safe, unless someone is stupid enough to dig it up someday.

The rest of the horrible things, we buried at sea. It was the best use for the Minoan navy in years. Asterius was convinced that would allow the poison to slowly decay, and harm no one. I would Hope he was right, but that thing is a liar. I knew that it was better to have those horrors resting in the sea than on the ground.

They took our commands, of course. All of their commanders had ended up in a burning pit, after they drank poison voluntarily and died. Sometimes after chopping their ropes right off. That burning pit was in the crater where Asterius' former paradise was formerly located, if only for convenience sake. There were so many bodies to provide a burial rite for. It made the tower stink for days, but it was unavoidable.

The Athenians chose to keep the Sun Eye. I hated the idea, and voted against it, but as a trophy it was a perfect choice. We selected three ships as another trophy. This was ironic, and perfect insofar as we also needed a way to get home. We also had some people and things we wished to have as guests on our journey.

They may have also taken our commands because Asterius was there, with us. I can understand their terror of him. They thought he was a god, then they thought they were going to be sacrificed to him, and then he shows up and tells everyone that's a big mistake and he actually helped save them. That's an unbelievable story, even if it is obviously true. But no one was going to say no to us. Well, almost no one.

"You can't have that." The queen had retaken her position. It had taken some work. She was groveling around until the Athenians took her bodily and dumped her in front of Chianten. He knew she was going to inevitably be queen, as Asterius had no intent or desire to be king, so he gave her wisdom that was so searing and devastating that she spent weeks living in our former camp, in tears.

She came out of that sane. It might have been the first time she was. She had lived a terrible life, largely not of her own choosing. But now she was telling us we couldn't have the wand. I had learned it was called this after Asterius tired of me calling it the tool. It was an amusing conversation that occurred at a time not worth relating.

"Now I find myself of two minds about that word." Asterius said, somewhere, doing something.

"Oh?" I went back to what I was doing. He kept talking, with some difficulty.

"I half expect it to start flashing and beeping when you do that now." I would have laughed, but my mouth was full. But I didn't relent.

"Rrrr.. It's a wand... You can also conduct a band with it. Well, better a dumb piece of metal…. Rrrr!" I had to answer this, and Asterius was both pleased and not while I did so.

"Ah, we use a staff sometimes for that. The.. wand would be more perfect for the role, I can see that now. Though your tool works fine for conducting me."

Very amusing, back to the court.

"And why not? You don't know how to use it and I've been using it all over." Asterius had it in his hands at that very moment. It had hardly left them except to make room for me.

"It's too precious."

"This kingdom has a poor track record of keeping precious things well." He meant so many things by this, but his mother felt the sting of these words for a particular reason. One might think the look on her son's face might have been the cause of her discomfort, but it was not that, though she was still racked with guilt over how her son had been treated. Rather than the glare of her son, it was the glare of the Sun. There was a large hole in the roof marking the trajectory of the top floor of the shorter tower as it fled from Miletta's arrow. The debris, broken furniture, and the corpses (so many corpses) were all cleaned up by this point, and the huge golden bull heads were already being melted down to help pay for the repairs, but the hole in the ceiling and a large crack in the floor remained. The court seemed spare without all of the furniture, but most of the people who used to sit in those chairs were dead, so no one was complaining. Except Asterius, of course.

"We are giving up the eye."

"It doesn't work. It gave up the magic smoke. It's a trophy now. That's all." Even with the crates of carefully packed scrolls Asterius and I had smuggled out of the ruins of the shorter tower, we had little hope of repairing the thing. It was beyond all of us.

"We might need it. All of those ghastly sources of radiation." This was a variation on the particle word I had learned a few days later. A continuous transmission of particles. No fun story for that one, I was shitting and I yelled my question out of the bathing room. Oh, that is a fun story. Also this was the first good point Elaía had made in hours. Well, against us.

"You have the alternative. The detector." I wanted Asterius to have the wand, he loved that thing, it was so much fun. The only thing he treasured more were those scrolls, which were being held in secret at the quarry by the masons. Most of them took after their old teacher, it turns out, and it was easy to find common ground with them. We trusted them with the secret. The masons seemed to be good at keeping secrets, even unnecessary ones. Elaía was unaware of that library; she must not have had a need to know. But she did know about the detector, and its downsides.

"It has to be moved around on a cart." It's true, it was large.

"Which is ideal for a kingdom with many possible sources of radiation to contain." This was a half truth, almost a lie. Asterius really wanted that wand.

"Fine, so long as that is the only marvelous wonder you decide to donate to a lot of savages." That she considered her own son to be one of those marvels made this statement into a lie the moment she said it, but her words functioned more as a point of rhetoric than a statement of truth, and everyone knew that.

"In material, yes." This was fully a lie. Asterius intended to do some targeted looting yet. His mother knew, so it wasn't really a lie, any more than her previous words were. "But not in personnel. I demand the use of the masons."

"No."

"I'm not going to trundle them onto the ship at spear point and tie them up like Ma'aht was. They can choose to come help rebuild Athens with Thesius and I, or not. We have a debt to pay to them, mother. You would not like being the person you would be right now if they had not saved us." I think he was giving himself entirely too little credit here, but it was useful for rhetorical purposes, so... Also, Elaía had the recent experience of being the person she was before we saved her, so this was a convincing argument.

228

"Fine, if they can come back when they are done." None of them ended up doing so. That's not a spoiler, there was no coercion, it was just much nicer in Athens.

"Agreed." Asterius was pretty sure they would want to stay in Athens. He was right.

Not all of the treasures we found were material. Some were... ok, calling them personnel is heartless when they were hostages. The ladies who had rowed us to shore were an assortment of conquests Androgeus had collected over the years. After his death, his father literally collected them, into a permanent retinue of mourners. We found them locked in a living chamber with but one tiny slit of a window. Most of them were stark raving mad.

Almost all of the preparations for our trip back to Athens were all wrapped up when Asterius and I found ourselves back at the berry patch, a lovely private place we had spent many happy hours at before we kicked down the door. It's been hardly mentioned, but, well, this is not pornography. But just as a for instance, the large container of oil Miletta had seen me take out of the camp was permanently stored here. We were preparing to use it, when I heard something. Or rather, I didn't.

"Wait, do you hear that?" It was a bad question. 'Do you not hear that?' would have been better, but who says that?

"I'm quite done with waiting, darling." Both of us were, but this was more pressing.

"No, really." I wasn't going to ignore this.

"I hear nothing."

"Exactly." Asterius got off all fours, and rose to his feet.

"Gods, now?" This was an exclamation I might have reached for in a few minutes, but it was a question. And not a happy one.

"Yes." I knew.

"Should we dress?" We didn't have a choice.

In the clearing before us there was a murmuration of birds. Thesius didn't know that lovely word, the ancient Greeks had no word thus, but it was beautiful. They gathered, in some amazing dance, which should have caused them all to collide together into a mass of feathers and broken wings, but instead they wove together perfectly without any mistakes whatsoever, and when they unwove the woman was standing there. She wore only her hair, that on her head, and there was a lot of it. It wasn't exactly a modest outfit, however.

"Thesius! Asterius! So delighted to meet you!" She seemed very happy indeed. So did we, which was embarrassing. Strangely, in a moment we would forget about this almost entirely, though it never ceased to be true throughout the conversation. "Hermes told me all about you, and the marvelous work you've done. Good to see so many things going according to plan." I thought back on Athena's plan, and my mouth moved without volition.

"Athena's plan went sideways." Totally horizontal.

"Yes, hers involved you stabbing that lovely ma… male person with a sword. Let me see, what did my plan involve you stabbing him with?" The answer was pointing right at her. We exchanged glances.

"How could you have planned that?!" Asterius said. It was a good question.

"My husband made that sword for him." I knew that, but I hadn't shared the specifics beyond 'the smith of the gods' to Asterius. He knew that now too. "Athena insisted upon the tab on the sheath. Getting him to leave it unbuttoned took some doing." How did they manage that? How did she know I had done that? "We are of the mind, darling. You figured that out already." It turns out, you don't have to ask questions out loud to a god. I should have known that by now.

"He also made me a knife. I could have hurt him with that." It was almost a lie.

"Don't almost lie to a god, even if I am your grandmother."

I fell right down. Asterius did too, without my shoulder to lean on.

"How?" My condition was making it hard to get up. I couldn't just flip onto my stomach and push myself to my feet as I usually do. Asterius gave me a hand up, though I felt like grabbing something else.

"Eros is my son. Your father and mother both fervently wished for a child. Well, your dad was shooting blanks." There was another term that did not involve firearms here that Aphrodite used in the original language, as only Asterius would have understood that metaphor, "So, we had to improvise. He took the guise of your father, and had the two of them share a very intimate dream. It wasn't even cheating, really. We evaluated whether they would be open to a fling, but I know better than to try and take honey from a bear." She was definitely referring to my dad here, my mom was almost hairless except for on her head. "Strange, you seemed to pick up some unusual traits. I've not seen a god of Hellea with body hair in some time. Usually rubs off on the kids too. I think that's because they based us on the Nile model so much, and they had this thing against hair." She stroked her amazing hair, which was every lovely color, but especially the ones you liked most. It was the color of Asterius' lighter belly fur, to my eyes. "I'm glad they didn't make us all bald." She smiled. The whole world smiled with her. That was actually both exhilarating, and terrifying. But Asterius was frowning.

"This seems strangely confessional, and given what I know of gods I feel like I may die at any second. Can I relax?" Well, except, you know. That was incapable of relaxing, on both of us.

"You will yet live." She said this with a laugh. It was a joke, but the fact she tore it out of his mind made it less funny to him, and I.

"Then tell me, I know he may be family, but why are you telling us this? These are things gods do not want their faithful to know. Or anyone but their high priests, for that matter." It was a question on my mind, as well. I had this creeping feeling we were verging on forbidden knowledge so many times of late. Is this a feeling you are having, as well?

"You have to share at least a little bit of stage direction with the players. I know that the first act required a lot of improv. You still managed a great show, Hermes was very impressed with you both." With everyone, really, but we knew that, and she knew that we knew.

"So, we are to follow this new plan, that we didn't know we were following all along? On what, faith?" I was so glad I had Asterius here to ask these questions, but I also felt like he was having to be Chiron for me, so I knew I had to ask the next question.

"If you had faith, Asterius, you would be poorly suited for the plan." That was neither a yes, or a no, and the more I thought about it, the more infuriating I found it. Rather than think more, I just asked.

"What is the plan?" It was burning me up, I had to know.

"I'm not sure." This was not the answer either of us expected. We also didn't know what to say in response. We stood there like fools, bobbing around, until she continued. "The plan precedes me. And I must conspire against myself to execute it. Such a bother."

"Then, what are we to do?!" Now I was infuriated. I had thought too much, about too many things, and gotten nowhere.

"Oh, are you feeling a tiny bit angry at me? Like you really don't know what's going on and you think I might not be telling you everything?" She laughed, like a chorus of cicada in the trees, delicate and yet overpowering. "Good! Then you really are getting that godhood experience, grandson. We spend every day being mad at each other, or being sure we are up to something on each other, and you know what, we usually are. We can only brilliantly reflect the people of clay, and show them how they would be at their utmost. We also reflect all of their foibles. So you can go tell that headache your town calls a goddess I've been calling with some plan of my own that stepped on hers, and you can have both her and I pissing right on you. And not in no fun sorta way." I wasn't into that, but she somehow made it sound like it could be fun. But not with my grandma.

Her tone softened, like butter in the heat of… let's go for a pan, "I can't tell you everything, even if you are my blood, and even if you stand there so boldly, one foot in the dirt and the other in the air." She threw her gracile and yet strong left hand to that air, and a stream of fine petals followed her up in a great spiral, before floating down around us in a perfumed haze. I almost forgot I actually had both feet firmly planted. And the thing I couldn't get to stop pointing so rudely. "'Cause then she might know, somehow. But what of my mind? Turns out, much the same." This was quite a thought. Should I not think that? "The plan is only safe elsewhere. Such is life."

"Do you live?" Asterius had a quick comeback. I was still halfway through that, being amazed at each statement in turn.

"Sort of?" She put her finger on her chin. Was she pondering the question, or him?

"Is sort of living, worth living?" This was a question Asterius had answered for himself, recently. He was curious about her answer.

"That is the question we are trying to answer. But that's almost like a spoiler, and I wouldn't want to suggest that time isn't a straight line, because if that were so, then who would have said it first? He, or I?" She was more like Hermes than Athena, all things considered. I had no idea who this fourth person was in the conversation, so I had to ask.

"Who?" I was terribly confused.

"Exactly!" I had no idea. You might have a better idea. "Look, we could talk all day, and maybe we did, and there is just too much to relate. But I really should be getting out of here."

"Wha?" This was not a word, so much as a general statement of confusion and disbelief. It could have been any one, but it was both of us. And then she was gone. Not even birds. Just gone. I could still smell her, though. The fact is, it would take me many more years than I had to live to understand what she had said. This is not true of Asterius. But, regardless, we had something to take care of, and a bottle of oil to do it with. The anticipation did make it so much more delightful, too.

Asterius had a few tokens of love to exchange, as well. The first was exchanged in the back garden at the palace. I should get on describing the back garden. If one were to look in the gate into faux paradise, the first thing you would see is a giant crater that stopped smoking a few weeks back when the last of the bodies were burnt. The explosion didn't cause smoke, or fire, it was primarily energetic, and yes Asterius had checked it with the wand and it was safe. No radiation. Then the tower, in the distance, and merging somewhat with the wall. Then, to the left side of the tower and extending along the back wall, is another garden that is twice the size of the one we destroyed. The Athenians had been spending a lot of time there. Why not, it was fun?

Asterius and I were lounging on a small hill with a cutout, for lounging. It had more of that maddeningly elaborate masonry, but it was comfy to lounge against. More so than to look at. I suppose it was more for lounging. He rose to his feet. So did I, I was thinking it was time for privacy. He was thinking it was time for publicity. Most everyone was here, it was a perfect moment.

"I have a question to ask of you." It was directed at me, but he was so loud it was clear he wanted everyone's attention. He got it, except the people who were enjoying the particularly steep sections of the stone fountain river that were on the other side of the pond.

"I love your questions." And everything else about him.

"This is not traditional. I mean, in Crete, if two me... males love each other as we do, they exchange ankle bracelets." I immediately saw the problem with this, but he continued for the audience, which numbered about 70 including staff and Elaía, who was on a tiny boat that could support only one person on a perfectly still body of water. She had such an improbable body of water available there, which is probably why she had such an impractical item. She was also wearing a skin tight wrap and one of those glass things over her eyes that causes you to see less of the sun. Bewildering fashion choices, these Cretans. Back to the show, the stage just had to be set a bit. "But, my legs don't work like yours do. I tried on some of the ankle bracelets back in the murder cave, but they always cut my legs up when I moved."

"You knew to try on the ankle bracelets?" I was surprised. The tradition in Crete is to have men and women who pair up to wear the bracelets on their wrists. Gives you room for both if necessary. "I didn't think you had a preference."

"Oh, I tried both. I wanted to keep my options open, the heart being fickle and all." He smiled his glorious smile. "But, I have an alternative." He held up his hand, and the simple ring on it.

"This was in my pile, long ago. I picked it because it fit, it was simple, and it had a utility to me. The backs of my hands aren't as tough as yours, rapping on that stone was wearing me down." His mom lifted her sun reducing glass things, and gave him such a look. I think it was love, but she was squinting. "When we kicked over the pile, its partner jumped out. Same type, different size. I grabbed it. Didn't know why. A few days ago I figured out why. I hope[12] we don't have to have it altered." He gave it to me. It was lovely, in its simplicity; a band of gold. I tried it on, the same finger as he, the one next to the thumb on the right hand. It fit perfectly.

"It is also traditional for me to actually ask the question before you do that."

"You know the answer, everyone here does. I love you so much. I feel like I always have. How could I say no?" And we kissed. Everyone cheered, except for Elaía, who would have probably spilled her wine, which she was still fond of. She did smile. How could she not? Asterius was her son, and he had bagged a prince.

---

12 In this case, a word that means thus was used in the original language in place of that word, hope: 1. To have an intention that the best possible course of events might occur.

Hope is so jealous, it is almost impossible to even describe this word, in the modern context. Throughout this text, and from now on, hope is this concept I just described. Hope is that other thing, that's barely worth mentioning, since it inserts itself in everything whether you like it or not.

235

Everyone seemed very impressed with Asterius and I. It felt odd, to be held in such high regard, by everyone. As we basked in their love after the proposal, Asterius and I overheard something that suggested this admiration was not universal. I think my childhood friend Estius felt a bit jealous of all this attention I was getting.

"I don't understand why everyone is pretending he is a big hero. He didn't kill anyone! Barely raised his axe. Spent the whole time kissing Asterius." This was all true. The standard of heroism we had been raised with emphasized killing. Also I had done, or not done, all of those things. He also didn't know that Asterius and I were reclined on the infuriating hill thing not twenty feet behind him, and if he had, I doubt he would have had the courage to say this aloud. We didn't have to defend our battle cuddling, it turns out.

"If he hadn't been there we would all be dead. Same with Asterius, and their love did keep them sane through that. They kept me sane. Now, this is a private spot, and you are wasting my mouth by using it to put down your foolishness. Shall we continue?" Estius and Egeria were still very much in love, and why not? So long as he kept his mouth shut, Estius was a fine man. As to their activities up to this point, honestly, we had no idea. His fashionably short skirt must also come with an almost inaudible moan. We quietly left to give, and find, more privacy.

There were other tokens of affection to exchange, in private. One night, in the warehouse, Asterius came upon something he thought I would like.

"You like knives?" I always did carry one, and it was marvelous, but it was more about what one can do with a knife. Lacking a quick way to relate this, I said:

"Sure." It was sufficient, he understood what I meant perfectly, and it saved a lot of time, unlike this explanation. But, you weren't there.

"Oh, this is a good one." He had pulled a small knife out of one of the many boxes that were stored in this space. It was a box that was not full of deadly horrors. We had been dumping those in the sea as well, as we came across them. A tool is a good thing to have, but an object of curiosity that has outlived its usefulness and yet can still easily kill you is best not to hold on to. This tool had not outlived its usefulness.

"Look, it can fold!" And it could unfold. This didn't impress me at this point. "Also, check this out." Asterius calmly walked over to the wall, and transformed a double headed axe into a hatchet in mere moments. The other half fell to the floor, and clanged on the stones. This did impress me. It impressed me a great deal.

"It can cut anything?" It was more a statement than a question, but I was still very impressed and I wasn't sure it could be true.

"Not anything, but almost. Here." He handed it to me. Quite a statement of trust, as I had no idea how to use it. Besides as a knife. That was obvious, it had a blade, albeit one with teeth like things on it, rather than a clean edge as I was used to.

"That's called a serration." It was a new word to me, and Asterius knew my question, and what I would want to know, before I asked it. Marvelous. Even more so than the knife. "It's not the secret. Look on the side." On the side, roughly where a thumb might depress while you were using the knife, was a red flower. It stood out from the rest of the knife, which was made of that odd orange metal, with those same decorations, except the blade which was a dull grey. It was so much more pleasant to see such decoration on something that wasn't a nightmare. I immediately figured it out, and went over and made a hatchet of my own. I noticed that the freshly cut edge was red hot.

"Somehow it figures out what material it is cutting and vibrates at exactly the right rate so it will pass right through. It's terrifically useful, but it's not a weapon, so it's here in a box." Not now. Now it was in my pocket. There was no doubt of where it was going to end up. He also explained that vibration word to me later in relation to the action of a harp string, but that is out of sequence, and difficult to write about. But now, in honor of the asynchrony of time, a few words from the Goddess of Love regarding knives.

"He also made me a knife. I could have hurt him with that." It was almost a lie.

"Don't almost lie to a god, even if I am your grandmother."

I fell right down. Asterius did too, without my shoulder to lean on.

"How?" My condition was making it hard to get up. I couldn't just flip onto my stomach and push myself to my feet as I usually do. Asterius gave me a hand up, though I felt like grabbing something else. Aphrodite felt like answering the knife question I hadn't asked first, which was annoying at the time, but makes sense now.

"You know that was unlikely. And he was trying to save you! I doubt he would have brought the sickle down on you." I could easily tell that Asterius hated that phrase, even on her immaculate lips. "But think, that knife. A sword has but one use," I thought of another, and she corrected herself, "I mean, you can chop at vines with it... Two uses. Anyhow, did you get any use out of that knife?"

And I thought about all the hundreds of times I had pulled out that knife over the past few months and done some minor handy thing with it. Cut some rope. Opened a sack. Spread some butter on bread. Whittled the neck of an instrument. Split some leather. Parted the seal on that amphora of oil. Such mundane things that they are hardly worth mentioning, especially within the context of a romantic adventure. And I realized that her husband had given me a tool that I could use for countless things besides murder. And I was immensely grateful for it. That was a sufficient reply from me, for her. Then she moved on with answering my actual question, but only sort of, because she didn't fully understand that either. Moving on.

We were more or less fully prepared for our voyage back. We had the ships half packed, and had even selected a fishing vessel to act as our herald, and go a few days ahead with the good news. Minoan ships sailing into the harbor had been very bad news in the past, and we didn't want to cause a panic. But there was one thing we had to take care of, yet.

Twenty Six

The Labyrinth had to go. I was not going to walk away from here while that murder cave stood, where it might swallow more lives away. It was a perfect temple for the darkness, and like any other uncontrollable thing that serves only to kill, it was not worth keeping under any circumstance. More or less everyone agreed. Our first attempt was simple. Thesius and I braved that stair, a lamp in each hand. I had a nice cylinder that threw light out the end of it now. It was rendered in silver and gold and was clearly labeled: 'Makes [Lighted/Light of] Things'. This almost seemed like a joke, but they were so dry back then I can't imagine it. We also had some accelerant in bottles I had rigged to catch fire when broken. We sprinted to the middle, threw it at the wooden roof, and took a few steps back to watch it catch. It went right out just after it did.

"I thought you said that stuff burns endlessly even without air?" Thesius was as confused as I.

"It has air built into it, I don't know how that happened."

"Let's try to figure it out outside." We didn't. It wasn't until the next attempt that we did.

My initial theory was that there was some sort of odd draft at the center of the structure that blew the accelerant out into the space. I thought we were lucky there wasn't a violent explosion. But I was wrong, so terribly wrong. I should have had more faith[13], but not really, because that thing sure had faith in me.

Our next attempt involved some more conventional accelerant, and a few more volunteers. The two of us had pinpointed the places in the maze with the least air movement. Thesius was surprisingly useful, as his nose had found most of them on his forced tour. Teltale's plans were also very useful, of course. We had a few volunteers, Theo and Juisephone, who has not come up yet. She was of the second

---

13 We will cover the double meaning of this word in the modern context, later. But, here is context you could use, if you wish.

sacrifice, and was very brave, and resourceful, and silent. We had four locations pinpointed. We made it to the central chamber.

"Do you hear that?" It could have been anyone. It was Theo.

"Is that…"

"No, not at all." Who else could those two be? Juisephone screamed. It was the first time I had heard her scream, and it was not without good reason.

I had just run into the room. But… it was not me. It was like of the darkness. It bore no clothes, and looked savage, and bloody. Its eyes were red fires in the blackness. It was an outline, but then an image of myself, torn and broken. It lacked genitals. But it still had my perfect sickles of death. It advanced upon us with frightening speed. I bodily picked up Theo, who was a bit overwhelmed, and carried him away from the path. It banked off the wall, and then stood, and bellowed into the chamber. This was what I was acting at. But it was real.

We made it out, all of us, somehow. Juisephone was the wisest of us. She went for the stair immediately after she screamed. I followed, carrying Theo. Thesius may have been the second wisest, though it is not a contest, when he left the eternal flame burning at full brightness at the bottom of the stair behind us. It was a tool, but it could hold back a god of darkness.

"Well, now we really have to burn that place down!" That could have been anyone. But only Thesius was unshaken enough by the experience to speak at that moment. But we had to have a plan. It took us a few days, but there are conversations worth mentioning.

"What is that thing?" We were at rest, at night for once. I wasn't fully used to it, sleeping at night, but I enjoyed any chance at novelty, and the novelty of my Thesius by my side would never escape me. We had a room in the palace, in the deceased head of the guard's quarters in the outer wall. It was pretty spare, as we spent little time there, but I had to insist upon one of the camp beds being moved in, for my comfort. After years of sleeping on stone, those cushions were intolerable. Thesius was also very much in favor of this choice, so it was an easy thing to insist upon. This was a good setting for this conversation. Some things I would prefer not to say before anyone but my love.

"It's a god." Or, the opposite of one.

"I thought you said their ritual was a comedy of errors? And you... we escaped. How did it work?" He shifted his position, with his back against me, and his head pressed against my chest. We had discovered that I could hiss words at a whisper's volume through my teeth one night, while he was trying to teach me how to whistle. This was a pleasant signal that he understood we had to talk of forbidden things. Perhaps even the gods won't hear, if we keep our words low and held close to our chests.

"They really believed in it. The ritual." I drew in a long breath. Hissing wasn't efficient, it was just quiet. His sigh of pleasure as we cuddled brought my mind to other things, and I may have released a few... low barks of joy. Thesius had made me so much more comfortable with my unique involuntary utterances, as they seemed to give him such joy in turn, but I still lacked good names for most of them. I gripped him tight, and I tried to focus. "That sincere belief seems to be the key. Also, they did that power stacking thing."

"What did they stack on?"

"The old god, I won't name it, was of death and harvest. This new one they were making was also so many other things. It made the invocation of the god sound like some sort of awful recipe."

"What was on the menu?" His curiosity struck me as odd, but then I realized it was of strategic significance. We had to kill that thing.

"Darkness. Violence. Imperfection. Silence. Discord. Sin. Evil... as in, literally the whole concept of evil." Thesius laughed, quietly. It was such an absurdity. "They also said it was lord of the underworld. I thought that job was already taken."

"Arbias didn't seem to think that thing was to supplant our gods..." I had noticed this too. I had been trying not to think of it.

"No, he seemed unsurprised to see me along side Hermes. It bothers me. What was I…" He squeezed me sharply when I associated myself with that thing. It would be best not to do so, he was right. "… that thing supposed to do?" He continued doing something wonderful to my forearms with his hands, but I was too lost in thought to truly enjoy it.

"Something awful, clearly." Anything so awful seemed so far away from us in that moment, even though I knew it was right downstairs.

"It worries me. It's as if that thing was crafted to order."

"Made? Like the centaurs? To some purpose?"

"No, like a god. They are all made to a purpose, always have been." If I had wanted a reply, this was not the pearl of wisdom to share. But all I wanted was his warmth, and his love, and my golden bear had so much of that to give, even when he was lost in thought.

"So we have a god of darkness, in the darkness, that wants to keep his home." This was Miletta. She was talking it out; such a useful habit.

"Yes." It could have been anyone. It was Thesius and I, simultaneously. All of us were in the swimming pool in the back garden, and mostly naked. That hardly mattered for the sake of the conversation, but it is fun.

"Can I shoot it?" We all looked at each other. Maybe? Or not?

"It seems too modeled on your design." This was Thesius, but it sounded like me. I was so proud of him.

"I was worried it was going to grab a bow out of the air, frankly." Juisephone had been forced to speak about her experience a lot, and she had grown. She wasn't at all bashful to bathe in public view anymore, for instance. Bathing wraps were available, of course, not that the Athenians cared.

"So, what?" I knew the answer, in that moment, even though I had asked the question. Answering like this would be too teachery, and so I waited for suggestions.

"We use another god on it?" That was my idea, but it was Mantes, who was sunning himself on mother's tiny raft, the one with the stuffed giraffe head mounted on it. I was relieved that I did not have to be the one who had voiced the idea, it seemed most unlike me.

So, we used another god on it. We gathered together in our grand procession, but this time we wore every bright color we could find. We brought out the drums, and the horns. And we prepared to play the merriest music we could imagine. The time the darkness had most seemed to leave that murder cave was when my beloved Thesius and I played music there. Well, there are gods of music... let's see if they can make a curtain call with us.

We descended into the darkness. I had distributed cylinder lamps to some in the band, others had lamps with contained flames, which hung off chains on their instruments. It really depended on whether you could play with one hand or not, we had plenty of those cylinder lamp things. They must have made them by the thousands, back in the day. Thesius and I took the lead. Oh, and we began playing before we descended, no sense in taking chances.

Once we got to the bottom it was a different place. The columns seemed to stretch out forever. I couldn't even see the walls, and these cylinder lamps had throw.

"Keep playing, the darkness is trying to unnerve us." Thesius was right. Even I was unnerved by this. We kept playing. The second song is when things changed.

It was there. But it wasn't there. It was in pain. But it was pain. It was death. But it was dying. It fell, and held its hands to its head, and cried out in agony. And then, there were gods. A few lovely women appeared. They seemed perfect blah blah blah. Glowing eyes too. One had a harp, and the other an aulos. They were dancing around that thing and playing along. I had a quick question, and I really hoped the one with the harp would answer because this was working.

"Would it be ok[14] if we burnt this horrible temple of death and darkness down around you? I mean, would you be ok?"

"Oh, we'll be fine. Fire is fun too. She's of the fire." But she did not precede it. She who was of the fire continued playing the aulos, thankfully.

We also had incendiaries. Did I not mention that? We threw them at the roof, and the band retreated up the stair. I ran through, one last time, and threw one on top of the roof inside the cave, from the hidden path. My dear Thesius was there already. He had run ahead as soon as the walls had reappeared, with a cylinder torch. We wanted to ensure the thing didn't try to run out the backdoor, and he had a spot of light on it. I handed him his eternal flame, and we kissed. Then we ran like hell because a cave on fire is immensely dangerous.

Thankfully, the roof did not collapse, that may have caused a catastrophe up above. Of the cave, not that damned Labyrinth Arbias built inside of it to make it kill people better. Not that it wasn't already good at that. The roof of the Labyrinth collapsed and all the stones were shattered. The darkness no longer had a perfect home to fester in, and the world was a better place for it.

14 This is a very modern word, but Crete had an equivalent. Asterius was disinclined to use it because he liked words and it seems so rushed. But they were very rushed.

Also, if you are a pedant, the joke in time is now here, but the joke is on you. Enjoy that. We did.

Final Chapter

The journey back was uneventful, except for one event. Two days in, Sinia was having another bout of sea sickness, when he fell over the side. He didn't even surface, even though he was an excellent swimmer. The dark god of death and harvest, the mad King of Minos, and all the accumulated madness of the ancients had slain but one of the band of Athens, and that was by time. But Poseidon took one of his own.

The crowd that awaited them did not seem pleased. Rather, panicked. The band sent a skiff ashore, with a few of the lost Athenians, and as the reunions and the tears even began Thesius was figuring it out.

"Our herald did not get through." At this moment, with the sort of irony that almost always suggests some sort of godly intervention, the herald ship came around the corner of the cape, into plain view of everyone. Its main mast was broken. The band had seen no bad weather at all, and that was the answer to the question both of our heroes had. But the irony was unending. First, a reunion.

"Boreo!" Thesius was already on his feet, and so was Asterius, not that he was steady upon them or even recognizable.

Oh, that, the disguise. Let's back up to another conversation.

"You can't go walking into Athens like that, Asterius." This was Thesius. No one else would dare criticize his walking, or his fashion. They were both just too impeccable. At the moment he was wearing a pleated skirt in a rainbow of colors with a cloth belt that tied in a fanciful fashion along the sides with ribbon, along with a light cape about his shoulders in purple. He had become fond of the outfit after the band's last performance, and it looked dashing on him.

"I can dress in a wrap, I look good!" Asterius did, and everyone agreed. He had been trying on a lot of outfits, when he wasn't busy taking them off again for Thesius.

"No, if it looks like we stole the god from Crete and brought him home we are going to be in trouble. Everyone will want a piece of us. A bloody one." This could have been Thesius, but it was Mantes. It was also very correct.

"So what?" Asterius was going, there was no stopping him. And how could he hide what he was? Thesius answered by holding up a leather mask. "I didn't know you were into that, darling." Thesius ignored this.

"As much as it reminds me of that creepy death party your mom threw, a mask is a good choice." Thesius knew that necessity comes before fashion.

"Look at me, Thesius, will a mask work?" Everyone had anticipated this question. It had been a topic of quiet discussion for days.

"A mask and lie will." It could have been many people, so many of the Athenians were so wise in many ways. It was Helea. She was dressed in a mixture of Athenian and Cretan finery. All of their fine party clothes had been found in a chamber next to where the head priest lived, before he voluntarily drank poison and died. Everyone had tried to not think about what he might have been doing with them. They seemed well kept.

"Not a lie. Something like a lie." Only Thesius and Asterius understood the distinction, or the need to bear it in mind. But, strangely, it was Eridice, who either was concealing her understanding or was speaking from a higher source. Everyone was a little surprised she had spoken at all, as she had a remarkable skill to disappear into the background that she used most of the time, and after they recovered Mantes continued with a truth and a falsehood.

"No, a full lie will be needed. But it's a costume, what damage could it cause?" His choice of the most simple costume possible at all times might damage his case, if everyone in attendance didn't know how unrelentingly wise he was. He could be naked and dirty and they would listen to him, before asking him what had happened.

"Well, he has to be a foreigner." This was Theo. It was a good, clever observation. Theo was full of those. He was also a bit more full of the belly than he had been in the hidden canyon. It turns out he rather liked the meat pies. He was still such a fearsome wrestler that he would be at the tip of any spear the band might throw, anyway.

"It would be good if we really only knew them for being big, cause, dang." This was Miletta, with some more charming slang most people didn't know. She collected the stuff. She had taken to collecting many things, including the fair and slight Cretan man who was holding onto her left hand. Helea was holding onto her right.

"How about a Vik? None of them come round, but we get their bronzeware sometimes through the chain. They seem to wear masks all the time." This could have been any Athenian, as they were all familiar with the bronzeware in question. It was very fun to look at. It was Miletta again. There hadn't even been a pause, there was just a lot of information to convey. Also she was just a bit more like Hermes all the time since she put on that thing, which she could not take off. Also, she was wearing clothes, of course, do you think that guy was sitting at the royal table eating food with his dangly bits all out and everything? It only objected to fashion during the binding process. Clothes had become another collectable for Miletta, and she was blindingly fashionable at the moment. She was not a blind hole in space.

"Leather masks with horns?" Asterius was skeptical, as he had not seen the bronzeware in question, but he had read of the Vik. Also, the mask had holes for his horns, it would have been more of a hood otherwise. Also, the Vik never wore leather masks with horns, just helmets with masks, and only in battle, which they were fond of depicting on bronzeware. Also, lies have lasting consequences, even necessary ones.

"Don't forget the shoes." Thesius had a whole outfit. The palace seamstress had been busy.

"I do not wear shoes." Asterius did not. Not that they even existed for his feet.

248

"When you must be seen by a crowd, now you do." Now they did exist, and Thesius had them in a box. Those must have taken longer to craft. They also had a leather apron thing that would cover his arms and most of his tail, most of the time. It was similar enough to his old skirt that it worked, but he insisted upon a modified version of a belt made with leather rather than metal to bind it, on the same model as his fanciful cloth belt. The belt comforted him. The Athenians knew it was best to spring this plan on Asterius after it was largely complete. They had voted in his absence, which is a touch unfair, but if he had been the deciding vote they would have included him. It was unanimous.

Back to Boreo.

"Boreo!" He was easy to pick out, but he wasn't the only person with darker skin in the crowd, not by far. That crowd was in jubilation, and was cheering about the return of their lost children. Everyone was filing down to the docks to see why they weren't bursting into flames and dying.

"Oh, my friend, I had thought I had lost you." Boreo was very happy to see Thesius. Somewhat less pleased with the leather giant that slowly followed him, but he seemed friendly.

"I found everyone else! And I found my love there. Meet Asterius." The leather giant waved.

"You always did like the big guys, dang." Apparently Boreo was familiar with this slang word too. He was correct. He also bore little resemblance to the baker family, who was from the Nile. In fact, the baker family was greeting their child back, Phyron, who had been in the last sacrifice. The shades of their skins matched, though not any other aspect of their faces, because they were from opposite sides of the continent. They had tears in their eyes and the names of foreign gods on their lips. They could be forgiven for this, by the Athenians anyway. The gods would have to work that out amongst themselves. Did you assume that the Merry Band of Athens was entirely white because they were Greek? Go look at a map, and check your assumptions, please. It was at this moment that Thesius noticed who Boreo was with, and was taken aback.

"You?... Are you ok? Did your mom get to the Heliopolis?" Thesius was speaking to a slightly older young man, who could probably be passed off as 17 or 18 as they never checked that.

"Your dad took care of us." Thesius and this man were both happy, on so many levels, by the events that were unfolding before them.

"Oh thank the gods, he redeemed himself." It was only half true, but Thesius didn't know it yet. At that very moment, before Thesius could ask why those two people were together, Latrius came running in, and made a beeline for him. He was very out of shape, and it took him a while, hand on knee, to get it out. It didn't help that he wasn't sure whether he was surrounded by ghosts or not.

"You father, Aegeus!" There was a lot more panting here than is depicted.

"Where is he, I want to share the news of my ultimate heroic victory with him!" Thesius was enthusiastic, and he had a lot of news to share.

"He threw himself from the cliffs, he thought the Minoans were attacking again, and he had failed us!" The gods do love their irony. Thesius did not like this, and the scene of shock, grief and horror that follows isn't worth relating. Before the tears were dry, Asterius was suggesting they flee to Thessaly to see Thesius' old teacher. Just to get away from the pain. So they did. It was a perfect idea.

A cart was procured. More like given, there was a lot of gratitude going around. As you know, the trip was boring, except it wasn't, because they had acres of privacy and oil. Once they found the privacy of nature, Asterius cast off his burdensome shoes immediately, and chose to carry them in the cart. He continued to use the staff he had procured, though.

"Don't know why I didn't think of this before. If I need to run, I can hold it with both hands, if I need to stand, I have something to lean on." He beamed down on his light, "And walking slowly is so much easier!"

Once they arrived, which was nearly a day later than the trip really called for, but what is a schedule, Chiron gave Asterius a thorough examination before they could talk. He was obviously in perfect health, Chiron was just immensely curious. There were greetings, and the like, but Chiron got down to business quickly. He had a question, and he wanted to ask it before Thesius had a chance to ask why he was merely curious, but not surprised, by Asterius. Most everyone found everything about him so surprising. Thesius had a remarkable quality to ask questions of Chiron that required a distraction to get out of, and he had no students at hand to provide one.

"And what of your goddess? Have you received congratulations from her?" Chiron cocked his head to the side, in the way he would when he had you pinned. Thesius hadn't considered it, but no. Was that odd?

"Well, no. I mean, Aphrodite... and Hermes did show up to see if a rescue was needed, but we had things handled. Uh... " Thesius now realized how weak this argument was.

"Because, though Asterius is clearly a lovely person, and this resolution is far better than even the vile lying whispers of Hope might have you believe could be possible... I was witness to the conditions of your mission. You were supposed to stab him with a sword, not what you ended up stabbing him with." Yup, he was pinned. Asterius burst out laughing; it rang like a bronze bell off the trees, and Thesius felt far less embarrassed. Just having him around made him feel so strong.

"We've made quite a habit of stabbing one another. I wonder if we keep trying, it will make up for the lack of a deadly result." His words were, themselves, like a laugh. Asterius was so clearly happy to be here, in the light, so far from all the places and people who had tortured him. In response to this joy, Thesius took his hand, and looked up at his smiling face, fangs and all.

"Oh yes, do fill me in on every intimate detail about something I can never enjoy myself. We could follow it up by rubbing gravel into my hooves, and perhaps then Asterius could cook me a meaty Cretan meal, every delicious morsel of which I would savor until it made me shit like a waterfall for two days." His words sounded grouchy, but Chiron was beaming. Both our heroes knew it was a rarity to be so in his favor that they could be blessed with his sarcasm.

"Maybe we should focus on making Aphrodite happy?" Both Asterius and Chiron were already nodding at this point, "She seemed delighted." She was also the speaker's grandma, so that helps.

"The two of them love each other, of course." Chiron tossed his hands in the air for emphasis. It was hard not to imagine flower petals, but there were none. "But they scheme against each other too. I would recommend blaming this on her somehow. Given the good resolution, well, Athena is wise. Aphrodite wouldn't be at all offended if you blamed her for a torrid love affair, either."

"Agreed." Asterius pressed his face against the end of his staff as he leaned upon it, and leered down upon him, "Love made me do it. That's our line." They both so wanted to run off into the woods and practice stabbing one another some more. But, they were interrupted: Thesius heard him first.

"A runner approaches." Asterius nodded his agreement, as he pulled on his leather mask. He had gotten so good at not catching his horns. Up, over the hill, came the runner. He was a youth, and was dressed as a messenger, with the customary band on his head to signify the protection of Hermes. This was probably his first job, Thesius had doubts his face had ever touched the shell. He stopped, caught his breath for a moment, and immediately upon seeing his golden locks, he called out.

"Hail, Thesius!"

Thesius was puzzled. 'He is here to say good things about me? An odd thing for a messenger to be sent to do.' He only thought this, but it was as good as if he had said it. It was at this moment the messenger noticed Thesius' company, in the way that people can be blind to extraordinary things. He fell right down, but then got up again.

"Oh, no... " Chiron groaned, as he buried his head in his hands.

The messenger dusted himself off, and continued with his message. "The people of Athens send their greetings and good tidings. By public lot, and in appreciation for your great act of heroism, Thesius, son of Aegeus and Aethra, has been elected as the new King of Athens. All hail his name! All hail Thesius, King of Athens!"

"What?" Thesius was lost in thought immediately. 'No... my father is the king. He killed himself, the fool he...' Asterius spoke up.

"Say that without the flourish, boy."

"You've been elected king! It's good... I'm bringing good news, right?" He shuffled uncomfortably.

"That's not true!" But it was. Thesius looked to his companion for some comfort, but his face was a blank slate beneath his mask. Chiron hid his face in his hands. "I can't be king... That's terrible!"

And that is the tale of how the Merry Band of Athens used the tools given to them to defeat an unborn god of death and darkness, and save themselves and all those who would have fallen before it, and how the gods were merely useful in cleaning up, mostly, except the gods who were critical to the plan, but did not know.

Join us for the next volume in the trilogy, Asterius & Thesius Tangle with the Hearts of Man

Afterword

I happened upon the story on a frosty afternoon, in the late fall of 2003. I had just finished class, and there wasn't enough time to go across campus to the lab to work on the work, so I went into the bookstore at the Ohio Union to do something I had precious little chance to do those days: waste some time. It was warm, and there was coffee and books, so I was at home. Sometimes I would half nap in the comfy chairs there in this hour, but today I browsed through the books for some random thing to read. The further away from molecular biology, the better. In the literature section, I came across a thick work of mythology, precariously balanced on the edge of the shelf. I reached for it more to save it than anything, but it also seemed a perfect choice so I grabbed it and went to find one of those comfy chairs.

The first few chapters didn't interest me much. The text was concerned with comparative mythology, with an emphasis on the distortions modern western archeology has introduced into the original text, sometimes out of misunderstanding, sometimes out of bias. A good bit of it was obvious in the way that an academic text can be, as it tries to set up its thesis. I flipped through, until I came upon a photo card later in the book that made me blush; a group of period works (vases, primarily) depicting Thesius and the Minotaur entangled together, though definitely not in combat, accompanied by a more modern sculpture that probably scandalized everyone that saw it, though at the time I did not know it was a modern sculpture. Well, this sparked my curiosity, so I read on through to find a wholly different take on the tale that, according to the text, was a common alternate telling at the time. It stuck firm in my memory as it was such a different, and more hopeful take; one that you have just read in long form. But there is also a bit of a mystery about it, and I pray you, the reader, may help me solve it. Here is this version of the tale of the Labyrinth, related as best I can from memory.

The City of Minos did call for endless revenge upon the People of Athens, for the loss of their prince and son.

And so, with every passing, they would send their youths, 7 and 7, to Minos to die in the Labyrinth, at the hand of a monster.

As the years passed, many were sent, but none returned.

Until the King Aegeus, his own son Thesius was selected in the dark lot.

But the goddess, Athena, had a different plan, and had him trained.

Armed with glorious implements. A sword, a lamp, and a knife.

These were secreted away in the maze, by the Minoan princess.

Thesius did enter the maze, to seek out the monster, but his wisdom did draw him to the air, and to the light.

He found himself in a secret place, and there he did see truth.

A voice in the darkness, led him forth, to the hidden exit.

There he found his brothers and sisters, alive!

The monster was not, and he had saved them.

The light and the string did bind them, and in love they triumphed.

Together in love, they led the Athenians back through the darkness, and took the palace for the light.

You see, I can't find any mention of this version of the tale anywhere now. Oh, I have found that scandalous early 1800's marble (Antonio Canova). That seems to exist, but the other works? Any single mention of a version of the story where Thesius and Asterius hook up in the end? Besides a few variants that suggest that Thesius brought Asterius back to Athens on a 'string', no sign. And I did spend some time looking, combing the internet and the library. I ended up crashing on a wall of slash fiction and disappointment. And that's where it would have stayed I think. After all, I doubted myself. Did I just dream it up, asleep in the chair, half holding the book with eyes closed and jaw slacked? I was overworked and undersleeped, so that's believable. But then this stupid (amazing) video game came out in the summer of all our discontent, and I found myself reliving it all again.

Hades, by SuperGiant, is probably a better work of fiction than this is. The way it tells so many branching narratives in one work, rather than depicting just one as this book does, is truly marvelous. Games may provide us with a better vision of time than any book could ever. It drew me in immediately, but a few hours into my play through I was shocked to find Asterius and Thesius fighting side by side in Elysium in flaming pink glory, as if the Asterius was indeed the hero (and the lover) I remembered from this alternate telling. I simply assumed this was someone else who was aware of this version of the tale, but I was disappointed to find it wasn't as I played on. It was more like the authors of the game script were righting a lot of wrongs in the mythos. It is true that Asterius being condemned for the horror he was subjected to by his father and his people seems even more unjust than Orpheus and Euridice being separated for all eternity just because he looked back.

But now the story was back with me, and it bothered me terribly. As a counterpart to the story of Cupid and Psyche, it has a beautiful symmetry. In one the divine is cast into darkness by a lack of trust and open communication between lovers, but in the other the divine is brought forth into the light by trust and communication that sees past physical differences. In one the simple act of being a couple is thwarted by the blinding glare of beauty, leading to a long and grueling punishment. In the other, the revolutionary act of loving another person who might seem unlovable, leads to a blinding act of heroism. Hades had shown me the great emotional power that lies in correcting the mythos, and writing those wrongs that live on in our collective mind. I had to put it down. For my own sanity this had to be made real, in some sense. I had to take Asterius out of that murder cave. He didn't belong there, no one does. If only I had known the extent of it.

And here it is. But then, I found there was more that flowed perfectly from this starting point. I have a lot more typing to do.

Made in the USA
Columbia, SC
12 May 2021